# Emma Taylor's Secret

*By*

*Andy Cooper*

Copyright © 2023 by - Andy Cooper - All Rights Reserved.

It is not legal to reproduce, duplicate, or transmit any part of this document in either electronic means or printed format. Recording of this publication is strictly prohibited.

*Dedicated to*

*Kay*

Cover Illustration by Lauren Prince

# About the Author

Andy Cooper lives in the north of England. He is a former BBC journalist. He now works as a freelance writer and journalist.

# Table of Contents

About the Author ................................................................... iii
Chapter One - Emma ............................................................ 1
Chapter Two - Dan................................................................. 6
Chapter Three - Emma .......................................................... 9
Chapter Four - Dan & Emma .............................................. 13
Chapter Five - Toby ............................................................. 13
Chapter Six - Jen .................................................................. 22
Chapter Seven - Maddy ....................................................... 26
Chapter Eight - Emma ......................................................... 31
Chapter Nine - Dan .............................................................. 34
Chapter Ten - Maddy ........................................................... 38
Chapter Eleven - Jen ............................................................ 44
Chapter Twelve - Emma ...................................................... 49
Chapter Thirteen - Toby....................................................... 56
Chapter Fourteen - Emma ................................................... 59
Chapter Fifteen - Jen ............................................................ 62
Chapter Sixteen - Dan .......................................................... 65
Chapter Seventeen - Maddy ................................................ 69
Chapter Eighteen - Emma ................................................... 74
Chapter Nineteen - Maddy .................................................. 80
Chapter Twenty - Dan.......................................................... 85
Chapter Twenty-One - Jen .................................................. 88
Chapter Twenty-Two - Emma ............................................ 95
Chapter Twenty-Three - Maddy ....................................... 102
Chapter Twenty-Four - Jen ............................................... 106

Chapter Twenty-Five - Emma & Dan .......................................................... 112
Chapter Twenty-Six - Toby ........................................................................ 117
Chapter Twenty-Seven - Jen ...................................................................... 123
Chapter Twenty-Eight - Emma ................................................................... 128
Chapter Twenty-Nine - Dan ....................................................................... 131
Chapter Thirty - Jen .................................................................................. 136
Chapter Thirty-One - Toby ........................................................................ 140
Chapter Thirty-Two - Emma ...................................................................... 144
Chapter Thirty-Three - Maddy ................................................................... 152
Chapter Thirty-Four - Toby ....................................................................... 161
Chapter Thirty-Five - Dan ......................................................................... 166
Chapter Thirty-Six - Maddy ....................................................................... 169
Chapter Thirty-Seven - Jen ........................................................................ 174
Chapter Thirty-Eight - Emma .................................................................... 179
Chapter Thirty-Nine - Maddy .................................................................... 183
Chapter Forty - Emma .............................................................................. 186
Chapter Forty-One - Dan .......................................................................... 192
Chapter Forty-Two - Maddy ...................................................................... 195
Chapter Forty-Three - Dan ........................................................................ 200
Chapter Forty-Four - Emma ...................................................................... 204
Chapter Forty-Five - Toby ......................................................................... 209
Chapter Forty-Six - PC Reynolds ............................................................... 213
Chapter Forty-Seven - Maddy .................................................................... 217
Chapter Forty-Eight - PC Reynolds ............................................................ 217
Chapter Forty-Nine - Toby ........................................................................ 225
Chapter Fifty - Maddy ............................................................................... 228
Chapter Fifty-One - PC Reynolds ............................................................... 234

Chapter Fifty-Two - Toby ............................................................... 237

Chapter Fifty-Three - PC Reynolds ............................................ 246

Chapter Fifty-Four - Maddy ........................................................ 253

Chapter Fifty-Five - PC Reynolds .............................................. 258

Chapter Fifty-Six - Dan ................................................................ 262

Chapter Fifty-Seven - Emma ...................................................... 269

Chapter Fifty-Eight - Maddy ....................................................... 270

Chapter Fifty-Nine - Toby ........................................................... 274

Chapter Sixty - PC Reynolds ...................................................... 277

Chapter Sixty-One - Maddy ........................................................ 280

Chapter Sixty-Two - PC Reynolds ............................................. 284

Chapter Sixty-Three - Emma ..................................................... 291

Chapter Sixty-Four - Maddy ....................................................... 292

Chapter Sixty-Five - Jen .............................................................. 296

Chapter Sixty-Six - Emma .......................................................... 299

Epilogue .......................................................................................... 307

# Chapter One
# Emma

A canvas stood on a pinewood easel in the middle of the room. Emma loved the way colours reacted, shapes emerged, intertwined and tricked the eye. Art could scoop up her imagination, take her off to a distant place - an escape. Sometimes fierce energy came from within, an energy full of vibrant ideas and it felt like she couldn't paint fast enough. But this wasn't one of those times. Today was another day when her past crowded in, disabling, almost paralysing, wrapping itself tightly around her.

She took a break. Nose pressed against the glass; her eyes so tightly focused on a single droplet of rain they almost hurt. The dull, dispiriting, grey Cumbrian morning felt like a metaphor. The window steamed up, and Emma could no longer see down the village's old stone street. With her index finger she traced a heart on the pane...and then, childishly, an arrow thrust through the middle.

Ms Higgins, Ms H, as they'd called their art teacher, always said; when inspiration leaves you make a cup of tea, go for a walk, leave it a day or two, if necessary, but wait. Wait, because *it* will return. There was a mirror behind the kettle, and she pulled one of her Emma faces - that's what her mother called them. She straightened her central parting with a little finger and admired new highlights. Her eyes were her 'thing' even she could see that. However hard she tried to avoid it; men would just fall into them. Some were swallowed up forever, others would eventually scramble out – but rarely undamaged. How long could she possess the magic? She was thirty-six and she heard the tick of the clock.

Emma prepared a second mug of tea for Toby. He occupied the room next to hers in the small but increasingly successful art gallery.

'Tea, Tobes?' She sauntered into his room.

'Oh yeah, sure, thanks, thanks a lot, yeah.' He thrust out an alien-looking clay-clad hand.

'Oh, bollocks, sorry, I'll wipe that. Bollocks, no cloth.' Toby was being Toby. He wiped his hand down his dishevelled stained jeans, which if not worn by him might have been considered artistic.

'How's it going?' Emma asked, dancing around him in order to admire his work.

'Well, I'm entering a different phase, I think,' he replied rather doubtfully.

On the stand was the start of a new sculpture. Toby would make up a proto-type in clay and then use it as his model before chipping away at a chunk of stone. The work was slow and painstaking, but Emma thought him quite brilliant. She walked slowly around his work, taking it all in with a critical artistic eye.

'What about that bit?' she teased, pointing to a piece of clay that had half broken off.

'Yeah, um, well, work in progress, you know?'

Toby could produce figures of people, animals, or, in this case, more abstract shapes. These shapes were particularly popular in the foyers of big corporations which were intent on impressing visitors, customers, and shareholders. Emma guessed he must make a very decent living, which was not easy for an artist of any kind, while she, on the other hand, only just made ends meet supported by a monthly cheque from her father. Guilt money on his part, she was sure.

What Emma liked most about Toby was that he loved her. He'd stumbled unwittingly into her eyes back when they were in school, and so far, for him, there had definitely been no way out. She knew it, and he knew she knew it. One of them couldn't do anything about it; the other didn't want him to. It felt good to be loved, and more importantly for Emma, in her current vulnerable state, it felt good to have someone who was willing to do almost anything to make her happy.

'And how are *you* getting on?' Toby asked, ruffling his mop of unruly brown hair, leaving small pieces of clay precariously balanced between curls. Emma carefully, intimately, removed a couple. Toby smiled awkwardly, and she could see and enjoy the shiver which ran through him. He rubbed his hands down his smock.

'I'm a bit stuck, actually," said Emma. "That's why I've gone walkabout again.'

'Hmm,' was all Toby returned. There was a brief silence as he rummaged for the right tool but not the right words. It was ok; they were comfortable with silence. Emma knew their relationship was one-sided. Her affections lay elsewhere. But despite that and the ongoing awkwardness on Toby's part, there was a bond between them borne from a shared history. She considered them firm and close friends.

'Right, well, um, I'm sure the super talented Emma Taylor will get going again in a minute,' said Toby, eventually, in that upbeat dismissive way he dealt with most problems. 'How are you settling into your new flat?' he asked.

She liked hearing her maiden name, Taylor. She'd only recently decided to use it again. 'Yeah, it's good. I'm good, all is good.' She was lying, of course, and it rather killed off any further conversation. As she turned to leave she heard Toby let out a long slow sigh under his breath. He always saw through her.

Back in her own studio, she put on a CD. She still used a CD player at work – very old-fashioned now in a world of streaming. U2's nineties hit, *Beautiful Day,* filled the room. But it didn't chase her mood away, and her mind drifted to an increasingly familiar place.

Her friend Steph had persuaded her to go to that party. She knew ***he*** would be there. The two girls spent all afternoon getting ready. Steph said the red dress looked best. She'd replied that he wasn't Chris de bloody Burgh and she preferred the blue one. She could still feel how that dress felt, how that day felt – even though it was more than twenty years ago. She could almost smell and taste it; the anticipation, excitement, and nerves - all wrapped up with a fear of failure. That's where it all began.


The afternoon shepherded in a party of school children. She'd agreed to this visit soon after starting at the art gallery some weeks back. The manager, a slim well-dressed woman with a penchant for dangly matching jewellery, liked to raise the community profile of the gallery. She'd explained to Emma that inviting children from the local primary school to meet the artists was one way of doing it. She clearly also hoped that by displaying the children's pictures – which were sent in as a thanks for the visit - their parents would come into the gallery and spend money, and they did. Emma wasn't quite sure what to expect, but she liked children and she'd set up her easel with a large piece of paper for them to collectively paint. They'd been told to arrive in their painting smocks, and there they all were - about a dozen seven-year-olds in old clothes, or shirts borrowed from their parents, looking baggy, excited, and very sweet.

'Now, first, imagine a shape and then think of your favourite colour. It's up to you where you put that shape. You can link it to someone else's shape, or you can put it on a clean part of the paper,' she said, to a sea of enthralled faces.

The session went well - the children seemed to enjoy themselves, and their teacher was happy – even though some of her charges collected more paint on their faces than found its way onto paper. But as the group was leaving, one little girl seemed reluctant to go - she was still making finishing touches.

'That's very good, but you'd better leave it for now,' said Emma.

'I love, love, love painting, it's so exciting,' said the little girl, her eyes wide open and sparkling. 'Every picture is different. Thank you, Emma, for showing us and letting us do this.'

Tears suddenly welled up in Emma's eyes. Was it because this little girl was so adorable, or that she instantly saw something of herself? As she gently ushered her out of the room to join the rest of the class, the single, soon-to-be-divorced, Emma, without a little girl of her own to collect from school – a little girl who might come running across the playground clutching the latest painting – knew there was a lot more to it.

She blew her nose, dabbed her eyes, and began tidying. Once more, she was drawn to the window. It had stopped raining, but, if anything, the day was even wilder. An elderly lady wrestled with an umbrella against a recalcitrant wind; a cyclist, clad in plastic, ducked into his task. Three buildings down from an ivy-covered old stone shop stood a rather shabby-looking garage. She hadn't been over there, not to that part of the village, not yet, not even to do her shopping. And so far, since her return to what she'd always called her real home, she'd only been to one of the village's two pubs, the one on what she called 'her' side of the street. He used the other one. And the garage was where *he* now worked.

# Chapter Two
# Dan

They were at it again - sexting. Dan sent his message and waited for a reply.

*'Yes, yes, YES!!'* his partner, Jen, texted back. A bit quick this morning, perhaps she had to get back to work? He put his coffee cup down on the oily garage floor and texted back a suitable reply.

Dan was sitting on three quad bike tyres tucked into his favourite corner of the workshop. Tools and parts of cars were scattered everywhere. The mechanics mostly knew where to find things; the rules of the workshop were somehow established by osmosis. Normally, when he was taking his break, he'd enjoy these exchanges with Jen. But today he was in an odd mood – and he knew why.

It was eighteen years ago when Emma left him, almost overnight, it seemed. Her Dad had a new job; the family was moving away; it would be impossible to keep things going, she'd said, and that was that. He'd thought it was the last he'd ever see of her. But now, apparently, she was back in the village. What did she want? Why had she returned? Why now? There'd been many times when he'd have given almost anything to see her again. But now, just when she'd chosen to beam back into his orbit, things were different; his life had changed.

Initially, after Emma left, he'd been angry. But when that anger subsided, he was just left feeling empty, clutching his insides. Over the years, other girls briefly flickered in and out of his life, but there was no one to compare. They weren't Emma; that was their problem, but also his problem. It had taken him a long time to reach some kind of equilibrium and move on. But, six years ago he'd met Jen. They were good together. They'd even talked about marriage – vaguely -

and starting a family. He liked the idea of becoming a dad. If men could get broody, then he was well on the way.

'Eh, Danny, you going to do any work today?' Asif shouted across the workshop.

'Yeah, yeah, yeah,' was all Dan could think of in reply.

He eyed the car he was working on. It was a Beamer – 7 Series. Sleek, black, predatory. It belonged to a retired businessman, who'd obviously made a fortune; either that or he was some kind of criminal mastermind. Dan often imagined the latter; he looked the type.

'Heh, Dan, did you know that Emma is back in the village? The one you used to have that thing with when we were at school,' threw back Asif.

'Yeah,' Dan replied, grumpily.

'Well?' prodded Asif. 'Are you going to call her, see her?'

'Just fuck off about it.' Asif got the message.

It had cost him his 'A' Levels. He regretted that. His father, who believed a man had to make himself and not rely upon the props of education, hadn't been much bothered. He'd always wanted him to get a "proper" job as soon as he was allowed to leave school. But it bothered Dan. They'd planned, he and Emma, to try to get to the same university. He knew he could and should have achieved more in life. If he had, if he'd gone to university, he might not be working in this garage – even if he was now the best mechanic by a mile.

'A hundred fucking miles,' he said out loud.

'It's five hundred miles, you prick, man if you're about to sing that Scottish song,' Asif shouted. Dan chucked an oily rag in his direction.

He put away his mug in the tiny kitchen – if you could even call it that. On the wall, just below a faded early two thousands oil stained girlie calendar, was a memo under a heading that said "Company Notices." The garage wanted a secretary who could also help with the accounts. That could be good for Jen, Dan thought. He took a picture on his phone and texted it to her.

A reluctant exhaust pipe now beckoned. But as Dan worked, his head just wouldn't shut up. What would Emma look like now? Would she have changed much? He'd changed. He'd filled out. His lean teenage body turned to muscle, with just the hint, surely only a hint, of a beer gut. What would she make of him? Necessity had re-drawn his ambitions and dreams. He now felt more grounded, more realistic, and more boring.

Of course, the great thing about Jen was that she was funny; they got on really, really, well, had a laugh together, sometimes, a lot of times, didn't they? Jen was more him - wasn't she? She hadn't done brilliantly at school either, but she was sharp in her own way. She did have an even sharper temper when goaded, but then he wasn't perfect either. He decided he'd give her a massive hug and more when he got home.

Just then, his thoughts were interrupted, and a rhythm had started up. It was Asif using two spanners as drumsticks on an old steel drum. He was generating a real beat. Dan stopped what he was doing and began playing air guitar. They were soon working up a sweat. Dan thought they had the beginnings of something new for the band.

'Where did that come from? It's good, let's remember it for rehearsal,' he said.

'Just sort of came out of my head,' said Asif. 'But I like your solo. Start thinking of some words, how about Emma, oh, Emma, Emma, Emma?'

'I told you – fuck off,' said Dan.

# Chapter Three
# Emma

Emma began working on her plan. ***The Plan*** - as she uninspiringly called it, and now underlined it, on a blank sheet of paper. Up to this point, she'd been going on instinct, answering to some unspecified force, a force she'd suppressed for too long. It was irresistible, driving her into this new phase of life where she had unfinished business, things to sort. Sometimes her past felt like a heavy rock tied around her neck, dragging her down. But if she was going to liberate herself, cut herself free, and be the person she wanted to be, she had to *do* things and get organised.

Step one of ***The Plan*** had been achieved, and she wrote it down: *returning home to the village*. She could tick that off, she was here, she was re-established. She now had her own rented flat as well as her new studio and much to her surprise - when she got on with it and worked without distraction - her painting, her work, was developing well.

But that was not the priority. Dan was the priority, well, one of them. She called step two of ***The Plan*** - verification. Yes, she'd loved Dan back then, and she believed and felt she'd always loved him – even when she was married to Roger. But what about now? Was she really just in love with a memory? Since her return to the village, she'd only seen Dan a couple of times from a distance. He still looked good, fit, handsome, hardly changed – at least viewed from 80 metres. He still felt like her hero. Dan was the one person she'd met so far in life who'd really understood her, got her, listened to her, and listened properly. Well, ok, apart from Toby, but that was different.

Maybe, like her, Dan would have a few faint age lines appearing around his eyes now. Back then, when they were teenagers, she'd teased him about whether his hair might fall out like his father's. It hadn't. He'd joked – or, at least, he said it was a joke – that she'd be on the plump side, like her mother. She wasn't. When she'd first seen him again out of her studio window her heart had skipped, her stomach had clenched. That had been a good sign. That's what love did to you. Wasn't it? It must be right? It felt right. But she needed to check. How could she verify her feelings for Dan until she'd at least spoken to him again? It was all such a long time ago.

Her thoughts were interrupted by Toby and a cup of coffee.

'Eleven o'clock already,' she said, quickly covering up her notes.

Toby sat down on a stool; he looked a bit awkward. Nothing unusual there, he often looked awkward. But Emma guessed he was about to say something significant. She waited with a fixed smile on her face.

'Hey Em, you do know that your old boyfriend, Dan, still lives in the village, don't you? He works over there in the garage. Some kind of grease-monkey mechanic type.'

'Er, yes,' said Emma, sounding awkward herself now.

'Well, um, you do know that he's got a partner. She's called Jen. Jen something.'

Emma tried not to react. But the news hit her in the midriff. No, she didn't know. Ridiculously it had not occurred to her that Dan would have someone else.

'Oh right, partner, you say, good for him. Are they, um, married?'

'No, I don't think so, just living together,' said Toby. 'I was talking to some of his mates in the pub.'

'You were?' She couldn't imagine Toby choosing to socialise with car mechanics. However, she could imagine Toby wanting to confirm bad news about Dan.

Emma held herself together, their conversation moved on, and Toby eventually went back to his studio.

So, her plan would need a bit of a rethink. Life wasn't going to be a fairy tale where the hero waited for years and years for his one true love. No surprise when she thought about it. After all, she hadn't. She'd been married. But, nevertheless, she was rattled. Today had started well, what with the sun shining, but clouds were gathering now. She began to think things through as calmly as she could. It wouldn't be right to split Dan away from this Jen *Whatserface* - not if they were truly happy together. If that were the case, she'd have to do the decent thing, wouldn't she, and withdraw gracefully? But maybe they weren't. Maybe Dan only thought he was happy. In any case, he surely couldn't be happy in the way they'd once been.

That afternoon she wandered back into Toby's room.

'Tobes?'

'Yep.'

'Fancy a drink in the White Swan tonight after we finish - just a quick one or two?'

'Er, yeah, I thought you didn't like the White Swan? I thought it was a bit, um, basic for you - what with all those mechanic types in there?'

'Well, you must like it if you were in there the other day. Anyway, worth a try, just to see what it's like.'

Emma had some make-up in her bag, enough to spruce herself up a little. She put her hair up, then down again, eventually settling for somewhere in between with dangly strands framing her face. It was also important, for artistic impression, to show the three diamond studs in her left ear. She'd rehearsed some lines – but discarded most of them. This first encounter had to go well, and she was as nervous as hell.

# Chapter Four
# Dan & Emma

There she was, in the pub, sitting with some bloke. Wasn't he that tosser from the art gallery, that sculptor? Dan quickly turned his back on them in order to close the pub's big heavy oak door. It bought him a moment; he must think quickly. Of course, he could just leave, but why should he? He crossed the pub aiming for the safe haven of a wooden stool next to the bar on the far side. Out of the corner of his eye he noticed Emma glance up at him. He made it across the stone floor, ordered a pint, grabbed a paper, and buried his head. He didn't want to speak to her, he wouldn't speak to her. But as he took his first gulp of beer, he did sneak another longer glance. Bloody hell, she looked fantastic. Who was he kidding? Of course he wanted to speak to her. He wanted to speak to her more than anything, but he wouldn't all the same. He'd just sit and wait for his mates.

Emma's heart missed a beat when Dan walked in. Toby noticed her glance up, and he shaped to look over his shoulder to see who it was.

'Don't look,' she hissed.

'Why?'

'He'll think I want to speak to him.'

'Who's him?'

'Dan.'

She watched Toby slowly close his open mouth. But he quickly resumed chatting away, even though it must have been obvious he was now struggling to hold her attention. Emma was vaguely aware he was going on about his next project, but she couldn't concentrate.

'I've sent off a bid …London…I don't suppose…it's quite a big one…,' Toby meandered on.

'That's great,' replied Emma.

'Well, it's not yet, I haven't got it. Do you know what, Emma? I'm not sure you're listening.' Toby finished his pint, abruptly got up, and headed for the toilet.

Dan was sitting just there, thought Emma, on his own. This was a chance. Suddenly she was heading over - sooner than she'd expected. Talk about grabbing the bull by the horns, she was riding it through the streets of Pamplona.

Dan glanced up from his paper and carefully placed his beer down on the table, pretending he hadn't just watched her walk across.

'Hi Dan, remember me?' she said. Her voice was posher.

'You're back then?' he replied.

'Well, yes, I have been for some weeks. I've been hoping I'd bump into you so that, well, you know, just to say hello.'

'Hello,' Dan said, returning to look at his paper.

'Dan, we need to talk, I've a lot to explain.'

'You could say that.'

'I know I left rather quickly, you know, back then.'

'Yep, you did.' He picked up his beer and took another swig.

'I should have given you a better explanation,' she said, sitting down on the stool next to him.

For a moment, he was lost for words. He put his glass down again, and because he couldn't look her in the eye, he addressed the polished wooden bar.

'Look, Emma, there's nothing to talk about, not here, not anywhere. It's all a very long time ago. I've got a new life now, and I wish you all the best. I'm not sure why you're back here, but if it's to mess with my head, or rake up the past, forget it. It's nice to see you and all that, but goodbye.'

Then he looked at her, into those eyes, and he felt his resolve begin to melt when he could see she was close to tears. Perhaps he'd been a bit abrupt. He was just about to speak to her again when she got up, turned on her heels, and walked towards the door – picking up Toby as he ambled out from the toilets. She linked their arms and pulled him towards the door. Toby looked a little surprised as he glanced back at his half-finished drink.

As they left the pub, Emma also looked back over her shoulder. Dan quickly looked down, making sure his head was buried firmly in his newspaper, but he wasn't reading a word.

# Chapter Five
# Toby

She'd been very drunk that night, but then so had he. Half the sixth form had been in the village hall for the gig. Most had pre-loaded. The band, Dan's band, was very good. And Dan? Well, he was the outstanding lead guitarist. All the girls idolised him; all the boys were envious but reluctantly admiring.

As he stared at the blank, rather grubby magnolia-coloured walls of his room, Toby recalled that even he'd decided, back then, that Dan Cartridge was a decent enough bloke. That was in spite of his jealousy, knowing that Dan was with the best girl in the school.

But Toby knew he'd also captured a small part of Emma back then. She would talk to him, just as she did now. He knew he was always rather awkward with her; the words just didn't come out right. But she never seemed to mind, and she confided in him, she was relaxed with him. They "got" each other. Maybe, she did use him somewhat as an easy, always available receptive ear for her troubles. But he didn't care, she was always so interesting, cute, funny, beguiling, and beautiful. Yes, recalled Toby, his eyes losing focus, they had been very drunk by the end of that night eighteen years ago.

His mobile phone pinged him back to the present. It was a text from Emma: *'Thanks for drink at the pub. Soz not myself. See you tomorrow, xx Em'*

He texted back a smiley face and then reached forward to put his phone down on the table. As he did so, his foot collided with an empty pizza box, which in turn bumped into a dirty plate from dinner, which nudged against yesterday's take-away cartons. He cracked open a second beer and thought back to earlier that evening,

It seemed to him that he was about to go through it all over again. Déjà vu. Once more, he would be the third player in a drama that was now entering its second act. All he could do, as before, was hang in there and hope that in the end, he'd triumph and win the girl in the final scene. From where he sat, on his battered, but nevertheless rather cool, leather sofa, it didn't seem very likely.

Toby eyed a third can, which he'd left on the table near the window. What he ought to do, rather than drink beer and succumb to this mood, was tidy up a bit. His mother was due to *Skype* him soon for her weekly chat. He placed the laptop where he thought she wouldn't see so much of the room. He definitely didn't want her to notice where the paint was peeling off the walls, nor the yellowed, slightly damp, net curtains - the ones which hid the black mildew gathering in the corners of the old draughty sash windows.

His mother – and there was only her left now - lived in the south, near Eastbourne, and she only came to visit about once a year. So, most of the time, the state of his flat wasn't an issue. Anyway, he was artistic, what should anyone expect?

The *Skype* call chime rang out and he jumped, even though he knew it was imminent.

'Hi, Mum.'

'Hi, dear, can you see me, ok?'

'Er, yes.'

'Can you hear me, ok?'

'Yes, otherwise I, er, wouldn't have answered you, would I?'

'Very funny, how are you?'

And so the conversation began. It was always like this until they warmed up. Toby got on pretty well with his mother, even though she did fuss a bit. But he wasn't feeling quite on top form this week, and his mother, who had a highly tuned antenna for these things, sussed him out straight away.

'Are you *really* alright, Toby?' she asked, peering into the camera like a scientist trying to examine a specimen more closely.

'Yeah, fine, well, sort of, yeah, ok, hmm.' There was a pause. He might as well tell her; she'd get it out of him anyway. 'Do you remember Emma from when we were at school?'

'Yes, vaguely, tallish, seemed nice, lovely hair. You had a big crush on her, didn't you? She left the area in something of a hurry, I seem to remember.'

'She's back.'

'What do you mean she's back, back where, back in your village?'

'Well yes, where else, um, back?' he waved his fingers in the air for quote marks.

He watched his mother pull away a bit from the screen. 'And are you happy, or upset, about this *being back*, this returning from obscurity, or wherever she's been?'

'Er, not sure really, a bit of both, I guess. She, um, sort of married some bloke, and now that's gone wrong, she's come back to the village. She works in the room next to mine at the gallery, actually. She's an artist - quite a good one too.'

'Well, that's nice,' said his mother, but she didn't sound too sure.

At the time, he recalled his mother didn't like Emma's family – especially her father. '*A very, very, rude man,*' she'd called him. But Toby knew his mother was always keen to help his love life. She'd become very excited a couple of times over the years with the few girlfriends he'd had. Sophie with the red hair - she'd liked her, even though she'd only met her once. None of his relationships lasted very long. His mother often grumbled that she wasn't ever going to have any grandchildren.

'The trouble is, I think she still has a sort of thing for that guy she was with before, a bloke called Dan,' said Toby.

'Oh, I see,' replied his mother, rather haughtily, even for her.

But then, more sympathetically, she said, 'Well, Toby, if you want to win her, you're going to have to fight. There can be none of your usual giving in. Every girl wants to be protected and wants to feel secure. Security is at the root of it, trust me. You've got better prospects, I'm sure, and that's what you can offer. What does this Dan chap do?'

'He's a garage mechanic,' said Toby.

'Good Lord. See what I mean.'

'He's a very good one, apparently,' Toby added generously.

'Well, that's as maybe, but remember, you're making very good money now,' his mother continued. 'Not that you spend any of it. You need to offer her a home. Start with tidying up that flat of yours. A bit of decorating wouldn't go amiss. You live in a lovely Georgian building, make the most of it. You could put that beer away for a start. I can see it behind you, Toby, how many have you had?'

He glanced back anxiously.

'Why don't you think of buying a house?' she continued. 'I can help a bit, and I'm sure that between us, we can put together enough money for a deposit. You could ask this Emma to help you look for the right property.'

'Whoa, whoa, slow down, Mum. I think you're, er, taking things a bit…you know…fast.' But it didn't stop her. His mother loved organising everybody's life.

The call ended some ten minutes later. He certainly felt better for it. Although his mother was a bit full-on, she knew him better than anyone, and she did have a point. He resolved to carry on trying – trying to win the girl of his dreams – it was the only option he had.

He must do two things. One: work harder at being more socially adept - he'd practice on people that didn't matter so much; try more small talk; try to be funny and amusing. Perhaps he'd join the *Facebook* and *Twitter* communities, he'd avoided all that stuff up to now. It was daft, really, because he knew that these days all artists needed a social media profile. If he could become more comfortable with other people, and be more gregarious, perhaps he'd relax a bit more with Emma. He'd then become a more interesting and confident person.

And, yes, Mother was right; the second thing he'd do was smarten up his place. He'd buy some new furniture and re-decorate. He wouldn't go for the idea of buying a new house, for now, that was too big a step. But, yes, perhaps Emma would come around and help him with the flat, she was good at colours. She could be in charge of his *new look*. Maybe, she'd also help do some of the work. He could chat with her, and they could have a laugh. People did, you know, laugh when they decorated a home together, in films anyway…and well, over time, maybe…just maybe?

The main thing, Toby reassured himself, was that Emma was back in his life. He'd show her that he was the type of bloke with whom she could settle down; dependable; secure; with prospects; with money. Dan just couldn't compete working in a garage – although, to be fair, and Toby always was, he probably made a decent, honest living…being skilled and all that.

Toby prided himself on not being a snob, he read the *Guardian*, for Christ's sake, and he was sure Emma wasn't either. But when all was said and done, people liked to have a bit of money. It oiled the wheels of life. You could go places – travel, buy stuff, get away for romantic weekends. He liked the idea of that.

But Toby also knew he'd have to play a long game. He'd not expected to get a second chance and certainly not expected Emma to come back home, not after her family moved so far away. He'd stagnated – it was time for things to change. Things hadn't been right in Toby's life for a long time.

He leant back, sipped his beer, let out a long slow breath, and remembered. Back then, that night when they were teenagers at school, it had felt right. Towards the end of that evening, he and Emma had left the gig early for a walk. She'd brought a bottle of whisky along for company. She'd had some kind of an argument with Dan, and she'd certainly drunk more than him during that evening - a lot more. She'd begun to sing, yes, that's what had happened, she'd started to sing, setting the dogs off as they tried to join in. That's why he'd had to get her off the main path.

What was it about her anyway? Had he just fixated on her? Was she just an obsession? Did he just want her because he couldn't have her? No, he knew it was more than that; he loved her completely back then, just as he did now. That night, that drunken night, Toby had taken her off the path across the cricket field to the old groundsman's hut. There was an old sofa in there. She'd kissed him. Yes, in her inebriated state, it was she who'd *wanted* him that night.

# Chapter Six
# Jen

Jen was cooking dinner when Dan arrived home from the pub at about seven, a little later than usual. She could tell he was in one of his moods by the way he threw his bag down in the corner. She'd been in this place before, and she decided to take things slowly.

'Hi hon, everything's cooking just nicely, you chill out,' she said brightly.

Dan grunted, grabbed a beer from the fridge, and slumped down at the kitchen table. But then, to her surprise, he seemed to recover himself.

He sniffed the air somewhat over dramatically. 'You're such a good cook,' he said, putting his beer down. 'My Nigella.'

It was all a bit awkward and staged as he wrapped his arms around her and gave her a peck on the cheek. But it made things better – sort of.

'Ere, watch it, or Nigella will chuck the whole bloody lot all over the floor if you're not careful, and then it'll be à la bloody carte with added fluff and dog biscuits,' she said.

Everything seemed ok over dinner. But as the evening wore on, it was obvious to Jen that Dan's mind was somewhere else.

'Look at that. I don't know how she's so slim eating a pudding-like that,' Jen said, as they watched their favourite cookery show on TV. 'She wants to have another think about wearing that,' and so on and so on. Jen joked and shouted out comments, much as she normally did, but Dan didn't banter back in his usual way.

A fear, which had nestled in the pit of her stomach earlier in the day, tightened its grip and now began to constrict her throat. She'd left work early, taking back some flexi-hours so she could go to the hairdressers – the fount of all village gossip. Di, the hairdresser, in her usual mouthy way, had blabbed on and on about how this girl Emma had come back to the village and how she and Dan used to have a big thing going on when they were at school. Di thought it was all highly amusing. Jen didn't. But she did manage to give a masterful performance to all the other women in the hairdressers of being relaxed and totally confident about 'her Dan.'

'You'll never guess what?' she said, looking at Dan as he stared off into the middle distance. 'I say, hello there, earth calling Dan, you'll never guess what?'

Dan still didn't seem to be listening. Jen persevered. 'I say, you'll never guess what they were gossiping about in the hairdressers while I was having my – oh, that looks nice – bloody, sodding hair done?' Her voice had grown louder. She had his attention now.

He looked up and smiled at her. 'Well, no, you're right there, I probably won't. In fact, I can pretty much guarantee that; and your hair looks great, by the way.'

A semi-decent recovery, she thought. 'Anyway, this girl Emma, or something, is back in the village, and you used to have a thing with her when you were kids.'

The smile disappeared from Dan's face.

'We were eighteen.'

'What?'

'We weren't kids, we were eighteen.'

'Well, pardon me, whatever. It's true, then, you did have a thing. Was it serious?'

'At the time, yeah, not now.'

'How serious?'

'Serious.'

'On a scale of one to ten serious.'

'Don't be ridiculous, it's all a long time ago. It means nothing now. No need for you to get all worried and insecure.'

'I'm not. I just wondered that's all,' she said, trying to sound nonchalant.

But Jen was not a secure person, however much she tried. If people crossed her, and made her feel vulnerable, the anger would well up like lava in a volcano. She could then begin to *think* things.

She took a sip of coffee. She couldn't let the subject go, not yet. 'Well, you know me, never one to worry - like bollocks, I'm not - but, whatever you say, the fact is that tonight you've come back home in a big mood and sat there with a cloud raining on your sweet little head, so it's maybe not surprising I'm a bit agitated.'

The heat was on now. Jen knew what she wanted; for him to tell her that he loved her, Jen, the girl who first came to live next door, then moved in with Dan Cartridge, mechanic, musician, and all-around decent bloke, well mostly. Anyway, *her* decent bloke.

For once Dan seemed to read her mind. He stood up, pulled his sweater straight, and then, somewhat dramatically, he went down on one knee. He said all the right words. He told her how he'd met Emma briefly in the pub and exactly what he'd said to her. Yes, it had bothered him a bit, but it was nothing to worry about. He told Jen he loved her, he did all the right things.

Only Jen still wasn't sure. There was something about his eyes. They weren't saying the same as the words which flowed so easily.

Later she lay in bed, unable to sleep, at what must have been three in the morning. The darkness pressed in and led to even darker thoughts. This Emma girl had to go, she had to be persuaded to leave, to go back to wherever she'd come from. Jen wasn't having people *coming back,* assuming they could just pick up where they left off. She imagined that was what this Emma was up to. She knew women and how they worked. She certainly needed to keep an eye on things from now on. She'd go for that secretarial job Dan had texted her about. Then she could be near Dan all day. First, though, she needed to know more about Emma. When she got the chance, perhaps she'd pay the art gallery a visit.

# Chapter Seven
# Maddy

Alone in her room, her sanctuary, Maddy carefully unfolded a single piece of paper. She'd learnt by heart what it said, but it didn't stop her studying the words over and over. Drawing up her knees, hugging them tightly, she looked across the bed at, Marmaduke, her care-worn companion. He stared back, loyally. One of his eyes was a bit wonky now, and a small piece of stuffing was coming out of his paw, but he'd been a friend for all of her eighteen years, and he helped her think.

She'd come across this document by chance one afternoon when her parents were out. She'd been looking in one of her mother's drawers for jewellery to match a new dress, and, right at the back, behind a couple of old boxes, she'd discovered an envelope with her name written on the front. She'd taken it out of the drawer, hoping her mother wouldn't see that it was missing. She didn't. Neither did she notice, in the days that followed, how her daughter shut down, barely spoke, closed in on herself.

Today was lovely and hot – especially so for the south of Scotland. A cooling breeze blew in through the window carrying the smell of newly cut grass. Her father had been busy. She decided to take the document and do her thinking on a bench at the bottom of the garden. She liked it there when it was warm enough.

'You alright?' said Mum, as Maddy walked into the kitchen, the document carefully hidden under her top.

'Yeah, fine – just going to sit in the garden for a bit, it's gorgeous.'

'Well, yes, if you like heat. I find it all rather stifling. It's at times like this I wish we lived in America and had air conditioning.'

'You can have air conditioning here, silly,' said Maddy. 'You just have to persuade Dad to spend the money – that is for the three days a year we actually need it.'

'Aye, so we won't be getting air conditioning then. We've only just paid for this new kitchen.'

After pouring herself a drink of water, Maddy went through the patio doors, across the neatly cut lawn, which felt cool and ticklish on her bare feet, past the roses, Dad's water feature, and into the secluded wooded area where she sat on the bench. From this spot, at the bottom of the garden, it was easy to imagine you were somewhere deep in the countryside. The rhododendrons grew everywhere, knotted, thick, and tangled like matted hair. You couldn't even see the house from where she sat. Behind her were fields, there was little or no traffic noise to be heard, just the birds singing love songs or sending warnings and threats to each other, she didn't know which. At this moment she felt sure of herself, which was good because a lot of the time she didn't. Maddy knew now, more than ever, that it was time to channel her seething anger, the hurt, and her sense of loss. It was time to act, make decisions. It was time to grow up.

There'd been a day shortly after her twelfth birthday, a day she'd never forget; a day when her world turned upside down; a day that changed her life forever. She remembered every detail. She'd been planning to meet up with a couple of friends. They were going to play a new CD – Lady Gaga – and talk about what they usually talked about – boys. She'd also planned to show off a new top, bought in a sale. It had blue and white horizontal stripes - she could still picture it.

But then Mum had asked her to come down to the sitting room for a chat. That usually meant she was in trouble, but she hadn't known about what. When she walked into the room, Dad was there too, with a load of papers on the coffee table in front of him. It had looked serious.

'Nothing to worry about, but we want to have an important talk,' Mum had said, immediately making her worry more than she ever had. Was one of them ill, with cancer or something?

'Now, you know how much we love you?' her mum had continued.

It got stranger and stranger. 'And, of course, we've always loved you since you were a baby. Only…only… we didn't really know you when you were a very, a very little baby.'

A sudden chill had shot through Maddy. She was quick, and she saw immediately where this conversation was heading. She'd sat in stunned silence, her head spinning, her world crumbling, as mum and occasionally dad, painfully, excruciatingly, explained that actually, they weren't really her mum and dad at all. They had brought her up and would always be her mum and dad - even though they weren't - and they would always be there to look after her, and nothing was going to change. They said it was just that she ought to know the truth now that she was nearly a teenager. Eventually, the word came out. The word that had resonated in her head ever since. Adoption. She was adopted.

Maddy – apparently, a name chosen by her real mother - grew up almost overnight. Somehow, even though 'nothing had changed,' everything had changed, and the bright, happy-go-lucky little girl, who loved chatting away, painting her mum and dad pictures, playing silly games, and telling silly stories, all but disappeared. In her place was a morose, sulky, secretive, withdrawn, introspective child who felt abandoned, left to fight her demons alone.

For several months she'd hated everyone, most of all herself, and she took it out on herself. She tried to make the pain go away by self-inflicting pain, just so she could feel *something*, something real. She had to hide the consequences from her parents and everyone else - the scars on her arms and the trauma she felt. Over time – mainly by shutting things down inside - she got through.

Her parents, seeing it from their eyrie, had called it a phase, and they made excuses to their friends and relatives, saying her moods were down to hormones and being a teenager. To some extent that was probably true. But Maddy knew, from that day onwards, she was no longer the same person. She wasn't who she thought she was, she was someone else, from somewhere else.

Looking back, she understood why it had been such a shattering experience at the time and why it was still. It wasn't that she didn't love her adoptive mum and dad. They did all have fun – sometimes - and basically, despite her sulks, door slamming, and long hours spent in her room avoiding them, avoiding life, they rubbed along as well as most teenagers and their parents.

But Maddy quickly came to the conclusion that a certain part of her life wouldn't and couldn't be shared with them. They didn't really want to talk about the adoption. Every attempt Maddy made to find out more, or to talk about her feelings, she was closed down. The subject was changed. Her parents were obviously hoping that she wouldn't let it bother her too much. To this day, it remained typical for them to avoid discussing any topic which was either too difficult, too embarrassing, or too real.

On top of the upset and loss of equilibrium, Maddy was also angry. Surprisingly, perhaps, not so much with her adoptive parents, who'd certainly kept their secret for too long, against all modern advice and protocol. After reading stuff online, she wasn't quite sure how that had been allowed to happen. Another mystery. No, she was mostly angry with her real mother – whoever she was. Why had she abandoned her? All Maddy was told was that she was a young woman who'd got into trouble and wasn't able to bring up a baby. Her parents said they didn't know her name and that, in any case, she'd probably have married since and changed her surname. For some reason, Maddy believed them and didn't press the issue. She didn't realise they were lying to preserve their mantra of what was *for the best*. She hadn't realised, until now, that the truth lay in the back of a drawer.

What obsessed Maddy now was why a mother, any mother, wouldn't have wanted to keep her baby if she possibly could. It was 1997 when she was born, not the 1890s. It wasn't as if single parents, if that was what her real mother was, were rare. They were no longer ostracised, sent to the workhouse, or anything like that. Each time Maddy tried to think through a rational explanation she dismissed it, with the underlying feeling that no loving mother would give her baby away.

Now, aged eighteen, Maddy needed some answers. She needed to confront life. It would take courage, patience, and time. She didn't want to get into something which was bigger than she could handle, so careful contemplation was required. And, for the past couple of weeks, she'd just, well, looked at her piece of paper and thought about what to do next.

As she sat on her bench, and the dappled sunshine played around her feet, she knew she'd made her decision. It was time. Time for the search to begin. Time to find out who she really was. She carefully unfolded the document - her birth certificate - and read it again.

**Registration District:** *Carlisle.* **Name(s) (if any):** *Madeleine, Rose.* **Sex:** *Girl.* **Name of Father:** *Not given.* **Name of Mother:** *Emma Taylor.*

# Chapter Eight
# Emma

Emma didn't hold out much hope. It was like looking for a needle in a haystack, trying to find some kind of family resemblance in the dozens of faces skipping across her screen. And she was assuming her baby had kept the name she'd given her - Madeleine. What might her daughter be into? There was Madeleine Fitzpatrick, a surfer; Maddy Green, who loved equestrian, she just didn't know, and she was driving herself insane imagining all the possibilities. Her online search was a key element of *The Plan:* Step one - come back to the village; two – validate feelings for Dan and win him back; three - find daughter, Madeleine, or Maddy - as she'd always called her.

Social media was like an illegal drug – it was so addictive. Emma didn't even know what she'd do if she ever found someone who might be Maddy. Direct contact was forbidden. She'd read that she would be allowed to send a letter via the charity or authority who'd handled her adoption. But she didn't even know who that was. She looked online to see what other information she could find in any news stories:

**'*The natural parents of adopted children are increasingly using Facebook and other social networking sites to track down their offspring, flouting the usual controls and safeguards.'***

Well, she hadn't done that last bit, she hadn't done anything wrong - yet. In any case, she was the one who'd been wronged in the first place. The one who'd felt she was given no choice but to give up her baby. She picked up a battered photo, the one she always carried around in her bag, the one of her pretty tiny little girl. What would she look like now? Now that she was eighteen.

*This was Emma's secret.*

A secret to everyone except her parents. It had been a secret for so long that she didn't even know why it should be kept a secret anymore. But it *was* a secret, a secret wrapped in guilt and shame. The shame was inexorable. It went to the very core of her. A shame that had grown and grown over the years in parallel to her sense of loss. She had been persuaded too easily to give away a part of herself. What young mother wouldn't suffer after handing over her lovely baby? Her Maddy. She felt the guilt deeply too. But she knew who should really be carrying all of that; it was her own father. He'd persuaded her, he'd pressured her, shamed her. He'd arranged everything.

It was a Saturday, and Emma was in her flat. She closed down her laptop and put the kettle on – that was enough for today. Her obsession must be kept under control. It had been the internet, with all its possibilities, which first ignited her urge, need, to find Maddy. That, and being back in her former home village close to her baby's father; and, of course, the fact that she was now separated from Roger.

Living with Roger had been like putting her whole life on hold, while she pretended to be someone else. For the first few years of their marriage it had worked. She'd had a decent clerical job in the same company as Roger, who worked as one of the firm's solicitors. They'd travelled into the office together, had lunch together, and come home together. She'd deliberately spent all her time focused on him so that she didn't have any time for herself. That was what she'd wanted at the time to help bury the memories - "move on" - as her father had implored – and it worked to a large degree. But she'd also buried her true self during those years. She'd not painted, for instance, that side of her life was closed down, stored away in a cupboard.

It was Roger who constructed their suburban existence. Badminton on a Tuesday; the cinema on Sundays; a meal out once a week, normally Thursdays; sex on a Friday night. They rubbed along ok, that is until Roger wanted to start a family. The very idea had snapped her out of her trance, she just knew that it wouldn't be right. It would be a betrayal, a betrayal of Maddy. Roger didn't know about Maddy. So, in the end, Roger had to go; and she had to go and move on.

For the next hour or so, she tidied up her flat before deciding she should change into some brighter clothes - it would help put her in a more positive mood. She'd promised to go into town with Toby to look at some new furniture for his place, she was going to help him do it up. She'd agreed because, well, she liked his company, and she also felt a bit guilty for using him in the pub the other night as a way of meeting Dan.

Dan? Yes, she thought, that went well. Not. Their awkward meeting had stalled her idea of getting back together and telling him, somehow, sometime, that he was the father of her child, a child she hadn't brought up and neither of them knew. But he had to be told at some point. It would mean sharing her secret, and even though Dan had the right to an equal share of that secret, the idea terrified her. What would he do? How would he react?

She must continue with *The Plan*. The lesson from her encounter the other night was not to be so impetuous. She should have waited before going over to talk to Dan. She should have let him see her laugh and joke with Toby in a relaxed way. She should have played with her hair more, like in one of those shampoo adverts, gained his attention, teased him a bit, and got him interested. Then, she could have been more laid back and natural later on. Anyway, there was no point in further analysing it. What should she do next?

# Chapter Nine
# Dan

Dan's head was a mess. Ever since that night in the pub, he'd not been able to get her out of his mind.

'Are you coming to the shops?' Jen asked.

'Yeah, I guess.'

'Well, you can't come in your bare socks, so you'd better put some shoes on.'

'Yeah, ok. Are we taking the dog?'

'What do you think?'

'Might as well give him a bit of a walk.'

'Well then, once you've got your shoes on, you could get the dog lead, couldn't you? Because, you see, I'm carrying this bag, yes, this bag, the one I'm holding in my hands right now - full of clothes for the charity shop.'

'What clothes?' Dan wasn't keeping up.

'The ones we talked about last night. I don't know, Dan, you're not with it. It's been like living with a, with a, I don't know, a…'

'A wonderful, hunky, attractive man,' Dan said, quickly jumping to his feet and planting a kiss on her cheek, trying to prevent things from entering dangerous territory again.

He knew he was struggling to be himself. He had to get over this, get back on an even keel. He collected the dog and the lead, put his shoes on, picked up his coat, and they were on their way.

Town was ten miles away from the village. It had a fairly decent collection of shops, even though some had closed down and either stood empty or were now charity shops, like the one they were going to visit.

In the car, Dan turned up the volume on the CD player preventing Jen from nattering away as she usually would. It meant he could think. Once more, he ran through that conversation he'd had with Emma on the night in the pub. It wasn't what they'd said to each other that bothered him; it was the resurrected memories of their time together and what they'd shared.

Physically, she'd hardly changed at all. If anything, she was even more attractive. Of course, she was a woman now, not a girl. Her skin was still so clear and soft, her hair shining, her clothes…Jen turned the CD off.

'So, what I was thinking, Danny boy, was that once we've been to the charity shop, we might take a look at that new three-piece suite. You know the one I told you about? It's got those extra scatter cushions I really like.'

'Err, ok, how much?' said Dan, snapping out of it and getting to what he thought was the essential point.

'Well, how much do you think? It's not going to be cheap, is it? Fifteen hundred quid at least, I should say, maybe two grand? We've got that five hundred, and we can put the rest on credit - they're offering nought per cent spread over four years.'

Dan should have responded with enthusiasm; he knew he should. But all he could think of was the cost. Four years of monthly payments. Cost and commitment, it scared him. More so now, which scared him even more.

'Yep, ok,' he said. He'd go through the motions and find a way of stalling things later. Jen had turned the music down and was warming to her theme.

'I also think some re-decoration might be in order, parts of our house look like they haven't been introduced to a paintbrush for twenty years.'

'Hello wall, I'm a paint brush,' interjected Dan, deploying a funny voice. 'Yeah, and I'd like to cover you with sloppy paint if that's all right?'

'Hmm, well, I'll have to think about that,' Jen played along. 'Being a wall, n'all, I'm a bit straight about these things, and I tend to get plastered on a Friday night, so I might not feel like it.'

This banter could have gone on for some time; it often did. Dan knew they clicked in their way when they tried. Their humour might not be everyone's cup of tea, but, in this and many ways, he knew they suited each other.

But their brief good moods were brought to a shuddering halt when they arrived in town. In the car park, Dan spotted Emma arriving with that Toby bloke – the tosser. His heart quickened. He'd be nonchalant.

'Hi Dan,' said Emma brightly as she walked past.

'Yeah, hi,' said Dan, morosely. And that was it.

But Jen noticed everything. 'Who was that with the sculptor chap from the art gallery?' she said after Emma and Toby had moved out of earshot.

'Just a friend of his.'

'It's that Emma girl, isn't it?'

'Yeah, I guess so.' Dan was struggling with his nonchalance.

'Blimey, Dan, she's beau-bloody-tea-full.'

Dan said nothing. He busied himself, letting the dog out of the back of the car and putting a lead on him. But he thought that, yes, yes, she was. This was going to be hard, so hard.

'Right, you ready, let's go and hit the shops? Charity shop first?' he said.

'I mean, why couldn't she look like some old bag lady or something? How am I supposed to compete with her?'

'I've told you, Jen, you're not competing. It's not about looks.' But that wasn't quite the right thing to say.

'Oh, thanks very much. What, you think I can't compete? I should give up? Maybe you're right, what's the point?' snapped Jen

Dan took her hand and gently squeezed it, hoping that would change the conversation. But there was no need, Jen stopped chatting, and they walked silently into town.

Dan decided he'd deploy the trick that only men seem to possess. When there's too much to think about, don't think at all. Put yourself into stasis, a void, it wasn't that hard. So, after a while, he managed to park all his Emma thoughts in some cerebral cul-de-sac and turn his mind to the charity concert he was setting up for the band.

'Can we stop and get some new guitar strings," he said, as they passed the music shop.

'More new strings?'

'Yeah, I'm starting a collection,' he snapped. 'Actually, Jen, you never guess what, the strings on a guitar need replacing every so often, otherwise, it begins to sound like shite.' He'd meant to come over in a light, sarcastic, jokey way, but it just sounded harsh, and Jen looked hurt. Dan pecked her on the cheek. But that didn't seem to go down too well, either.

# Chapter Ten
# Maddy

She'd been quite happy to let things pile up, but Maddy decided it was time to tidy her room. There were clothes everywhere, mostly on the floor, while assorted compacts and tubes of make-up were scattered across her dressing table. On the bed, old magazines covered half-finished homework. It was a mess, but she had seen worse at her friends' houses. After spending half an hour methodically putting things away in their rightful places - she picked up her mobile.

'Hi Amy, it's me, any chance you could come over? I need to talk?' Amy said she would be around shortly, she was just finishing her tea.

Maddy spent most of her time in her room these days, either on her phone or on her PC, so tonight was not unusual. Occasionally in the evenings she watched television downstairs with Mum and Dad, but they often preferred documentaries, which definitely weren't her thing. Her room felt like HQ – her place to plan. Top of the agenda now was this summer's school holiday, which would be the longest she'd ever had, sandwiched as it was between the end of 'A' levels and university.

The doorbell rang, and Maddy raced downstairs. 'It's for me,' she shouted in the general direction of the lounge.

'Who is it?' asked Mum.

'Just Amy, we're going to try on some clothes.'

Amy jumped through the door looking like she was bursting to start asking questions straight away. Maddy quickly put a finger to her lips and they both rushed back upstairs. Maddy had pinched a can of beer from her dad's stack, and she now poured it into two glasses, then she opened a large packet of crisps and put on some music. They were set.

'Well, go on, what is it?' said Amy, expectantly.

'It's a secret.'

Amy looked at her wide-eyed, waiting for more. But Maddy couldn't speak.

'Right...sooo, you said it's a secret,' prompted Amy. 'Maddy, are you going to tell me what it is, or just leave me dangling in the air, so I actually, literally, go totally bonkers trying to think what it could be?

'It's a big secret,' said Maddy.

'Right.' Amy gestured for her to continue.

'It's like the bloody biggest you've ever heard so far, and you absolutely mustn't tell anyone.'

'Cross my heart and hope to die,' said Amy.

'You will, if you tell anyone, you absolutely fucking will.'

Now that it had come to the moment, Maddy was struggling to get her words out - *the* word. She hadn't told anyone, ever, that she was adopted. She'd carried the secret, and her shame and pain, for the past six years. It had been a burden, there was no doubt about that – made all the greater by trying to pretend to both her parents and her friends - not always successfully - that she was fine.

But if she was now going to *come out*, so to speak, it was only right that Amy should be the first to know, her best friend since their very first day of senior school. Amy had bumped into her at break time – literally. Maddy hadn't been looking where she was going, and they'd both almost tumbled to the ground before untangling themselves and bursting into a fit of giggles. From then on, they were mates. They did everything together. Yes, there were always other friends in their group, but Maddy and Amy were inseparable. It helped that they lived close to each other, so popping around to one another's houses was a fairly common occurrence.

Amy had also been there when she'd gone through that awful time when she'd felt worthless and alone. She hadn't felt able to tell Amy what the real problem was, so she'd made something up about a boy. Amy had stopped her hurting herself. She'd helped give her back some self-respect, some self-worth, simply by being there, by being her friend. She was better now, and Amy had helped. That was friendship.

By now, Amy was slowly swaying backwards and forward as if trying to give Maddy the momentum to speak. Several times Maddy opened her mouth like a fish gasping for air, but nothing came out. Then with a big effort, she managed it.

'I'm adopted!' she said in a burst. It was out. It was said. It was done.

'You're what?'

'I'm adopted.'

'Oh-My-God,' Amy spoke the words slowly. 'You can't be.'

'What do you mean I can't be?'

'Well, what about, what about…your mum and dad?'

'They're not my mum and dad – not my proper mum and dad, anyway.'

'So, who is…who are your mum and dad?'

'I know my mum's name, and I think I know where she lives, but I don't know who my father is. I'm not even sure that my mother, my real mother, knows.'

Maddy studied Amy's reaction as she sat there, hand over mouth, eyes popping out of her head. Amy swept back her mane of black hair and slid her hands slowly down her face.

'Well, that's the bombshell of all bombshells, Maddy. Jesus. What can I say?' she said.

Maddy suddenly started to sob and shake all over. The emotion took her by surprise. It was as if the sheer effort of telling her friend, of getting it out, had taken its toll. She collapsed onto the bed, hugged Amy, and wept uncontrollably for several minutes.

'Maddy, it's OK. Why didn't you tell me?' asked Amy.

'I…I was afraid you wouldn't like me, that no one would,' said Maddy, her voice steadying a little. Actually, she didn't really think that anymore, but it sounded better than saying she'd been ashamed.

'Of course I would, what difference does it make? You're still you. How long have you known?'

'Since I was twelve.'

'Oh-my-god,' said Amy again. 'Is that what it was all about when you were, you know, doing that stuff to yourself?'

'Yes, I guess it was,' replied Maddy, rubbing her bare arms. 'Anyway, now that you know, you mustn't tell anyone. I don't want anyone to know, they'll think I'm a right bloody loser.'

'They won't, Maddy, of course, they won't. But, yes, I've told you I will never say anything. And I really, really, mean I will never say anything.'

Maddy dried her eyes with a small cotton handkerchief and managed to compose herself.

'Good. Now I need you to help me. Look at this.'

Maddy handed Amy a printed sheet.

'I think that's her. It's a village in Cumbria, where my birth was registered, and that's her name.'

'It *is* her,' said Amy. 'You look like her, just like her, don't you see it?'

'Well, yes, of course, I see it. Scary, isn't it? Anyway, she looks like she's doing ok, not some poor, destitute person who couldn't afford to bring up a child. She's an artist, you don't get to be an artist – not one who makes their own living in a studio - unless you're from some kind of posh middle-class family,'

"Well, to be fair, you don't know that,' said Amy. 'And it was eighteen years ago.' She looked at the printout from the website and then back at Maddy as if taking it all in.

Maddy continued: 'So, what I'm going to do is this; I'm going to go to this village and spy on her. I'm going to find out more about my mother. You know, what type of a person she is. Is she nice? Is she horrible? If I can, I'll try to find out the story of why I was dumped. Why *did* she get rid of me, Amy? Apparently, she's not allowed to see me unless I want it, so I guess I can't blame her for not tracking me down. But I want to know more about her before I decide if I should reveal myself.'

'You won't have to. One look at you, and she'll know,' said Amy, looking at the picture again. "She looks like your elder sister."

'Yes, well, I've thought of that. I'm going to change my hair, the cut and the colour, or get a wig, or something, so that I don't look so much like her. And I'll wear thick-rimmed glasses instead. I can get a pair off the net, which just has plain glass in them. And, well, I'll just hope for the best. In any case, I'll keep out of her way. I'll collect information from people who know her in the village.'

'Right, er, so how are you going to live?'

'Well, I've got some savings, but look, I've been trawling through websites, and there's a job in the local garage as a secretary/accounts sort of person. I've applied for it. If I get the job, I'll be able to afford a flat or a room somewhere. And it'll give me a reason to be there.'

'Ok,' said Amy. She still looked doubtful. 'What do you want me to do?'

'I want you, Amy darling, to cover for me. I'm going to tell Mum and Dad that I'm spending four weeks of the summer with your family in Cornwall. You know, at your uncle's farm, where we went after our exams when we were sixteen? We did it before, and my parents spoke to your mum and stuff. I bet they won't feel the need to do that again, and as long as you're convincing, it'll be fine. They don't really want me hanging around the house all the time, anyway. I'll turn off GPS on my phone as a precaution, not that they understand all that, and they'll never know.'

'But you won't get that job if you can only work there for a few weeks.'

'I know, but I won't tell *them* that, will I?'

'And what if you don't get the job?'

'I'll think of something else. As I said, I've got some savings. Anyway, I *will* get the job. Who would they rather go for, me, or literally anyone else?' Maddy jumped off the bed, stretched her arms out, and twirled around. It was a good show of confidence, even if she didn't really feel it. She thought her plan was as flaky as, well, a flaky thing. But at least it was a plan – so she was going to go with it and hope for the best.

# Chapter Eleven
# Jen

Barney knew it was time for his walk. His tale wagged, his ears were pinned back, and his bright eyes looked up expectantly at Jen.

'Go on then. Go and get your lead. I'm not getting it for you, lazy sausage,' she said. Barney scampered off and returned with the lead between his teeth, his tail wagging ever faster.

'Just taking the dog out for a walk, Dan,' she shouted up the stairs. She heard some kind of grunt. Dan was having a bath.

Jen and Barney made for the woods. They didn't go that way often, but she needed a long walk today. It would be a chance to clear her head.

The woods stretched out before her. It was early summer, the leaves were a vivid fresh green, and the undergrowth was still relatively low. It was warm, clouds scuttled across the sky on an energetic breeze, and the light dipped in and out of the trees as though someone was playing with a switch.

The woods ran for about three miles between the village and a neighbouring hamlet. There were paths crisscrossing each other throughout, some were well-trodden, others less well-used. It was quite wild in places, and wild was what Jen wanted today. Barney didn't take much notice of the paths. He leapt off into the bracken, chasing some imaginary animals. Sometimes he'd go after a real live one, such as a rabbit, but, thankfully, he rarely ever caught anything.

As she walked, Jen began taking stock of her life – as she often did. She knew she was a worrier, but often when she thought things through, she realised that she didn't really have anything much to worry about. And logic told her this recent business with Dan was all a fuss about nothing, just her mind, fuelled by her insecurities, making five out of two plus two. An old girlfriend had come back to the village – so what? She'd quizzed Dan about it, and he'd said all the right things. Obviously, he'd been a bit thrown for a few days – what with old memories clouding back in – but he'd soon settle down, and it'd all blow over, rather like the clouds. Maybe, they could even be friends with this Emma. She seemed quite keen on that sculpture guy from the gallery, so perhaps they could do things as couples. They'd go to dinner at each other's houses and talk about holidays and furniture and eventually babies and stuff.

She walked on. Suddenly, she was aware of heavy footsteps behind her. They were coming at speed. Someone running. She looked around anxiously. But there was no need to worry, it was only Asif from the garage, out on a jog.

'Hi Jen, how's it going?' he said, coming to a stop, breathing heavily, whilst resting his hands on his knees.

'Yeah, I'm ok, Asif. You gave me quite a start there. It made me think for a moment whether I should be out in the woods on my own. Barney would do nothing to protect me,' she laughed a little nervously.

'I think you'd beat me off in a fight,' Asif responded, looking exhausted.

She was hurt by the remark. Asif noticed the awkwardness and spent the next five minutes trying to extricate himself from any suggestion that she was in any way bigger and stronger than him. He mainly just dug himself deeper into a hole until, eventually, he clearly decided it was best to cut his losses and continue his run.

'Tell Dan I'm OK for the rehearsal tonight,' he shouted over his shoulder as he sped off.

Feeling somewhat depressed now, Jen embraced a fresh set of doubts and insecurities which were now whirring around her head. Why would Dan stay with fat old her when little Miss Perfect was back and probably available? He'd said he loved her for who she was. But did he? The dark thoughts were clouding in again. She instinctively didn't like this, Emma. She guessed she was the sort of girl who was used to getting her own way, the sort of girl who would just walk all over you to win your man. No feelings, just a ruthless type, determined to get what she wanted.

Jen thought about the job she'd applied for at the garage and the idea of being closer to Dan – not just to keep an eye on him, but to be closer in every way. But she'd yet to follow through with her other thought of going into the gallery to find out more about Emma. Perhaps she'd revise that idea and go right in there and confront her. Give her a *"this town ain't big enough for the both of us"* speech. She smiled at how silly that sounded. But some version of it could happen. Action was certainly required.

As she walked on the path closed in and it was slow going. It occurred to her just then that she hadn't seen Barney for a while and she called out his name. The undergrowth was getting thicker and thicker, she had to trample it down. Clearly, no one had been this way for some considerable time. Then she heard a bark, it was Barney's bark – but some distance off to her left. The only way to get over there would be to plough through the bracken.

'Barney, Barney, where are you, daft dog?' she called.

She was answered by another bark, but it wasn't his normal friendly bark. This was the bark he made when he wanted you to look at something. Jen decided to take the plunge into the bracken. If Barney wouldn't come to her, she'd have to try to find him. She kept calling his name.

After about ten minutes of struggling through the undergrowth, with Barney's bark becoming louder and louder, she came across a clearing and a bit of a hollow in the ground. Jen negotiated her way around it and realised she was actually in a spot right next to the cricket pitch. Then she spotted Barney. He was running in and out of an old hut that was set back from the field under a canopy of trees.

"Sshh, Barney, for heaven's sake," she called out to the dog.

He ran over to her, but then he ran back again into the hut. It was like an old *Lassie* film she'd watched as a kid; the dog clearly wanted her to follow. At first, she just peered into the hut, then she tested the floor, it seemed ok, and she crept inside. The hut didn't look like it was used for storage anymore, and she remembered that a new groundsman's shed had been built over the other side of the pitch, next to the pavilion. Dan played for the cricket team now and again when they were short, so she'd had the dubious pleasure of watching a few games. They took too long – the best part was the tea.

Once inside the hut, Jen could see a jumble of old tools stacked up in a corner, there were some old cricket stumps and a rather distressed cricket pad. The only furniture was a big old sofa next to a small chest of drawers. On the floor was a tatty old piece of carpet or the remains of a rug. One of the windows was broken, and thin spindly branches from an intruding tree were exploring the roof space. But then she noticed the oddest thing – hanging on a hook was her Dan's old coat. So, that was why Barney was so excited. It was a coat he still wore when he was working out of doors or taking Barney for a walk. One of the pockets was ripped – she would recognise it anywhere. Dan must have been in here recently, she thought. How weird. She wondered why? Jen was about to go back out again, but something made her stay, sit down on the sofa, and take a look in the small chest of drawers. There was nothing much in the first two drawers. But the bottom one was full of stuff. She pulled everything out to take a proper look. There were a couple of old cricket balls, some clothes, and a load of old cricket scorecards, which had turned brown over time. Surprisingly everything was pretty dry, the whole hut seemed to be reasonably water-tight. Right at the back of the drawer was a plastic carrier bag. Jen pulled it out and felt inside. She extracted an old hard-backed, slightly dusty book. Its cover was a pretty pattern of faded blue and red flowers. Jen opened the book and quickly realised it was some sort of diary. She began to read.

# Chapter Twelve
# Emma

Emma was rather pleased with it. A half-finished pseudo-landscape in vivid shades of red, purple, and yellow. Over the weekend, one of her paintings had sold for eight hundred pounds, which had given her new impetus. But, even though her creative, artistic juices were flowing nicely, she'd earmarked the second half of this Monday morning to write a letter. Of course, no one wrote letters these days, they seemed so old-fashioned now. But Emma had thought it through. E-mails and social media were risky - they could be seen by an inquisitive partner; in any case, she didn't have Dan's mobile phone number, or an e-mail address. So, yes, a letter would be the best way to say what she wanted to say.

She looked out of the window across to the garage. An elderly lady hung onto her headscarf as she struggled up the street. Dan would be in there, she thought, working away on someone's car, so near but still so far away. She blew a kiss hoping the wind would carry it home, but before it was cleared for take-off, her heart sank. The memory of that *chance* meeting in the pub was still too raw, an unmitigated disaster – not only with Dan - but also with Toby. To make amends to Toby she'd since spent quite a bit of time with him. They'd bought things for his flat together, followed by a meal out. This evening they were meeting up again to plan to decorate his place. It was a good thing that Toby was getting his life more organised, thought Emma. She could help with that; she was good at organising - perhaps she could organise him a girlfriend. That's what he really needed.

Around eleven o'clock, she sat down with a single sheet of A4. '*Dear Dan.*' Too formal. She tore it up, deposited it in the bin, and started again. This time she wrote: '*The Gallery, just a little way from you...*' and then *'Hi, Dan.'* That was better, far more relaxed, and with a sense of fun. God, how she needed a sense of fun back in her life - back in her life *with* Dan.

So many dreams. He a rock star, she a groupie painting pictures and selling work along the way. His music, her art, that's what everyone said. She'd known it probably wouldn't turn out that way – but dreaming was dreaming.

'*Hi, Dan,*' she wrote. But what next? How much should she tell him? Well, the answer to that question was obvious – everything - but when and how? Would it be easier to put it all in this letter? Or would it be better to use the letter to arrange a meeting and then tell him face to face? What if he didn't agree to a meeting? Perhaps she could entice him along by saying she had something very important to tell him.

The news that he was father to an eighteen-year-old daughter would come as a total bolt from the blue for Dan. She imagined that for him, it must have been bad enough that she'd left, disappeared, all those years ago, but discovering she'd left carrying *their* baby would be an incredibly difficult pill for him to swallow. Pity, she thought, she hadn't been swallowing **the** pill at the time.

She'd been in a state of utter shock in those final few weeks before her family left the village. She'd bought a second testing kit to eliminate any doubt. There was none. She was pregnant. Not surprisingly, it took her days to pluck up the courage to tell her parents. She prioritised them ahead of Dan. She shouldn't have, she knew now, but back then, she was still very young and living at home.

After she'd broken the news, her mum had just wept. She'd wept an awful lot. Her father, however, hit the roof. That wasn't what she'd expected at all. Up to that point, they'd always been very supportive parents, giving lots of their time and wanting the best for her. Yes, she knew they'd be shocked, but she assumed that after an initial reaction, they'd come around and, at the very least, be pleased with the thought of becoming grandparents. Then she'd imagined she would somehow live with Dan – maybe marry him - and even though they were only eighteen, they'd live happily ever after. After all, dreaming was dreaming.

But her father had become incandescent, angrier than she'd ever seen him. He'd called her a slut; he said he couldn't believe what she'd done to her parents, that she'd thrown her life away. Her father had always been quite domineering, but normally she could manipulate him and get her own way. Not then, she'd never seen him like that. It was horrible. It had gone on all weekend. Her father wanted her to have an abortion. He'd scared her, he'd bullied her, he'd shouted at her. But she didn't consider it for a moment. Difficult though it was, pushing back against an avalanche of anger and emotion, she'd stood up to her father. It was her baby, her decision to make, and only her decision. But the onslaught exhausted her, and her defences were weakened. Eventually, after many arguments, lots and lots of tears, and, to her eternal regret, her parents persuaded her that if she insisted on having a child, she must give it up for adoption. They'd said the baby would have a more stable life with an older more mature couple. At the time, in her turmoil, she'd seen some logic behind it. It was true what her father said that having to care for a child would have affected, certainly delayed, university and her chances of a career, and also put an awful lot of strain on her parents. How feeble and immoral those excuses felt now.

Everything happened just before her 'A' Level exams, and she'd been away from school for three weeks, revising. That had been a relief; at least she hadn't had to face anyone – not even Dan. He'd called her on the phone several times, and with a supreme effort, she'd managed to chat to him, briefly and in a reasonably normal way, with her mother hovering near the phone the whole time. She'd explained to Dan that she had lots of schoolwork to do and they couldn't meet up for a while. He wasn't happy about not seeing her, but he'd said he understood that she was more concerned about exams than he was. In any case, there was still a little awkwardness between them after a big row two months or so earlier. She'd got drunk the night that happened. Toby had walked her home – at least she thought he had - she couldn't remember much.

The row was about nothing, really. Dan had asked her to come to a concert in another town – about a hundred miles away - to support him and his band. She'd said she couldn't because her dad didn't want her to stay away. He'd said she shouldn't always do what her dad wanted - how prophetic that statement turned out to be.

About ten days after that weekend from hell, her father had come home with another bombshell - he'd volunteered for a transfer at work. It was all going to happen quickly, and they were to move house. Move to another area. He told her she shouldn't tell Dan anything, as it would only complicate things. In fact, he'd tried to ban her from seeing him. She'd hated her father even more for that and, again, went against him. She did see Dan for one last time. A day she'd never forget.

They'd met at the end of study leave, and she'd decided there was only one thing to do. She didn't want to lie – just not tell the *full* truth. As someone once said, it was called 'being economical.' They'd met at the cricket ground. It was a nice day, so they'd sat on a bench near the hut. Emma told him her family was moving house - moving away – and that it was all her father's fault. She'd said they could try to keep seeing each other – but given the distance involved, it wasn't really practical. So, she'd said that even though she still loved him they should end things. It'd been great, she'd said, quite coldly, but all good things had to come to an end. She'd been matter-of-fact about it, just to get through the conversation – even though it was the opposite of what she'd really felt. How he hadn't seen through her, she'd never know. It was quite an act on her part, but she was a good actress.

Dan had at first been angry, and then he'd cried. He'd actually gone down on his knees and begged. He'd said she should come and live with his family. But she'd just repeated what she had to say, almost on autopilot. Looking back, it was like she'd been brainwashed by her father. The message fixed in her mind was to cut and run.

She began to write:

*Hi Dan,*

*I've wanted to write this letter and talk to you for so long. I'm sorry we didn't hit it off the other night in the bar - I'd wanted to arrange for us to meet and chat. Please read this letter now and listen to what I have to say with an open mind.*

It wasn't a bad start. It didn't explain why she hadn't written or been in touch over all those years. But there wasn't really an adequate explanation for that. Every time she'd thought about doing it, the story had become more and more complicated. First, she'd had their baby, followed by the deep trauma of the adoption, and then she'd gone to university and got a job where she'd met and eventually married Roger. At the end of the day, it was always easier not to say anything. The painful memories flooding back now were a reminder of why she'd trained herself to bury them in the first place. She put down her pen and stared straight ahead, her eyes slipped out of focus, and a tear crept down her cheek.

That day they came for Maddy would stay in her mind forever, although, strangely, she couldn't remember much of the detail - just the utter despair. Her family had been in their new house for nearly a year by then. She recalled staying in her room and staring at the wall for hours and hours on end. Her father had said it was best if she wasn't there for the handover, so she'd said goodbye to Maddy earlier. Her father had handled everything, so she'd felt he could handle that terrible transaction too. It meant she didn't meet, or know anything about, the couple who adopted Maddy. She didn't want to know then, and she'd never asked since. She remembered the mumble of conversation downstairs – and not a murmur from Maddy – she was such a good girl she slept through the whole thing. Then doors had slammed; a car had driven away, a car with her baby inside. She'd just stared at her wall.

It had taken her months and months to recover any semblance of normality as she struggled with the guilt, shame, and regrets. She should have acted differently over Dan. She should have acted differently over the baby. She should have dealt with her father. How had she let him influence her decisions? He'd argued that she had her whole life ahead of her; that she had talent as an artist; that she had a place at university; that she'd have been away from Dan a lot of the time anyway. She was at a crossroads, he'd said, and she had to take the right turn. So, she'd gone along with it. It was for the best. Her parents kept on impressing upon her that it was, indeed, very much 'for the best.'

*Hi Dan,*

*I've wanted to write this letter and talk to you for so long. I'm sorry we didn't hit it off the other night in the bar - I'd wanted to arrange for us to meet again and have a longer chat. Please read this letter now and listen to what I have to say with an open mind.*

*You meant everything to me back then when we were together – and you still do. It must have seemed very odd and cruel for me to have left you so suddenly all those years ago. What we had was special, very special, and the memories of that time still warm my heart today. If I could turn the clock back, I would.*

*Dan, all I can say now is that I was under the influence of my father, in a way which seems both ludicrous and pathetic now. The adult Emma cannot believe how stupid and naïve I was as a teenager.*

*Over the years, I wanted to get in touch with you to better explain what happened. But I met and married Roger – which, again, seemed a good idea at the time, but turned out to be a disaster. We're getting divorced. So, I hope you can see that the right moment never arose – until now.*

*Now I am back in the village – I'm back for you. I know you are in another relationship, and I totally respect that. I will not cause trouble. But if there is any hope for us, please, please, give it some thought. At least let's meet and talk about it.*

*All my love, forever,*

*Emma. xxxxx*

She left the gallery's number on the end of the letter - it was, maybe, best not to give him her mobile number yet - in case he stored it on his phone and it was seen.

She'd made the decision not to tell him about the baby in the letter. That had to be right. She hoped he'd at least agree to meet up, then she could tell him how much she loved him face to face, how she wanted them to get back together and then find their child.

# Chapter Thirteen
# Toby

He moved the bowl of nibbles, they looked better on the side table. A bottle of wine was open. Should it be? It might be better to put the screw cap back on again. Toby didn't want to give the impression he was trying to get her tipsy, although he didn't mind if she did. He decided it was best to keep the wine in the fridge and ask after she arrived. He'd tidied the flat, but he was now worried it looked too tidy, so he re-arranged the cushions in a more random way.

He shouldn't be this nervous. He really shouldn't. After all, he talked to Emma every day – they were good friends. That recent meal out they'd enjoyed had been good, a real laugh. For once, he'd been relatively relaxed, and she seemed to like his sense of humour. She certainly appreciated his views on art, and there'd been something else. They'd had quite a long chat about politics and the state of the world, something they'd never have done as teenagers. They agreed on most things. She described herself as a good-hearted left-winger, just as he was. That was important, he thought, to have similar views about life.

He put some music on. It was too slow. If he was going to have music it needed to be heavier. He'd let her choose.

Before he could worry anymore the doorbell rang.

'Alright?' said Emma, cheerfully, as he gestured for her to come in.

'Err, yeah, I guess so, well sort of, you know. You?'

'I'm ok, Tobes, really quite ok.'

'Drink?' he asked, then quickly added, 'Not that it matters if you don't, I mean, I know it's a weekday, and we've both got work in the morning. And...'

She came over, put her first finger across his lips, and then stroked his cheek. His heart leapt, he could have kissed her there and then.

'Tobes, stop talking, I'd totally love a drink. Pour me a big fat glass of white wine.'

I love her, I love her, I love her, thought Toby, as he went to the fridge to fetch the wine. He took a deep breath and managed to pour some without spilling. Then they chatted about the day, sipped the wine, poured another glass each, and, at last, Toby began to calm down.

'So?' said Emma. 'What do you want to do about this place?'

'Well, my mother thinks I should move out and buy a little house. I could probably afford it with some help from her.'

He let the comment hang in the air for a while, hoping that Emma would be impressed by the fact that he had the means to provide a home. She just sat, nodding, quietly turning over the pages in a brochure of paint colours.

'But I think maybe it's probably a bit soon to do that,' he continued. 'So, I just thought I'd give this place a bit of a spruce-up with some paint and stuff. I've spoken to the landlord and he's more than ok about it, which is not surprising, I don't suppose he'd ever get off his fat backside to do anything for these places. Anyway, you're the artist, the colour expert, what would suit the flat, and me?'

'Let's see,' she said. 'What colour are your eyes?'

She looked straight at him, and he blushed. He stared back into her eyes and was once again a totally lost soul.

Emma turned away. He noticed she'd slightly reddened. He was sure that he had too. Then, she turned to a page in the brochure showing shades of blue, and they discussed the various merits.

Toby thought the evening was going rather well, but then after about an hour, and with no warning, Emma said she'd better go and quickly gathered up her things.

'I hope I've been of some help, but I'm not really sure I have. I think I just came for some free wine,' she laughed.

'Not at all, Em, you've, er, been a great help, I think? I know what I'll get now. Do you, er, think you might help me with the actual painting? Say next weekend?'

'Can't do Sunday evening, I thought I'd go to that charity concert Dan is doing in the village, but Saturday and Sunday earlier in the day until about four-ish would be fine,' With that, she gave him a peck on the cheek, and she was off, leaving Toby flushed but bereft.

# Chapter Fourteen
# Emma

The stars were out, it was a beautiful night. Emma spotted the plough; it was the only constellation she knew. There were millions and millions of twinkling dots, all so far away, and all of them were just a little bit fuzzy. Maybe she should get some glasses after all, it was probably all that close work on her paintings.

From Toby's place, she crossed to the other side of the village, but before turning for home, she took a short detour. From her bag, she pulled out the letter she'd written earlier in the day. Its very presence had been nagging away all the time she was at Toby's, as though it had a beating heart of its own. It was why she'd had to get away, even earlier than she'd planned. Emma looked around her to check there were no witnesses, and then she dropped it through the letterbox of the garage. It was marked strictly personal and addressed to Dan Cartridge.

What would he make of it? She was beyond anxious about it. Everything depended on it, everything could backfire, and everything could go wrong. She didn't really have a *Plan B*. Would she feel that she had to quit the village again? Where would she go? She'd miss Toby. She quickly ushered any thoughts of leaving out of her head, this was no time for negativity.

She thought Toby had been a bit odd tonight, even more jumpy and nervous than usual. In fact, the whole evening had made her a little unsettled. Perhaps it was the way he'd looked right into her eyes and the way it had made her blush. It reminded her of that drunken night all those years ago after she'd argued with Dan. She vaguely remembered kissing Toby under a lamppost. But her mind was blank after that. She'd woken up the next day in her own bed, so he'd clearly got her home safely - luckily, her parents had been away. That was all there'd ever really been between them. She was sure Toby understood that they couldn't be more than just good friends. But the way he'd looked at her this evening, well, it was a bit intense. Mind you, she thought, it sounded as though he'd be quite a good prospect for someone; a successful artist who was beginning to get commissions from all over the country; someone who could afford a home and everything that went with that. It was certainly an appealing prospect – settling down, this time with the right man. Her parents had told her that they'd married in their early twenties, bought a house by twenty-five, and had her by the age of twenty-seven. These days it was so much harder for young people to get started. At least she wasn't saddled with a massive university debt, unlike graduates now.

Emma turned into her street. It was cold, and she wrapped her big thick cardigan around her. And then she saw it. Her eyesight was not a problem now. It was as clear as day.

Gary, the community policeman, was very sympathetic, but he said there probably wasn't anything much the police could do unless a witness emerged. He said he'd put out an appeal in the morning.

'It might be that your flat has been mistaken for someone else's. Are you sure you can't think of why anyone would do this?' he asked.

'No, I have no idea, I really have no idea,' said Emma, tearfully. 'Anyway, thanks so much for coming out. I'll be ok.'

Her neighbour, Sue, was standing by to offer further consolation as PC Harris got back into his car. Emma didn't know Sue very well. She'd knocked on her door in a distressed state, and she'd been a great help.

As PC Harris's car drove off they both turned. A succinct lacerating message was written across the window in what appeared to be bright red lipstick. It was there for every passer-by to see:

*"Go, you bitch, Go."*

When Emma had first seen it, she'd stood rock still for probably five minutes, unable to move, her heart thumping. She'd had trauma and upset in her life before, but at least her father's actions were meant to be in her interest. This was different. This had to be the single most horrible thing anyone had ever done to her.

Back in her flat, Emma rang Toby. It was still only about ten-thirty, so she hoped he'd still be up. 'Toby, you'll never guess what's happened.' Emma began. She told him about the graffiti and how she'd called the police, and about the kindness of her neighbour.

'I'm coming round,' said Toby.

'No, no, there's no need, I'm fine,' said Emma.

But there was no putting him off, and within a few minutes, he'd arrived on her doorstep, breathless after running over. To her slight surprise, Toby hugged her, she sobbed into his shoulder.

After another glass of wine and a full description from Emma of what had happened, Toby said, 'Well, my conclusion, Em, is that the police chap is right. It's, er, nothing to do with you. Who could hate you? Who could want you to go? You've only just arrived back here.'

Through the increasing haze of several glasses of wine, a thought was taking hold in Emma's mind. She knew who.

# Chapter Fifteen
# Jen

Jen knew she shouldn't have done it. She now lay in bed, rigid, thinking, panicking, regretting. Dan, who'd been late back from band rehearsal smelling of sweat, beer, and toothpaste, had crept in beside her. He hadn't said anything and probably assumed she was asleep. That's how she wanted it, she wouldn't hold it together if there was contact between them, of any sort. Given time, she could handle guilt, but at the moment it consumed her. Not so much because of what she'd done, she was glad about that, the bitch deserved it, but in case she was caught and would have to pay a price.

It was the diary she'd found in the old groundsman's hut which had got to her, eaten into her. She'd hidden it at the bottom of her tights and sock drawer and, until tonight, had only glanced at a couple of pages. But with Dan out for the evening, she had no longer been able to resist its' pull.

**This is the diary of Emma Taylor, Summer 1998.**

That's how it had begun, the very first page set the tone:

**What a night. Tonight, it was our first time.**

Every detail was in there, surrounded by little drawings of hearts and lips! Jen felt she couldn't bear to read it, yet she had been drawn to read it. The things he'd said to Emma, he still said now to her. The things he did then, he still did now.

**I thought I'd gone to heaven - I love him so much.**

I wish *you* would go to heaven, Jen had thought.

**We can meet here whenever we want. It's our sanctuary.**

62

She'd thought of how she'd seen Dan's old coat in that cricket hut. He must have been there – to meet her again. Their ***special place***.

None of it should have bothered Jen, it was schoolgirl stuff, all a long time ago, and she shouldn't be so suspicious about Dan. But it did, and she was.

**Our souls met; our bodies entwined – became one.**

After an hour of reading, she couldn't take any more; she'd jumped in the car and driven around to Emma's flat – she knew where she lived because she'd already followed her home one night. It was a relatively quiet road, and nobody was about. All the lights had been off, even though it was dusk, so she'd assumed Emma must be out. That had ruled out a one-to-one confrontation, but she'd had another idea. A lipstick could be very versatile.

At the time, she hadn't really cared about being seen or whether Emma might later discover it was her. In fact, she'd rather hoped she did. But now, back under the warmth of her duvet, she felt the cold chill of reality. You wouldn't need to be Sherlock Holmes to work out the guilty party. What would happen now? The police? Dan would kick her out for sure, and it would all be over. But if Emma remained a threat, it might all be over soon, in any case. She had to persuade Emma to leave the village.

Another hour ticked by with everything going around and around in her head. Dan was snoring now, so Jen decided to get up. She crept downstairs, avoiding the stair with the creak. She'd left the diary pushed under the sofa. That was another thing that had been keeping her awake; it needed to be in a safer place. She picked up a magazine, wrapped it around the diary, sat on the chair, and began to read some more. If Dan came down, which was unlikely, he'd think she was simply reading the magazine because she couldn't sleep. He was used to her getting up in the middle of the night. She was a worrier, so she often pottered about, or read for a while.

*'Tonight, I made the hut look really romantic. I picked some wildflowers and lit some candles. I had a bottle of wine open, and I rigged up the portable CD player, and it was playing Celine Dion. When he arrived, he was all sweaty, I think he'd run over... so I took all his clothes off. He was in a bit of a rush after that, but I made him do everything nice and slow. What a night – again?!!! He's my man, my very special, special man, and I want him forever...'*

Jen couldn't stop, but each page just made her feel more and more depressed, more and more hopeless, helpless, and, yes, angry. This was *her* man. How dare this woman have a part of him, have a claim on him? The diary entries detailed their nights in the cricket hut and all the other things they did together. Emma had also written about conversations on music, art, school, their hopes, and ambitions. It was all there, page after page.

After another hour, she put the diary down, and her mind began working through what she should do next. Did she have any chance of getting away with the lipstick episode? Maybe not, but if she was asked about it, she'd feign ignorance and claim her innocence. The first thing she needed to do in the morning was get rid of the offending weapon – the lipstick. She hid the diary at the bottom of a basket of washing. She knew for certain that Dan wouldn't look in there. She'd put it back in that old tin box under her bed tomorrow. Jen tip-toed back upstairs, Dan was still snoring away, it was three in the morning, and sleep eventually overtook her.

# Chapter Sixteen
# Dan

'Heh, Dan, how do you think it went last night, man?' asked Asif, as Dan shambled into work.

'Yeah, we were good – apart from one or two songs where we need to tighten up a bit.'

'Well, we'd better get it together on time.'

'Yeah, we'll be fine – let's have another rehearsal on Thursday night, and then I reckon we'll be concert ready.'

As well as Asif on drums, and Dan as lead guitar and vocals, there were two other members of the band. They'd first got together at school, but had only re-formed the band six months ago. They played rhythm and blues – old Eric Clapton stuff and other cover versions – but also some of Dan's new material. It was all a bit '70s, but it went down well in the pubs with both older drinkers, who recognised material from the first time around, as well as a younger crowd.

Dan loved it, the music, being in a band, the performing. He'd written one or two new songs for this upcoming concert, and he was nervous about how they'd go down.

He put his overalls on and popped his head around the office door to have a word with the boss. 'Tom, Jen just wanted me to check when she might hear about her application for the secretary job?' he said with a grin.

Tom looked up. It was hard to tell for a moment whether he was going to chastise or help. But then Dan detected a twinkle in his eyes.

'You can tell her she'll definitely be getting an interview,' replied Tom. 'I tried several times to ring her yesterday, maybe the number's wrong, so in the end, I put a letter in the post.' He paused for a moment, licking his narrow, slightly indigo lips. It was as if he was weighing up whether to say any more. 'I've only had three applicants,' he added at last.

'Oh, right, cool,' said Dan, cautiously wondering how far he could push this conversation. Tom continued. 'Yeah, one's a girl from Scotland, believe it or not. I'm not sure how she got to hear about the job, I only advertised locally? The other is Marjorie from the village shop.' Tom smiled, and his eyebrows shot up to the ceiling.

'Marjorie, right,' said Dan refusing to get drawn into the merits of mad Marjorie from the shop. He was going to play this straight. 'And, err, do we know much else about this other girl?'

'I'm not saying anymore, so away with you, man,' scolded Tom with a wave of his hand.

Dan was planning to give Jen some help for this job interview. He knew the way Tom's mind worked, or at least he thought he did. Even though the job was part secretary, part accountant, he thought Tom would want applicants to have some interest in, and knowledge of, cars. Dan was going to bring Jen in on Sunday, talk her through the basics of how a car worked, and explain all the engine parts. Mind you, she'd watched him stripping down their own cars so often - when they were first going out - she must know a fair amount already.

He was pleased Jen was applying for this job. Her current role at the call centre was a bit dull and not very well paid. The thought of her working in the same place as him wasn't a worry. Not really. It'd be good to meet up at tea breaks and lunchtimes and to see her when he had to pop in and out of the office with paperwork. But then a thought flashed across his mind – Emma. He tried to dismiss it straight away. That wasn't going anywhere, that wouldn't happen. And, in fact, if Jen was nearby, it would help make sure it didn't happen. In any case, he thought with a start, because genuinely, the thought hadn't struck him before - what made him think that Emma was still interested in him? Ok, she'd come over that night in the pub, but that was just to have a chat and to apologise for her disappearing act all those years ago.

He picked up his job card, and, curiously, a handwritten letter, which had been placed in his pigeonhole. The writing looked familiar; it was odd to get a letter at work - he'd look at it during his break.

The first job was just a routine service on a Vauxhall, which Dan could almost do with his eyes closed. The garage's new apprentice, Dean, was helping him. "Helping" had to be placed in inverted commas, but everyone had to start somewhere. He'd been new once, too.

'Deano, check the brakes for me, mate,' he said. He knew he'd have to re-check them, but it was time to put the lad on the spot a bit.

'Aye, will do,' said Deano, in his usual laid-back casual way. It didn't seem to matter how much he cocked up; nothing could affect Deano's mood. His mind was always somewhere else – probably on that girl, he was going out with. As soon as he got the chance, he was on his phone texting her back and forward and putting stuff on *Instagram* or *Twitter*. The rest of the time, he'd have his earphones on, listening to music. He hadn't said much to anyone – even though he'd been at the garage for about a month now. Dan found him annoying, but he couldn't actually say if he liked him or not, he just didn't know him.

'You coming to see my band on Sunday - we're playing in The Swan?' Dan asked.

'Yeah, could do if Mo wants to come,' replied Deano. Mo came from a neighbouring village and usually rode over on her motorbike wearing leather.

'I reckon Mo would like our music, rhythm, and blues stuff. She looks like the sort of girl who'd go for that,' said Dan.

Deano just shrugged in a non-committal way.

'I'll take that as a maybe,' concluded Dan under his breath.

Nights in the pub weren't what they used to be; people didn't come out like they once did. But this concert was for charity, and that might help attract a decent crowd.

At eleven o'clock, Dan took a break. He made a cup of tea and hid himself in his usual corner of the garage. He decided now was a good time to open that mysterious letter.

# Chapter Seventeen
# Maddy

Bright sunshine dissected the room. Shafts of golden light collided with millions of microscopic dust particles, dancing in the air, or revealed as a thick coating on the rather ugly Victorian furniture. Mum would never have allowed it, thought Maddy, as she lay back on her bed. She'd have been waving her feather duster about. It made her feel homesick thinking of her mum. She still thought of her as "mum," she always would - whatever happened now. Lying beside her was a big hairy cat rolling around playfully, inviting a tickle. He was a welcome guest; it made her feel better about things. The cat luxuriated in the sun, and Maddy buried her hand in his thick, soft fur. At first, he didn't seem to mind, but then he folded his paws around her hand and gnawed at her fingers.

'Hey, you're rough, you are,' she scolded, pulling her hand away.

Maddy had arrived at her digs the previous afternoon. She'd travelled down on the London train as far as Carlisle, and then she'd taken another local train and then a bus. The whole journey had lasted more than three hours. She'd booked online into a small neat red-stoned guest house on the edge of the village. It was quite reasonably priced. The money left to her by her grandma could fund her stay, but if she could also find a job, well, all the better. More importantly, the job would give her a reason to be in the village. It would be a good cover story.

She looked again at the letter she'd received from the garage inviting her for an interview on Monday. She'd been surprised to get this far, but on the other hand, why not? The cat waved a paw at the letter, she pulled it away and placed it back in her handbag.

'It's not for you,' she scolded. The cat began licking a paw, pretending not to care.

The guest house was a bed and breakfast, which would usually mean vacating the room during daytime hours, but her landlady said she didn't mind if Maddy stayed in, as long as she made her own bed. So, here she was at eleven o'clock in the morning, whiling away some time – time to think.

The big hairy cat stretched itself out and rolled over, all in one movement. It seemed very comfortable, as, no doubt, it did anywhere in the house. It clearly had the run of the place.

'Ooo, you're beautiful, aren't you?' Maddy said, stroking its' head. The cat purred even louder.

'Anyway, puss-cat, it's time I got on.' She picked up her phone and dialled a familiar number.

'Hey, Amy, it's me,' she whispered.

'I know,' replied Amy, rather taking the wind out of her conspiratorial hushed tones.

'Ah, right, of course, you do. How's things?'

'Well, *things* are ok so far. No phone calls or anything, if that's what you mean? You do realise I've got to stay in the bloody house most of the time for fear that your parents will see me – given that we're supposed to be on my uncle's farm?'

'Well, yeah, but remember they're going away themselves tomorrow for three weeks in Italy, so just hold tight, please, please, Amy darling.'

They talked for another five minutes or so in order to nail down their story and cover as many possible scenarios as they could. Then Amy raised a potential problem.

'You're using your real name, aren't you?' she asked.

'Yes, I have to because the garage will want to see identification, and I'll have to give them my national insurance number if I get the job.'

'It's just that you said your original mother gave you your Christian name.'

'I know, I've thought about that. But I've got no choice. It's a risk, but I'll have to go with it. It is a fairly ordinary name, after all. There are lots of Madeleines in the world. In any case, I'm pretending to be older than I am.'

That concern aside, Maddy couldn't believe how well everything had gone. Her parents had seemed delighted at the idea that she was going to visit Amy's uncle in Cornwall. Amy had been with her when they'd explained the plan. And, as she'd suspected, they didn't bother to get in touch with Amy's parents to check that everything was ok. Maddy had guessed correctly that, true to type, they'd always avoid an awkward conversation if they could. In fact, so untroubled were they by the prospect of Maddy going away they'd immediately booked the Italy trip the very next day.

'Well, if you're not here, we might as well get away ourselves,' Mum had explained.

Reassured by the chat with Amy, Maddy prepared to go out. She checked herself in the mirror on the old dark wooden dresser. What an extraordinary sight – she wasn't used to her new look - bright red hair which she'd had cut short with variable jagged lengths and a fringe, which partially overlapped a new pair of heavy framed glasses. It was all part of her disguise. In one sense, she didn't require one because no one in the village knew her, but she and Amy had been very struck by how much she took after her mother. With this look, she could, hopefully, get away with it. She texted Amy a selfie, and a reply quickly pinged back that she looked brilliant – followed by the obligatory smiley face and a thumb's up emoticon.

There was a knock at the door. 'I wondered if you'd like some lunch?' said Mrs Stewart, the landlady, poking her head into the room. 'Sebastian, come out of there,' she said to the cat, ushering him off the bed and out of the room.

'Oh, that's very sweet, but no, I'll be fine, thank you very much,' replied Maddy.

'Remind me again, how long are you thinking of staying?' inquired Mrs Stewart. 'Only I might get an inquiry from other potential guests.'

Maddy had been through everything with Mrs Stewart the previous evening, but it obviously hadn't sunk in. 'I'm here for at least a week, but I might be here for longer, maybe three or four weeks after that - if you have space, of course. I won't know about the possibility of a longer stay until next week.'

She'd kept things fairly vague up to now, and maybe it was bothering Mrs Stewart, who said, 'Only, you're very young dear, are you sure everything is alright?'

'Oh, yes, fine. It's just that I have some friends here, and we might be going off to stay somewhere else, but I won't know until next week.' She was finding lying easier and easier.

'I am actually older than I look,' she said, quickly, hoping this would reassure Mrs Stewart. 'I'm 21.'

Mrs Stewart seemed to accept that and left. Maddy wasn't totally sure if she had put her mind at rest, but everything seemed ok for now.

She picked up her interview letter again. All in all, she decided, she'd put together a very impressive application. She'd tried to tailor it just right. She'd said she had some experience of secretarial work, which was sort of true as she'd had a placement through the school which had turned into a few weeks of paid work in last year's summer holidays. But she didn't want to sound too clever, so she'd played down her academic qualifications a bit. Anyway, it had done the trick, much to Amy's surprise. Now, until the interview, she had a few days free to carry out some undercover research. She would try to find out a bit more about Emma Taylor – what was she really like?

# Chapter Eighteen
# Emma

She'd not heard from Dan. He must have read her letter by now. Rising panic fought with rationality. What if he really didn't want to see her; the rejection would cut her to shreds. But she'd only sent the letter a few days ago and he must have been up to his eyes practising for tonight's concert.

For the third time, Emma changed her outfit, her room a tumble of clothes, jewellery, and make-up bags. She reinstated her original look; a pair of tight jeans and a simple white top. It seemed her vacillating emotions blighted clear thinking on anything. She didn't want to look as though she'd made too much effort; on the other hand, she didn't want to look as though she'd made no effort at all.

Perhaps, she should have left her mobile number, and then he could have texted? Then again, maybe he wouldn't have wanted to risk a text reply being found on his phone. The whole secrecy thing made her rather uncomfortable. She didn't want to be the *other* woman; she wanted to be *the* woman.

She put on a brightly coloured big-beaded necklace, and then she tried a matching flower in her hair. No, too much. How about just a clip? In the end, she decided to put her hair up in a casual, scrunched-up last-minute sort of style. It took her ages to get it just right, especially the few carefully placed strands that had to look like they'd just been left behind.

She'd argued with herself over the last three days about whether to go to the gig at all. In the end, the bold get-things-done-and-be-out-there Emma had won. She was going.

Some make-up was required – subtle but significant. All the time, her stomach was tight with butterflies. She took another sip of white wine to try to calm down. She knew it would be awkward because Jen Whatserface would definitely be there, so there was little chance that Dan would come over and talk to her. Not unless he'd immediately given Jen the push after receiving her letter – but that was too much to hope for!

The deciding factor in her bold-Emma versus chicken-Emma argument was that it would show support. She'd always been there to support Dan when they were first together, every gig, everywhere, well almost, apart from that one time which had caused that row, anyway, and she would be there for him now.

She was going alone, but she didn't mind that. Toby hadn't mentioned the concert when she'd helped him with the decorating, so she hadn't either, assuming he'd either forgotten or didn't want to go. She smiled at the thought of him; Toby had been so funny with paint all over his nose. In fact, there was almost more paint on his face and clothes than there was on the wall. They'd done quite a good job of his flat. Saturday ended with a bottle of wine and a Chinese takeaway. Toby was relaxing a bit with her and didn't seem quite so awkward. He could be so funny sometimes – not always intentionally.

Emma wrenched herself away from the mirror, satisfied, just about. She picked up a couple of photographs she'd been looking at. They were of her and Dan back in ninety-eight. He had his arm around her, though she remembered he'd actually slipped his hand up the back of her top and was fiddling with her bra strap. Randy sod.

It wasn't until the end of the first song that she convinced herself that Dan had noticed her. She was sitting on a bar stool, quite a way back, trying to look discreet but directly in his eye-line. The woman she'd seen Dan with in town - who must be his partner, Jen - was giving it everything down at the front, whooping and clapping whenever she could. All a bit over the top thought Emma - this early in the evening, at any rate. Dan was shyly acknowledging the applause from that first number when he clearly glanced up and looked right at her. He smiled a little and nodded in her direction. He did, he honestly did.

And then Dan said, 'This is a song I wrote when I was younger. It's called *'This Time it's For You.'*

Emma's heart was pounding. He'd written that song for her. She would swear to anyone later that he looked straight at her as he sang it. Jen wouldn't have noticed, she was too busy shaking her head, looking at the floor, hair all over her face. Emma flushed, so sure was she of Dan's connection, and then, feeling too embarrassed, she also looked down to the floor. A bashful shy smile played on her lips.

At the interval, Emma honestly didn't know what to expect next. She hoped for some kind of contact from Dan, but she knew it was going to be difficult for him, even assuming she'd read things correctly.

'Hi, it's Emma, isn't it, I thought I recognised you?'

Emma turned. She was facing a big lump of a girl who was overflowing an obliging blouse. Fortunately, before she had time to respond, the girl helped her out. 'It's Carla, Carla Smith, remember me?'

'Yes, of course, great to see you again,' said Emma, spluttering into action.

The conversation ebbed and flowed through all the '*What are you doing now?*' stuff and '*What happened to you after leaving school?*' Back then, Carla had been a friend, well, more like just another classmate. As far as Emma was concerned, they'd never been close. In fact, she was beginning to remember, with every moment, just how irritating Carla could be.

'And what about Dan? It must seem funny you seeing him again after all this time?' inquired Carla, evil lurking behind her eyes, blatantly fishing.

Emma knew this question was coming; in fact, she was surprised it had taken all of two minutes to surface. Carla had never been known for tact. 'Especially now that he's moved on from you and is set up with Jen. But I expect you've moved on too, haven't you?' added Carla.

Emma decided to dodge the question and use the situation to her advantage. 'So, you know Jen, then?'

'Oh, yeah, we're great friends,' said Carla. 'We go to Zumba together on a Tuesday evening. Haven't you met her yet?'

'No, I've not had the chance. What's she...?' But before she could finish the sentence, Carla was waving for Jen to come over.

Oh, my god, thought Emma, what a nightmare, one which hadn't occurred to her? Now the woman she suspected of writing a hate message on her window, the woman who had her man, at least for now, the woman she'd least like to spend time with in the whole world, was coming over.

'Hey Carla, how you doing? Great, aren't they?' Jen said, waving vaguely in the direction of the stage, blanking Emma.

'Yeah, brilliant. Jen, have you met Emma, we went to school together but I haven't seen her for years?'

'No, well, only in passing, hi, pleased to meet you,' said Jen, with a beaming smile and eyes that remained elusive.

'Pleased to meet you too,' Emma lied. They exchanged a few comments about how good the band was, and Jen emphasised how '*her*' Dan was the star. Emma nodded politely, and then during a brief pause in the conversation, she managed to excuse herself. She shot off towards the toilets, pushing past a red-haired girl who seemed to block her path.

'Bitch,' she muttered under her breath, not at the girl, but because of Jen. It was time to go and powder her nose, mop her brow, and re-group.

When she came out, some ten minutes later, there was another shock. She bumped straight into Dan, almost knocking a pint of beer out of his hand.

'Hey, fuck, watch it there,' said Dan.

'Oh, sorry,' said Emma.

'Oh, it's you,' said Dan, brushing some splashes of beer from his shirt with his spare hand.

'Yeah, I'm loving the concert, really great,' said Emma, more awkwardly than she wanted.

'Thanks, yeah, well, yes, no, I mean, I think it's going, well, ok, anyway,' said Dan.

There was a pause. Then they both tried to say something at once and then they both laughed.

'Listen,' said Dan in a hushed voice. 'I agree we need to talk; it'd be cool to catch up and go through old times.' His tone was completely different from the night in the pub. The letter had worked. 'I'll ring you at the gallery, will they put me through?'

'Um, yes, no problem, there's an extension in my room. That'd be great.'

She glanced across the room to see whether the Jen woman had noticed. But she was engrossed in a conversation, so she reached for

Dan's hand and squeezed it. He didn't pull it away, and he squeezed back.

The rest of the evening passed in a blur. Emma was so happy. Her heart was singing, her pulse was racing, and as more wine flowed to her head, she danced along to the music, full of wonderful thoughts. Everything was going to be alright. She was sure.

# Chapter Nineteen
# Maddy

Maddy had seen everything. Sat to one side of the make-shift stage, she'd watched her mother like a wily fox in the shadows. How cool she'd looked, how young she'd looked, how coy she'd looked. And then, in the end, how happy she'd looked. Maddy had seen a poster for the concert the day before and thought it might be interesting and possibly productive to go. She wouldn't stay late because her job interview was the following day. So, she'd arrived at the pub quite early and bought herself a drink. She hoped she might see her mother but thought it unlikely.

The last few days had been spent trying to gather background information, but it hadn't been easy. Maddy had visited the art gallery a couple of times and looked around without actually going upstairs to the studios. She didn't want to accidentally on purpose, or even accidentally not on purpose, bump into her mother – not at this stage. Instead, she'd engaged in an awkward conversation with the gallery manager asking rather too many questions about the artists. It was actually very difficult to find out about someone without it being too obvious. How did they do it on those private detective shows on the telly? It always seemed so easy.

So, what did she know so far? That her mother had only recently returned to the village; that she was an abstract artist; that she had an exhibition coming up; and that she was good friends with a sculptor, who also worked at the gallery, called Toby. She didn't know how 'good friends' they were – and …err… that was about it.

She'd also followed her mother home – at some distance. It was the first time she'd seen her in the flesh, even if it was from behind. It had felt incredibly odd to Maddy to think that this woman, walking about eighty metres or so ahead, was actually *her* mother. What had been even more surreal was that her mother, Emma Taylor, a professional artist, etc., etc., was totally unaware that her own daughter was lurking just behind. For all Maddy knew, Emma Taylor didn't even know that her daughter was still alive – and probably didn't care. She hadn't cared much eighteen years ago.

But when Maddy had walked past Emma's place, she'd noticed something rather strange. It was obvious that some kind of message had been written and then rubbed out on the window - there were still marks and an outline of the words. Maddy had walked back past again to see if she could read what it said – taking care, of course, not to be spotted. She could just about make out the words '*go*' and '*home,*' and she'd caught her breath. My god, she'd thought, she's not very popular around here.

The band was warming up when she arrived in the pub, checking the sound system, calling out 'one-two, one-two.' She wasn't going to drink any alcohol, as she wanted to keep a clear head. She was just going to observe things and, to be honest, see if there were any nice boys in this village. If she was going to live here for a while, then she might as well see if she could acquire a boyfriend for the duration. She'd finished with Harry about six months ago, he was just too wet. He would not get on with things, despite encouragement, and to her embarrassment at the time, but massive relief now, she was one of the few so-called 'cool' girls in the school – as far as she could tell – who hadn't, gone all the way. She didn't mind, though, she'd been brought up to be careful, there was plenty of time in her life, and, anyway, university was bound to throw up a better standard than Harry. But now, on the other hand, if she was here in this village, away from home for a bit, well, maybe it was time to grow up. As she mulled all this over, her mother, her real mother, walked in.

Maddy's heart leapt. It was the first time she'd seen her this close. She was looking good. She could easily pass for someone in her late twenties. Just how young was she when she became a parent? Maddy's adoptive mother was fifty-six, so it felt totally weird to look at this woman, who could pass for her sister, and think that they were mother and daughter. Another point occurred - following on from her earlier train of thought about getting a boyfriend - that's what can happen to a teenage girl who isn't careful.

She had a real air of confidence, this Emma Taylor, thought Maddy, as Emma sat next to the bar on just about the last stool available. It was difficult for Maddy to put her finger on why. Perhaps it was the way she'd glided across the floor, quickly making a decision on where to sit, with a self-awareness that demonstrated she knew she was attracting admiring or jealous glances? Maddy watched her intensely, while making sure her mother didn't notice the scrutiny. Maddy decided that, although she couldn't but admire this woman on the bar stool, it didn't alter her prevailing opinion; she couldn't love a woman who, so obviously, hadn't loved her. Being this close hadn't reduced the distance between them.

Then something caught her attention during the band's second song. She noticed that her mother's eyes were glued on the lead guitarist, and how she then flushed, smiled shyly, and seemed embarrassed. She wondered if anyone else had spotted it. Certainly not that head-banging woman down the front, who'd been all over the same singer after the first song. It probably didn't mean anything, but it was fascinating this people-watching thing.

In the interval, Maddy went to buy herself another drink, and as she stood at the bar, a guy, who was also waiting to be served, said hi and introduced himself as Deano. He said that he hadn't noticed her in the village before.

'No, you can tell from my accent that I'm not from around these parts,' replied Maddy, exaggerating her soft Scottish tones.

They chatted for a while. Deano said he worked in the garage, and Maddy told him she had an interview there the next day. Deano seemed delighted.

'Oh, you'll love it,' he said. 'Well, actually, you probably won't. Tom, the boss, is a bit hard work. But all of us mechanics are a laugh.'

Maddy quickly decided that, although he was quite good-looking, he wasn't someone she was interested in and she made her excuses. As she came back across the bar, her mother was hopping off her stool and heading for the loo. They were on a collision course.

'Ooops, sorry,' said Maddy as Emma brushed past in something of a hurry.

Her mother gave her a half smile, but then Maddy was sure she heard her mutter the word "bitch." Charming, she thought, what a horrid woman, so rude? It was a fascinating insight and not very encouraging.

The band was taking a break for about half an hour, and, back at her table, Maddy reflected on what it was she wanted from this experiment. The idea, of course, was to find out more about her mother - to find out if she actually wanted to reveal herself and establish a relationship. But what else did she need to know? Well, first, answers to the big questions of why she'd been dumped as a baby and whether her mother had ever loved her. But it was also important to find out as much as possible about what sort of person her mother was now. Although this chance meeting tonight had been interesting and possibly revealing, she needed more.

Then she noticed something even stranger. Her mother had come out of the toilet and was talking to the band leader. And then they squeezed each other's hands. Maddy was sure the band leader was with the woman down the front. Something very odd was definitely going on there.

All the more reason to find someone who knew her mother really well and do it in a plausible, casual way. It was going to be tricky, very tricky, and she probably hadn't thought it through carefully enough. She needed that job. If she was going to find out more, she needed a reason to be in the village and a way to meet more people. The job would buy her time.

# Chapter Twenty
# Dan

The letter was stunning. Not because it hadn't occurred to him that Emma might want to see him again. He wasn't being cocky; he knew what they had before had been special. But the tone and boldness of the letter had knocked Dan off his feet. Several lines were lodged firmly in his head.

*'You meant everything to me back then when we were together - and you still do.'* And *'I'm back for you.'*

That's what she'd said. Fucking hell! Amazing. But what to do next? That was the question, and it was one that, for now, he couldn't answer. Jen had been so good for him. But he also felt he wanted Emma. It was a bit of a nightmare, but nevertheless an exciting one.

'Concentrate, Dan, concentrate,' he muttered to himself as he plugged in his guitar. 'You don't want to screw this up, not in front of all these people.' The concert was due to start in a couple of minutes.

'Hey Dan, we're going to knock 'em dead, man,' said Asif, high-fiving him.

'You just play the fucking drums and don't get too carried away,' Dan replied.

'No worries, man. And you just remember the words,' laughed Asif, adding, 'It looks like we've got a good crowd in.'

Dan looked around the bar. She wasn't there. It had been a lovely warm bank holiday and for once everyone seemed to be in a good mood, and rather thirsty. There was certainly a good atmosphere in the old bar.

And then in *she* walked, looking great, looking cool. Jen had her arms looped around his neck at the time and was whispering in his ear, so she didn't see, which was probably just as well. He kissed Jen on the cheek. She was great, always really supportive. Like Emma used to be – like Emma still was, or so it seemed.

His own composition, *This Time It's for You,* was the second song. He'd always planned to sing it, whether *she* was there or not, but as he began to belt it out, he knew exactly what the lyrics would mean to her. His eyes locked onto Emma, and he just sang to her. He couldn't stop himself. He hadn't planned to do that. He didn't really know where it came from, this urge to lay himself bare in this way. Luckily, Jen was oblivious, head-banging away just in front of him.

A cacophony of thoughts, a kind of running background commentary, chuntered through his mind as he sang and his fingers raced across the guitar. It was madness, these feelings, but there she was, loving the music, just like she used to.

The concert was going brilliantly, and when they came to the interval, there was a rapturous round of applause, cheering, and whooping – mainly from Jen.

'What do you think, brilliant isn't it?' said Asif, climbing off his stool and manoeuvring around his drums.

'Yeah, great. It's going well. But I screwed up a bit a couple of times,' said Dan. 'I got totally the wrong chord at one point, I lost concentration, did you notice? Do you think *they* noticed?'

'Nah, no problem, man, chill, it's brilliant,' Asif assured him. 'Stop thinking about that, Emma.'

Dan glanced across the pub, oh my God, Jen was now talking to Emma. It was too late to do anything about it. He watched in horror for a moment, frozen to the spot. But the conversation didn't seem to last long, and Emma soon went off to the loo. He hoped no damage was done.

Dan went to the bar, and friends and people he didn't know slapped him on the back as he squeezed through. Then, as he returned to the stage with a pint, out of the ladies' loo popped Emma and they nearly collided.

Before his mind had really worked out what to do, he was talking to her and saying that they ought to meet and that he'd ring her. And then she'd squeezed his hand, and he'd squeezed hers back, and there…it was done, they'd made a connection.

It was too late to undo anything now. He was on a path. He didn't know where it was going to lead, or whether he should be on it. Well, of course, he knew he shouldn't be on it, not if he had an ounce of loyalty to Jen. But it was almost like he'd jumped aboard a non-stop train, and there was no getting off. The main problem was, he didn't want to.

# Chapter Twenty-One
# Jen

A hangover was inescapable. It was what it was. However much you tried to deal with it – a shower, consuming lots of water, coffee, a big fried breakfast, headache pills, hair-of-the-dog, tiger-balm – it lingered, it nagged, sometimes a little, sometimes a lot. Jen's was mid-range. She could probably cope with it as long as nothing bad happened and no-one annoyed her too much. Dan had been a help so far, creeping about, being very quiet and very gentle. He'd already brought her a nice hot cup of tea, and he'd only opened the curtains a tiny bit. He'd kissed her on the top of her forehead, which was a good decision on his part, as her mouth felt and tasted like the bottom of a parrot's cage.

As she lay in bed, slowly recuperating, she had to admit that although drinking more than a bottle of wine may have seemed a good idea at the time, it was now feeling like something of an own goal. She had a job interview in three hours' time.

She glanced at the clock. It was seven - plenty of time to pull herself together. She sipped her tea. She could hear Dan singing to himself in the shower; it sounded like one of his own numbers from last night. The concert went really well. Brilliantly, in fact. They'd raised more than five hundred pounds for charity; the pub had been full; people really liked the music, and the landlord wanted them to put on another gig in a month's time. It was a great night, and Jen had had a ball. She always was going to have a ball. She wasn't going to let the presence of that woman put her off. What was she doing there anyway? The concert had nothing to do with her. And being introduced – OMG - that had been bizarre. She could kill bloody Carla for calling her over like that – still, she'd played it cool, and their chat had been mercifully brief.

She stretched a leg out from under the duvet and carefully reached down to the floor. Then the other ventured out, and she gradually sat up on the side of the bed. Each stage taken very slowly. She hoped the pain in her head would go away soon. As she sat for a moment and took stock, it occurred to her that it had been nearly a week now since she'd left her lipstick-written message on Emma Taylor's window, and, so far, nothing. No knock on the door, no police officer, no awkward questions, nothing. She might, just might, have got away with it. As far as she could tell, Dan didn't know about it; and there was no suggestion from her brief chat with Miss Arty-Farty that she suspected her. So, all things considered, that was a big relief. She allowed herself a small inward smile as she staggered to the bathroom, passing Dan on the landing.

As the shower's hot water washed over her, Jen thought through how she'd have to remain very much on her guard. Keeping her temper was going to be difficult. The bloody woman was still here, still putting herself about in all her glory, still sitting up there on her bar stool, looking pert, alluring, and tempting. Dan had obviously noticed her, and although he hadn't said anything, Jen could tell throughout the concert that he'd been aware of her presence. For starters, he'd repeatedly looked over in her direction. She'd noticed him alright, despite doing her groupie head-banging thing down the front.

Nearly three hours later, she made the short walk to the garage for the interview. Dan had been working there for a couple of hours by then. She gave him a little wave as his head emerged from under a car.

'Y'alright, Deano?' she asked in the reception area. She'd met Deano a couple of times before. He seemed to be organising things and was a little flustered.

'Yeah, fine, you're to wait in here until the other interview is finished. I'm supposed to apologise to you that you've got to share the room with another candidate who's arrived a bit early. This is Maddy,' he said, opening the door to an office.

'Hi, Maddy, I'm Jen.'

'Pleased to meet you, Jen.'

Maddy seemed a rather serious girl of maybe twenty, with red hair, a pair of thick-rimmed glasses, and an obvious Scottish accent. Jen immediately noticed that Maddy was much more smartly dressed. Damn, she thought, another mistake. She picked up a magazine to read.

'Did I see you at the concert in the pub last night?' asked Maddy, breaking a short silence.

'Oh yeah, were you there too? Good, wasn't it?'

'Yeah, I thought it was cool, not bad at all, actually. Are you, err, with the main singer?'

'What, you mean, Dan? Yes, we're together.' This girl was a nosey bitch, thought Jen. 'He works here at the garage too, which is how I got to know about the vacancy,' she added, wishing she hadn't. Mentioning the job seemed to bring an awkward silence. But the red-haired nosey Scottish one wasn't going to be put off for too long.

'Do you live in the village?' she asked.

'Just down the road. But you don't, I'm guessing, I've not seen you about.'

'No, I'm from Scotland, but I fancy living somewhere else for a bit.'

Jen thought she seemed quite young, this girl, to be setting up on her own. But then she remembered that she, herself, had only been about twenty-three when she'd moved to the village, principally to get away from her parents.

They chatted about this and that for the next half an hour or so, and Jen decided that she actually quite liked this girl. She had a really good dry sense of humour. Jen put her inquisitiveness down to just being friendly. She was also obviously very bright - which was a worry in terms of the job unless, of course, she proved to be too intelligent and that put Tom off.

Eventually, another woman, who Jen recognised from the village shop, came out of Tom's office. She and Maddy both smiled at her as Tom followed her out.

'Err, Miss, um, well, err, Jen, would you like to come in now?' said Tom, awkwardly.

Tom's office was even smaller than the waiting room. She had to stand to one side while he shuffled around and sat behind an old shabby-looking wooden desk. Next to him was a plump, round-faced woman with very stiff dark hair shaped in a bob. Jen didn't know her. She was so tightly squeezed into the available space it looked as though she'd never get out. Jen sat down on a slightly rickety old wooden chair in front of the desk. She folded her hands in her lap and smiled her best smile.

'This is Mrs Kingston, she's from Kingston's Employment Agency, and she's helping with the interviews,' said Tom, rather proudly.

Jen hadn't anticipated an outsider – this might be more difficult than she thought. She'd assumed – what with Dan working at the garage - that she'd just have a low-key chat with Tom and be a bit of a shoe-in. But Tom had obviously decided to do things properly.

'I wonder if I might start, Miss Clark?' said the woman. 'Can you run through your CV, highlighting any relevant previous experience and also your motivational objectives in applying for this role?'

She thought she answered the first part of the question, although it was all surprisingly formal. But "motivational objectives" what were they when they were at home? She improvised as best she could. She could hardly say that it was because she wanted to keep an eye on her boyfriend, so she talked about how the job was just around the corner from where she lived. But that was obviously not the right thing to say.

'So, the job is, err, handy,' said Mrs Kingston, sniffily, making a note. She glanced down at Jen's CV. 'I see you failed Maths GCSE,' she said before adding, 'Is there anything, other than the, err, convenience, which makes you want this job?'

Jen struggled a bit and said something about knowing the people who worked at the garage and how that would help her fit in.

'Yes, I was coming to that,' said Mrs Kingston. Tom just sat there, wasn't he going to ask anything? 'How do you think it's going to work, being so close to your boyfriend? Do you not think there's a risk of bringing problems from home into the workplace?' asked Mrs Kingston.

Jen was beginning to think that, if anything, her connection to Dan was going to work against her. This wasn't going at all well.

'And what about children?' Tom suddenly butted in. 'I was talking to Dan the other week, and he said you were thinking of starting a family.'

This was news to Jen.

'I'm afraid you can't ask that question, Tom – it would be against the Equal Opportunities Act,' interjected Mrs Kingston. 'I'm so sorry about that, Miss Clark, please ignore the question.' Tom looked quite sheepish.

'No problem,' said Jen, storing away the error – in case she needed to use it in her favour.

The interview staggered on. Not once did they ask her about cars, and that was about the only thing on which she'd done any homework. Dan had taken her into the garage after work and talked her through a whole load of car stuff. Not much of it had sunk in, but she was disappointed not to be asked anything. At the end of the interview she was promised a quick decision and thanked for her application. As she left the room, closing the door behind her, she smiled weakly at the red-haired girl and raised her eyes to the sky.

Dan was waiting outside the office. 'Well, how did it go?'

'Not good. They kept asking me tricky questions about money and invoices and about my motivational objectives.'

Dan assured her that she'd be fine, but she'd already convinced herself that she'd blown it.

She kissed Dan on the cheek and began to walk home. If she didn't get this job, and, frankly, she wasn't optimistic now, she couldn't keep an eye on Dan at work, and well, then, she had two options; trust him or step up her attempts to drive away that Emma woman. Perhaps she could do a bit of both.

Then she had another thought. That strange woman from the village shop wasn't going to get the job, was she? It would go to Miss Scotty Red-head, that Maddy, so, what if she made friends with her? Maybe she could be persuaded to tell her about Dan and any untoward comings and goings at the garage. She certainly seemed to have an aptitude for enquiry. Jen decided to pop home but return to the village for some shopping in about forty-five minutes. The Maddy girl should have finished her interview by then. She could sort of bump into her, and they could then go for a cup of coffee and have a chat.

# Chapter Twenty-Two
# Emma

'Hey, Em, the flat is still looking great,' Toby called out from his studio as Emma arrived for work.

'What, even after one whole day?' she replied.

'Yep, amazing, isn't it? I haven't managed to wreck it, throw red wine all over the walls, or set fire to the place.'

'You're slipping.'

'Thanks again for helping at the weekend.'

'No probs. The concert at the pub was good, by the way,' she added, talking over her shoulder as she entered her room.

'Oh right, ok, yes, um, good. I err, just spent the rest of the day tidying things up.'

Emma knew the concert might be a slightly awkward topic, so she didn't elaborate, but she did want to talk to him about it later. She'd decided she needed to be straight with Toby - making it clear where her affections lay. Now that she and Dan had, well, made a connection. That would be the right thing to do. Toby was her friend, and she wanted to keep it that way. They'd seen a lot of each other lately, and after spending the weekend together painting his place, it was obvious he still doted on her. He had a right to know that being a very good friend was as far as things would go. Ambiguity was the route to misunderstanding, and misunderstanding was the route to hurt feelings.

She settled into her studio and looked at the work she'd started last week. It was built around various shades of purple and was half-finished. She walked around the room, stalking her easel, looking at the painting from various different angles. She could already see three or four changes she wanted to make and was surprised she hadn't spotted them before. This was often the case. A few days away from a piece of work often seemed to reset the mind and give a clearer perspective of what one wanted to achieve.

'Hey Em, you'll never guess what?' Toby chirped from his room.

Emma walked back around and stood in the doorway, leaning against the frame. She noticed that Toby looked slightly different. He'd had his hair cut and, although he was wearing his usual plaster-splattered smock, underneath were those new jeans she'd helped him buy. They fitted rather well.

'I've got this new commission from a company in London,' he announced, holding his hammer up in one hand and a chisel in the other – rather like he was celebrating scoring a goal. He looked about ten years old and rather cute.

'Oh Toby, that's fantastic, well done.' Emma was genuinely pleased. 'What's it for?'

'They want something abstract, but it has to be big and curvy and subtly incorporate a small company logo. Other than that, the brief is very vague, it'll be up to me to design it.'

'And who are they?'

'Miller and Highfield. You've probably never heard of them, but they're a big stock-broking firm. They're mega-successful, and they're paying incredible money.'

'Fantastic. How did they come to hear about you?'

'One of their directors saw the work I did for the County Council. He was on holiday in The Lakes.'

'We should celebrate. How about dinner? I can do Thursday at my place? I'll cook something special,' said Emma before she could double check with herself whether that was actually a good idea - especially in view of her intention to make her feelings towards Toby clear. On the other hand, maybe the dinner would be a good time to do that.

'How incredible is incredible money?' asked Emma. It was an impertinent question, but she was intrigued, and she thought she'd push her luck. Toby, as always, was an open book.

'Twenty thousand, believe it or not, plus expenses for travelling to any meetings, measuring, moving the work down, and all that kind of, err stuff. How about that? And, I reckon, it'll only take me about two months to complete. I've already started some drawings, and I'll go down to present them in the next week or so.'

Later, back in her room, Emma was reflecting that Toby's career was really taking off. She wasn't doing too badly herself – another of her medium-sized two hundred and fifty-pound paintings had sold over the weekend – but she couldn't compete with Toby. She still needed that monthly cheque from her father.

She picked up a brush and dipped it into the bright magenta-coloured paint she'd mixed on her pallet. Still no phone call from Dan; she'd been hoping he would have grabbed the initiative and rung her this morning. Perhaps he'd got cold feet? Perhaps he couldn't get away? Perhaps the connection she felt at the concert hadn't been quite what she thought?

By the middle of the afternoon, despite frequently staring at the phone, imploring it to ring, warning Sally the manager downstairs that she was expecting a call and asking her to check the line, the phone remained distressingly silent. She was becoming despondent.

She began to think of a new plan, just in case Dan didn't, or felt he couldn't, get in touch. She wouldn't give up, that was for sure. But her mind began to explore a rather dark alley previously hidden from view. If this Jen Whatserface was going to try to intimidate her, then maybe she should fight back? What could she do? Well, she might find out where Jen worked, and then she could think of a way to make a complaint against her. She knew from her own failed marriage that pressures at work could often lead to pressures at home. One partner was knocked off balance by something which preoccupied their mind. The other partner would try to be supportive, but after a time, they'd become irritated that they weren't getting as much attention as normal. That's what had happened the time Roger thought his job was on the line. He'd had this bully of a boss who kept picking holes in the legal briefs he wrote. Roger was a stickler for doing everything properly, for being squeaky clean. In a commercial company that didn't always go down too well, especially if it came up against the ambitions of the directors. Roger had been in a right state about it for ages and ages, and Emma unfairly eventually became fed up. One evening she'd tetchily told Roger to either resign and preserve his principles, or shut up and keep taking his rather lucrative salary. They'd not had a row – Roger didn't have rows - but he went very quiet and sulky for a time. In the end, Roger came to realise she was right, and they couldn't risk a period of him being out of work, which would have meant failing to meet their rather large monthly mortgage payments. Roger wouldn't risk anything very much. She remembered they'd had sex again that Friday night after several months of abstinence.

So, yes, she could give Jen some of her own medicine; rock the boat a bit – unless, of course, Dan called. Or, she reminded herself - unless, of course, Dan told her that he was totally happy with Jen. Then she'd back off, of course she would. That would be the right thing to do.

Emma finished the top right-hand corner of the painting. She was pleased with her work and stood back to admire it. As she did so, she noticed, out of the corner of her eye, a girl with eccentrically dyed red hair and thick-rimmed glasses looking at some paintings in the corridor. It was rare for the public to come upstairs. She could only see her profile, but this girl looked vaguely familiar. Emma thought maybe she'd seen her somewhere before? She turned back to her painting, but her foot caught in the easel pulling the leg away. Before she could react, her painting, the easel, and a small pot of paint had fallen in a heap on the floor. The paint had splashed all over her picture.

'Bollocks,' she screamed, 'bollocks, bollocks, shit, shit.' The expletives flowed. Toby rushed around from his room having heard the commotion.

'Oh Em, what have you done? Let me help, we'll sort it. I can clean this mess up, and you'll be able to repair your picture. It's not ruined, honest, poor you, what a calamity?'

Emma just stood there with her hand over her mouth as Toby busied himself re-building the easel and re-instating the painting. His calm quickly calmed her, and she was able to pull herself together. Any spilt paint could easily be scraped off, and the picture over-painted. This was just like Toby, she thought, riding in, her knight in shining armour, helping to sort things. He really was an angel.

'Oh, don't worry, Tobes,' she said at last. 'I'll clean up the rest.'

She fetched a cloth from the small sink in the corner of her room and began cleaning the floor. It was as she bent down, she noticed that the red-haired girl was still standing in the corridor. Oh dear, she thought, she must have heard everything.

'Can I help you?' asked Emma, a little tartly.

'Well, actually,' said the girl, in what seemed a Scottish accent, 'I was hoping to talk to Toby. Have I come at a bad time?' She only half turned her face from looking at the paintings on the wall, which Emma thought rather rude.

'No, it's a brilliant time, probably one of the best times ever,' She quickly added a forced smile, hoping the girl would understand her humour. But the girl didn't see it; she was still staring at the pictures on the wall.

Toby instantly defused the situation. 'You'll be fine, Em,' he said, and turning towards the girl, he grinned enthusiastically, 'what can I do for you?'

As Emma closed her door, she heard the girl say, 'Well, I'm really interested in sculpture, and I wondered if I could, maybe, spend some time with you looking at your work and learn a few things?'

Toby was being his usual affable self, always willing to help anyone.

Cheeky cow. 'I'm really good at sculpture,' Emma mimicked under her breath.

Just then, the phone rang.

It must be Dan, thought Emma, with alarm. She chucked the cloth in the sink, quickly wiped her hands, double-checked the door was closed, took a deep breath, and picked up the phone.

'Hi, Emma Taylor,' she said brightly.

'Hello dear,' said her mother.

'Oh, it's you. Hi Mum'

'Well, you don't sound very pleased to hear from me,'

'No, it's good,' said Emma, recovering herself. 'It's just that I was, um, expecting another call.'

Emma's mother then explained that she and her father were travelling up to Scotland for a week's break and thought that they'd pop in to see Emma on the way.

'That would be lovely,' said Emma, immediately dreading the thought of it. She could tolerate seeing her mother, but her father invariably cast a cloud. He couldn't and wouldn't be forgiven.

# Chapter Twenty-Three
# Maddy

Maddy was feeling pretty pleased with herself. She'd have preferred it if Emma hadn't seen her at the gallery yesterday. But she'd managed to keep her head down and not look her in the eye. Toby had been really nice, and he'd been more than willing to help with her request for work experience. In fact, he seemed flattered that she wanted to spend time with him.

So this morning, in the absence of artistic clothing, she'd put on her scruffiest pair of jeans and her oldest t-shirt. She'd pinned up her bright red hair in an interesting artistic way and put on some bright red lipstick. The gallery was about a quarter of a mile from her lodgings along a country road. There wasn't a pavement, so she walked along the road, stepping into the grass verge whenever a car passed. A cheeky red-breasted robin seemed to follow her. Every ten yards, or so, he'd fly over her head, land on a twig, and serenade her with a new song. Or maybe, it was just the new verse of an old song.

As she made her way along, she reflected on the job interview from the day before. It had all gone rather well, she thought. She felt she'd impressed with her IT skills and her ideas on how to re-organise the filing. After the interview, as she'd walked across the village square, she'd bumped into Jen - the other woman who'd been interviewed. At Jen's suggestion, they'd gone to the village café - it had all seemed a bit contrived, and Maddy didn't think their meeting a coincidence.

They'd talked about how their respective interviews had gone, and Jen had been very frank. She seemed very put out that the interview hadn't unfolded as she'd hoped. Apparently, she'd spent time researching car mechanics because she thought Tom would ask her about that. Thank goodness he hadn't, thought Maddy, she didn't know the difference between one end of a car and the other. By the end of their chat Jen seemed to think they were now firm friends – heaven knows why – and she'd insisted they meet up again the following week, whatever happened, whoever got the job. Maddy didn't mind. Jen might know something about her mother.

She rounded the last bend and began the slow climb into the village. On her left was a field of oil seed rape. The brilliant yellow crop was blowing in the wind, and the smell of the pollen was quite overpowering.

When she got to the gallery, she crept up the stairs because she wanted to reach Toby's room without being spotted by her mother again. It was ok; Emma's room was empty, while Toby's door was half open, and he could be seen pummelling a lump of clay on the bench.

'Hi Toby,' she said, smiling brightly as she walked briskly into his room, quietly closing the door behind her.

'Oh, err, hi, um, Maddy. You ok? Lovely day. We should be out basking, sunbathing, or whatever, rather than being stuck in here,' he replied, wiping clay off his hands down the front of his smock.

Maddy had decided that today would be all about building a rapport with Toby. He wasn't going to reveal anything very much until he relaxed and trusted her. Though from what she'd seen of him so far, she wasn't sure if Toby ever truly relaxed, he seemed edgy most of the time.

'So, what are you doing?' asked Maddy, perching herself on a stool.

'I'm, err, sort of, preparing some clay to make a prototype model for my latest sculpture,'

'Oh right.'

'Yep, it's going to be a creation for a stock-broking firm to sit in their entrance foyer. The end sculpture will be about four-foot-high and made of stone. I'll do it at my workshop, which is basically an old garage I've converted. I use it for the bigger jobs. I'm going to the quarry to choose a piece of stone the week after next,' he paused to sip some coffee. 'Oh, sorry, do you want a cup?' he asked.

'No, I'm fine,' said Maddy.

Toby continued: 'So, err, because I need to get my design approved - and I obviously can't take a bloody great piece of stone down on the train to London - I'm going to make a model out of clay. It'll be about eighteen inches high. It's called a maquette and, along with these drawings, it'll give them a good idea of what the finished sculpture will look like.'

'So, what's all that metal wire and mesh for?' asked Maddy, pointing to a structure on the bench.

'Well, that's my inner scaffold. I will build the clay on top of that rather than have a solid piece. If it was solid, not hollow, it would be way more expensive and more likely to crack. I'm using self-drying clay, which won't need firing. That reduces the risk of cracking too.'

Maddy was impressed and fascinated in equal measure. She'd worked with clay a bit in art classes at school, but nothing very complicated. She'd once tried to make a cat for her mother, but it had come out looking more like a dog, and its tail fell off in the kiln. She watched Toby work, occasionally asking him more questions about the tools he was using. But mostly she told herself to keep quiet so that he could concentrate, which was hard.

She also found herself studying Toby himself. She liked what she saw. He had a ruffled mop of hair, which stuck up in all the right places, probably three days' growth of beard, and a dishevelled artistic look. He was quite tall – certainly over six foot, which meant he looked a little awkward bending over his work. But he was slim and fit, and although you wouldn't describe him as muscular, he was, well, normal. The only thing she could put in the negative column was that he seemed a bit awkward socially, but, actually, she found that rather endearing. It made him seem a bit vulnerable, and that appealed to her. She thought that age-wise he was maybe twenty-eight, possibly thirty. If she was pretending to be twenty-two, or twenty-three, then there was hardly any age gap at all. Yes, she could quite fancy this Toby, she thought. In fact, she did quite fancy him.

Her daydreams were interrupted by a call on her mobile. She recognised the garage's number.

'Just a minute,' she said, before scuttling out of the studio and almost jogging downstairs.

'Hi, Maddy here. I'm just walking outside, and then I can talk privately,' she updated.

'Ok, no worries, dear,' said a voice. It was Tom, the garage owner.

'Right, sorry about that. I can talk now.'

'Well, I've good news for you, Maddy. You've got the job; can you start next Monday?'

# Chapter Twenty-Four
# Jen

Her heart leapt into her mouth as soon as she saw the letter on the mat. It *had* to be from the garage. Jen was home a little early, and Barney was, as usual, very pleased to see her. He'd run to the door barking, jumping up at her, and furiously wagging his tale.

'Hello, Barney, Barney, Barney,' she said, rubbing the dog's head. 'Now get down and let me sort this mail.'

She put aside two bills and a charity letter, which left her clutching the hand-written brown envelope with its smudge of engine oil across the front. She was suddenly overtaken by nerves. Should she wait until Dan came home before opening it? No, she'd make herself a cup of tea, get settled, and then see what it had to say. She must face the truth. For the umpteenth time, she told herself it didn't really matter, one way or the other. And, in any case, she did now have a Plan B for keeping an eye on Dan – using Maddy as her unsuspecting spy.

'Yes, I'll take you out for a W.A.L.K in a moment, Barney.' Barney must have learnt how to spell because he rushed off to get his lead. His tail seemed to be wagging ever faster.

Jen made her mug of tea, cut herself a large slice of cake, and sat down with her letter. Why hadn't Tom simply phoned her? After all it wasn't as though he didn't know her. They'd sung carols together in the pub at Christmas, and she chatted to him every time she went in. Just then, a headline in the local paper, which lay on the kitchen table, caught her eye:

VANDAL ATTACK ON VILLAGE HOME.

Jen caught her breath and quickly unfolded the paper. There was a picture of Emma's flat. The story was only a few paragraphs long, and, to her relief, it didn't say much. The last paragraph detailed how the police were continuing their inquiries, appealing for witnesses, but, at this stage, they didn't know who might be responsible for what was described as "offensive graffiti." Thank goodness for that, no news was good news. A police sergeant was quoted as saying that the attack had caused the householder *"a good deal of distress"* and seemed to be *"totally unprovoked."* Well, good, distress was what she'd wanted to achieve. But the officer had got it wrong; the attack was very much provoked.

Her train of thought led to thinking about Emma's diary, the catalyst for her vandalism. She hadn't read any more for a couple of days. The last session had upset her again. And she knew that if she read any more, it would become increasingly difficult not to confront Dan. There was also the risk that she might, again, do something stupid against that *other* woman. Jen knew she couldn't trust herself if her temper was up.

She sipped some tea. Right, it was time to bite the bullet and open the letter. She read it twice, just to be sure, then she chucked it down on the table, walked to the kitchen sink, banged her fist on the sideboard, and sat back down. Not only had she been rejected, but Tom had written, *"I'm afraid we felt you weren't up to the standard required."*

Standard required? What was he talking about? It was just a basic secretarial role, answering the phones and doing a few invoices. She could have done the job with her eyes closed. It didn't matter, she'd told herself, but actually, it did matter. She was hurt, annoyed, and insulted. Tom clearly hadn't used the hired-in HR woman to write the rejection letter – it was just typical blunt, plain speaking put your foot in it, Tom. Well, stuff him, she thought, as her blood pressure surged up the scale.

Just at that point, Dan came in through the back door. He chucked his bag down in the corner, patted Barney, who was still holding the lead in his mouth, looked at Jen, and said, 'Oh, you've heard then?'

'What do you mean *I've* heard, how have *you* heard?' she replied in an obviously agitated voice.

'Tom pulled me to one side just to warn me,' replied Dan, nervously.

'So, how long have you known?'

'Since about lunchtime.'

'So, bloody Tom, who didn't have the guts to ring me and tell me straight, has already told you. Whatever happened to the concept of confidentiality? What about telling the bloody candidate first?'

Dan just shrugged. This was not the response she wanted. She wanted sympathy, she wanted support. She got neither.

'I didn't want his bloody rotten job, anyway,' continued Jen. 'Mind you, I might have stood a chance if you hadn't told me the interview would be all about cars. It wasn't. They wanted to know about bloody spreadsheets and finance programmes and motivational fucking objectives.'

'Well, I just thought that Tom being Tom, he'd stick to the basics. I didn't know he was going to bring in that HR woman. I'm sorry if I was wrong, and I'm really sorry you didn't get the job.'

'Who did get it then?' asked Jen, calming down a little, but she knew the answer. 'I presume it wasn't that strange woman from the Co-op, so it must have been the girl, Maddy,' she said.

'Is that her name, Maddy? How do you know that? I just heard it went to someone else, someone young, and she starts next week.'

'Well, as part of the incompetence of the whole event,' Jen continued, 'they made the candidates wait in the same room, and I got talking to Maddy. Actually, to be fair, she's very nice and probably quite bright. But she's only about fourteen, well, twenty at most. And she can't have anything like the experience I've got.'

Jen paused for breath and squeezed in a sip of tea. 'I can't believe you knew from lunchtime. When were you going to tell me? You could have rung me, sent a text, come home early.'

'Tom told me not to tell you.'

'Oh, did he? And I suppose your first loyalty is to Tom and not me, which comes as no surprise in the current set-up.'

'What do you mean by that?'

'You know exactly what I mean.'

'Well, if I knew what you meant, I wouldn't have asked, would I?'

They were both almost shouting now. This was building up out of Jen's control, and she knew it. Barney had shot off to sit in his basket.

'You, your head is so full of that, Emma, you probably haven't any room left to spare me a thought.'

'Oh, so, that's it, is it?' replied Dan, turning an even brighter shade of red. Jen knew she could provoke him to this state, and, for reasons which weren't totally worked out, she'd deliberately done so. She knew she'd regret it later. She just mustn't mention the diary.

'Let me tell you once more. There's nothing in it. Ok?' said Dan, turning his back on her and washing his hands in the sink.

'And I suppose you haven't met her down in the cricket hut, then?' blurted out Jen before she could stop herself. Careful, careful, her inner voice implored. Don't mention the diary.

'What?'

'You heard.'

'No, I haven't, why would you say that?' He was really shouting now.

'Because, Dan, dearest, I found your old coat in there.'

Dan paused and in a more measured voice he said, 'So, let me get this straight. You found my old coat in the cricket hut, and you immediately thought that I must have met Emma. How did you jump to that conclusion? You're mad, totally bloody mad. I can't be doing with this.'

With that, he stormed out of the back door, slamming it behind him. Barney cowered in his basket. Jen began to cry.

Things hadn't gone at all well.

The only consolation, Jen thought, was that he'd left without asking why she'd been in the hut and why she might suspect they'd met there. She didn't want him to know she'd taken and read some of Emma's diary. It would just make her look bad, make her look petty and suspicious and jealous, which, by the way, she knew she was. If he knew she'd seen Emma's diary he'd go totally ballistic.

Jen began sorting some dishes, after that she would do the laundry. Household chores were always an answer to stress. But then the obvious occurred to her; maybe Dan didn't know about the diary, why would he? That was a more positive thought. Anyway, she decided, calming down a bit, he'd be back soon. This was the way their arguments went. They could be quite ferocious, but they were usually over quickly. And sometimes, the making up again meant it was almost worth having the argument in the first place. There was no reason to think this tiff would be any different.

# Chapter Twenty-Five
# Emma & Dan

Chopped carrots and beetroot - an odd combination but extremely colourful, and that was the effect she wanted. Emma finished putting the casserole together and placed it in the oven on medium heat. She was quite looking forward to an evening with Toby. She wanted to know more about his new commission and how he was going to approach the job. Mapping out a design, when your starting point was a blank sheet of paper, was always exciting.

She was, however, a little nervous. Her plan to put Toby straight about the platonic nature of their relationship would take tact, diplomacy, and a lot of wine. She wasn't at all sure how he'd take it. He'd been very supportive these past few weeks, and they'd spent a lot of time together. He'd helped her settle into the gallery; given advise about setting up as a self-employed person; about tax, VAT, and all those tricky business issues. He'd been a rock. But at the end of the day, Toby was Toby. He wasn't Dan, her Dan.

The doorbell rang. That was odd. Toby wasn't due for a while. She quickly checked in the mirror, swept up a strand of hair, and then peered through the peephole. It was Dan!


He'd been on auto-pilot after slamming the door and storming out. Dan was angry. If Jen was so worried about him and Emma, then he'd give her something to worry about. He decided to go straight around to Emma's flat, and, well, anything could happen. He hadn't been quite sure of the logic in his actions. Logic hadn't come into it. He'd just wanted to see Emma, talk to her, and be with her. So, before he knew it, he'd arrived outside her flat and rung the bell. Here he was, no turning back, he'd taken a massive step back into a past life, knowing it could shape his future life in a way he couldn't predict. But the temptation to find out where he stood with Emma was too great. His stomach churned, his throat tightened, and he was sweating a little – partly from the walk over, partly from anticipation. He took out a scruffy old handkerchief and mopped his brow. He wished he had a clean one. He wished he had some aftershave on, or something. He felt hot and sweaty and more than bothered. He gave his hair a ruffle and rubbed his half-stubbly face. Then the door opened, and there she was.

'Dan!'

'Hi.'

'I, I thought you were going to call me?'

'I was, but I, I needed to see you. Can I come in?'

'Yes, of course. It's lovely to see you.'

Emma stepped to one side and let him in, closing the door. There wasn't a lot of room in the hallway, and he found himself very close to her. He could smell her perfume; her eyes sparkled up at him.

When he thought about it later, Dan wasn't sure who made the first move. They just seemed to move in unison into each other's arms. Dan carried Emma backwards into the lounge and lowered her onto the sofa. There were no words, just arms, and legs, gasps, passionate kisses. Dan felt the tension of the past few days melt away. The big question weighing on his mind - whether he still loved her - was swept to one side and replaced by another much easier question; did he want her? In this moment, this moment when instinct and lust were taking over from reason, the answer seemed obvious. It felt like it ought to be right – it felt like unfinished business. She could be his again.

It was all happening so quickly; Emma hadn't time to think, and normally she liked to have time to think. But actually, she didn't care now – she was just going to let things happen. It was such a massive relief to hold him so tightly after wanting him so much - it overwhelmed her. She'd been so lonely, and she hadn't fully realised how the loneliness, the emptiness, the bitterness, had burned into her soul. But it all seemed to fall away in this moment of, yes, that's what it was, happiness – a happiness which brought tears to her eyes. Right now, she wanted him like she'd never wanted him before. Never mind her resolve to talk things through, to explain things, to make sure they were still right for each other, she just plain wanted him, needed him, it had been so long. He was on top of her, she didn't care, she wanted him there. If they made love now, she'd have him back. He'd be hers again, just like he used to be. Only this time, she wouldn't let him go. She began pushing herself up against his heavy weight; she could feel his body respond. She increased the eagerness and passion of her kisses.

But inside, Dan knew something was not quite right. He tried to dismiss it – that feeling which was now taking hold; he fought it, tried to push it back, but it was no use. Everything was happening too fast. His body was more than willing, he absolutely ached for her, but all of a sudden, his mind seemed to, well, have a mind of its own. He really *did* need to talk to her first. He needed to get his own thoughts in order. It was hard to fight against his instincts and the intensity of the moment. But he needed to know more about why she'd left and broken things off, not contacting him again, until now? And then, of course, there was Jen. Jen was suddenly foremost in his thoughts. He realised what the uncomfortable feeling was – guilt. Emma wanted him – no doubt about that – and he felt euphoric, almost giddy about that - but he needed to regain control. He backed off, kneeling on the floor beside her.

Emma instantly felt bereft. She was still happy deep down, but that delicious feeling of abandonment disappeared as quickly as it had arrived. For a few moments, she was gripped by a sense of loss. Things weren't going to happen in the way she'd thought just seconds before. But surely, she had won him back – hadn't she? She must keep calm, stick to the plan, she mustn't mess things up. She sat up a bit on the sofa and propped herself up on one elbow. She wanted to ask him what the matter was, why he'd pulled away. But, instead, hiding her disappointment and frustration and trying to sound relaxed, she said, 'Well, hello, it's nice to meet you again after all these years.'

He laughed, 'You could say that. What happened there? I'm sorry, I just couldn't help myself.'

'Don't worry, neither could I, we never could, remember?'

'That's true.'

Emma straightened her clothes and put back some of her hair in the clips she was wearing.

'I'm so glad you're here,' she said, softly touching his arm.

'Well, yes, that was obvious. But you, err, did say we should talk. And I think we must do that first.'

'And we must. We just haven't had the chance.' She kissed him tenderly on the lips, but she detected a barrier building between them again.

Just then, the doorbell rang. 'Oh my god, Toby,' Emma blurted out. She had genuinely been lost in the moment and completely forgotten he was coming for dinner. 'He's early.'

'Typical,' said Dan. 'Timing was never his speciality.'

'No, don't, I invited him. He's coming to dinner to celebrate a new commission - a sculpture.'

'Well, if I'm interrupting anything between you?' said Dan, getting to his feet and pulling his t-shirt straight.

'No, nothing like that, we're just good friends, genuinely just good friends. Dan, I'm yours, like I said in the letter. You need to know that. I can send him away.'

'No, no, no, you must, err, go ahead with your plans, I shouldn't have come bursting in uninvited. Anyway, I must get back.' Dan got up and edged towards the door. 'Oh,' he said, pausing, 'Is it ok if he knows I'm here, I could go out the back way?'

'No, not at all,' said Emma. 'In fact, I want him to know about us. Look, we will talk soon. Great to see you – even this briefly.' Their awkwardness was reaching record levels, much to Emma's regret.

'I'll err, sort something,' replied Dan, vaguely.

Emma opened the door. Toby was standing there, looking quite cool for Toby, holding a bunch of flowers and a bottle of wine.

'Just good friends, huh?' she heard Dan mutter under his breath. She playfully kicked his shin, but not too hard.

'Hi, Toby,' said Emma. 'Um, Dan is just leaving. He just sort of popped around. You remember Dan from school? Well, yes, of course, you do, you live in the same village. It's me who's trying to get to know everyone again, re-establish old ties.' She was blabbering.

She kissed Dan on the lips. 'Come back around again soon,' she said. It was all deliberately done in front of Toby. Dan looked a little awkward. But nowhere near as awkward, stunned, and angry as Toby, who had a face like thunder.

# Chapter Twenty-Six
# Toby

Toby just felt stupid, standing on the doorstep clutching his flowers and wine as she openly kissed Dan, as if it was a perfectly normal thing to do.

'Hi, come in, Toby,' Emma said, as Toby looked over his shoulder to watch Dan disappearing down the path. 'Great to see you, just slip your shoes off and take a seat, I'll pour you a glass of wine. Fancy that, everything happening at once,' she said with a rather awkward false-sounding chuckle. She was obviously embarrassed by what had just happened. She should be, thought Toby, as he handed over the flowers and wine.

'Oh, they're lovely, how sweet, you're an angel,' she kissed him on the cheek. Not the lips for him, he noted.

Once inside, Emma went off to the kitchen to fetch him a glass of wine. 'I'll drink mine while I'm preparing if you don't mind,' she said, hovering in the doorway. 'You just relax. I'm a bit behind.'

No surprise there, Toby said to himself, noticing that the cushions on the sofa were all over the place, rather like her hair. Emma saw his glance and she casually went over and straightened them out. Normally, Toby would have offered to help prepare the meal, but he still wasn't able to speak. He needed time to take it all in.

He'd genuinely thought they'd been making progress. He'd become much more relaxed with her. He'd even smartened up his own image, as well as his flat. She'd helped him choose some of his new clothes. Now *that* was a boyfriend/girlfriend thing to do – wasn't it? Apparently, not. He'd imagined that this dinner – which was at her invitation, after all, could have been the start of something. He'd got the new commission, and she'd seemed delighted. Who could fail to be impressed? Emma had left a bottle of wine on the table, so he topped his glass up, downed it in one, and topped it up again.

'Have you got any problems with garlic?' she called from the kitchen.

Garlic, for heaven's sake, that was proof, as if he needed any more, that he wasn't going to get close to her tonight.

He'd have to say something, she'd asked him a question. 'No, um, that's fine and, err, dandy,' he said. Where did 'dandy' come from? He told himself to get a grip.

'Why don't you choose some music? Put on anything you like?'

'Ok,' he said, re-filling his glass of wine - again.

He chose some Stevie Wonder – they both liked the seventies and eighties music – and the rhythm of *Superstition* filled the room.

'Any more news about your commission?' she asked as she clanked about with various pots and pans.

'Only that I'm going to go down to London the week after next to talk to them about it and show them a model. Things should be tickety-boo from there.'

'Tickety-boo?' she teased him, poking her head around the door frame.

Bollocks, where did tickety-boo come from? Thought Toby, horrified.

'That's great then,' she continued. 'It's all moving really quickly.'

Toby tried to sound normal, telling himself that he mustn't sulk. After all, he shouldn't really have been surprised about Dan. It was obvious from that occasion in the pub that something was going on, or was about to go on. Come to think of it, what exactly *was* going on? Had Dan left his partner? Was he about to leave his partner? Did his partner even know? Was this going to be one of those secret affairs people had? He didn't think they'd get away with that in a small village, even if he decided to keep his mouth shut about what he'd just witnessed.

'Voila!' said Emma, standing in the doorway with two steaming plates, which she put down on the table. Chicken breasts were smothered in a variety of delicious-looking vegetables. He'd already smelt the garlic from two metres away.

'I thought that as we are both artists, I would make a really colourful dish,' said Emma brightly.

'It looks lively, I mean lovely,' replied Toby, who was beginning to feel the effects of what must now have been four glasses of wine.

They tucked in, saying nothing for the first couple of mouthfuls, and then Emma said, 'That err, um, visit by Dan,'

'Yes,' replied Toby, cautiously, knowing and dreading what was to come.

'Well, actually, that's the first time he's been round.'

'Right'

'I mean, I wouldn't want you to think I'd been carrying on with him without telling you. After all, you're one of my best friends.'

'Ok.'

Emma continued: 'Were you, err, surprised?'

'A bit.' There was another brief silence.

'And, um, are you upset?' she asked, tentatively, adding, 'I hope you're still my friend.'

Toby put his knife and fork down, took hold of her hand, and looked her in the eyes. Those beautiful eyes. For once, he felt totally together, not nervous in her company at all - maybe it was the wine? He wasn't entirely sure what he was going to say, but he knew it was time to unburden himself.

'Emma, I love you. I love you every minute of every day. I love you when we're together; I love you when we're not together. I love every inch of you, everything you say, everything you do.'

'Toby, don't,' she said, but he couldn't stop now.

'I have loved you since we were both fifteen. I have worshipped you. I always hoped you would come back one day. I couldn't believe it when you did, and I adore you more than ever. I have helped and supported you whenever possible. Do you think I would do all that because I *just* wanted to be a friend?'

He knew it was probably the most eloquent and heartfelt thing he'd ever said.

She pulled her hand away and was now staring into her meal, unable, it seemed, to look back at him.

He hadn't finished yet. 'I thought, stupidly, obviously, that we had a bit of a thing developing. I know I'm, err, a bit, um, awkward sometimes and that I don't look as great as the almighty Dan.'

'Don't be silly, Toby, you're fine, you're lovely,' she interjected.

'But I thought we had, we have, a connection.'

'We do,' said Emma. 'We do, you're not just *one* of my best friends, you *are* my best friend, you're so important to me. I wouldn't have been able to settle back here without you. You've helped me so much, Toby. I know it sounds stupid, but I love you too, just not in the way you want, not in the way I love Dan.'

'Well, you wanted me on *that* night,' Toby fired back, sounding petulant. 'You were, um, all over me then, you couldn't get enough of me.' There he'd said it.

'What night?' she paused. 'Oh, *that* night. Toby, I can't even remember most of *that* night. We were very drunk, well I certainly was, and it was a long time ago. You shouldn't have read anything into it.'

'Well, maybe not, but my theory is that it showed, it shows, that deep down you do love me. We'd be great together, Em, you know we would.' He clasped her hand again, and he noticed there were tears in her eyes now.

'I'm sorry, Toby, I'm so sorry,' she said.

'Dan's with someone else, I told you - that Jen,' continued Toby. 'What are you going to do about that?'

Emma held her head in her hands: 'I don't know, I don't know, it's up to him, I suppose. I've just said what I feel. It's up to him now.'

Tears were welling up in her eyes, and Toby got up to fetch her a tissue. His instinct was to stay and comfort her, but he knew that would be ridiculous. 'I think I'd better go. It'd be for the best,' he said.

'No, don't Toby, don't. I don't want that; I don't want to ruin the evening.'

That was just a bit more than Toby could take, but he kept his voice steady. 'You don't want to ruin the evening? Em, the evening was ruined for me, I'm afraid, as soon as I saw you two together. I can't help it. I'm going. Thanks for cooking for me and all, but it's best I go.'

He put his shoes and jacket on, opened and then slammed the door… just as he heard Stevie Wonder sing, *I Just Called to Say I Love You.*

# Chapter Twenty-Seven
# Jen

When Jen heard the door, she was filled with relief. Thank God, she thought, he was back. He hadn't been long. Probably, he'd just been for a walk to cool off. That's what usually happened. As he walked into the kitchen, Jen almost threw herself at him.

'I'm so sorry,' she said, putting her arms around his neck.

'No, I'm sorry. You've had a big disappointment with the job. I should be more supportive,' replied Dan.

'And I shouldn't have said those things. I know you did your best for me. I should be smarter - then, maybe, I'd have got the job,' replied Jen.

'You are smart, you're very smart. I don't know what Tom is thinking of, hiring some girl who won't know one end of a car from another. What happens when I want to make an order? Have I got to sit there and explain every part? Sod that. In my book, she can sink or swim.'

'Where have you been, anyway?' asked Jen casually.

'Oh, just for a walk,' said Dan, going over to Barney to give him a stroke. 'And I should have taken you, shouldn't I? You'll be bursting?'

'Well, why don't you just take him for a bit of a spin around the block so he can do his business, and I'll get some dinner on,' said Jen.

Things were returning to normal, she thought. That was a relief.

After dinner, they snuggled up on the sofa together to watch a film. That didn't always happen. Then Dan suggested they go to bed early. Jen thought that maybe, she was in for a lively night. She was right. That hadn't happened for some time, either. Perhaps, they should have a row more often.

Dan shot off to work in the morning, a little later than usual, and Jen tidied up the bedroom - there were a few clothes chucked on the floor. She didn't have to be at work for another hour, so there was no rush. She picked up Dan's shirt – and then her heart leapt, and her stomach lurched. She slowly pulled off a long auburn hair, and then another, and a third. The bastard, she thought. He had been with *her*. That's why he came back all steamed up. He wasn't away long enough to *do* anything with her, so he came back all revved up and settled for second best.

She sat down on the bed. At this moment, she was too angry to be upset. She'd absolutely have to have a word with that woman now. This whole thing was way out of hand. There wasn't a moment to lose.

'Hi, it's Jen,' she said on the phone to Heather, the supervisor at her office. 'I'm afraid I won't be in work today. I've got a bit of a temperature. I'm sure it's nothing, but I'm not feeling great.'

Heather was, as usual, succinct: 'Ok, take care,' was all she said before cutting her off.

Jen waited until ten, and then she walked over to the art gallery. It was a nice summer's day with a clear blue sky. The village was being itself. The postman emptying the pillar box; the baker unloading bread for the bakery; and the butcher, Bob, arriving on his bike. All very idyllic, a typical northern English village, but Jen wasn't feeling idyllic. She adored where she lived, she loved her life, and that was the trouble, she didn't want it ruined. Everything had been going brilliantly, and now this woman, this tart, was threatening to screw things up.

She marched into the gallery and spoke to the woman in the shop, who was arranging some cards on a display rack.

'Excuse me. Do you know where I can find Emma? I think her second name is Taylor.'

'Yeah, sure, she'll be in her studio upstairs. Does she know you?'

'Oh yes,' said Jen, turning on her heel and heading for the stairs.

And there she was, in the studio at the end, fiddling about with some paint pots. Her hair was scraped back in a ponytail. She was wearing a tight T-shirt and jeans. She was so slim – the bitch. Jen took it all in. She didn't bother to knock on the open door, she just walked in and shut it behind her.

'Excuse me,' said Emma, looking startled. 'Can I help you?'

'Can *you* help me?' Jen mimicked. 'You can stop helping yourself to my boyfriend, that's for sure.'

'I don't know what you mean. How dare you come barging in? Get out.' Emma was holding up one of her paintbrushes as though protecting herself.

Jen closed the door and took hold of the handle behind her. 'So, do you deny that you've been seeing my Dan? That you saw him last night, that you're trying to pull him away from me?'

'I don't confirm or deny anything. Not to you, anyway. I'll say it again – before I ring down to the manager - will you please get out!'

Jen stayed where she was. 'So, it's true then. If it wasn't, you'd deny it. Now, listen to me because I'm saying this nice and clear for you. Either you give him up, or something very, very, horrible is going to happen to you. Have you got it?'

Jen wasn't sure why she'd said that. She knew it sounded ridiculous, as though she was in an episode of some TV soap opera, but the words just came out. If they sounded threatening, well, in that moment, she didn't care. The sweat was dripping off her, and she found herself shaking from head to toe.

'I'd be very careful if I were you, threatening me like that,' Emma said.

Jen could see that her voice and body were shaking as well. Emma put down her paintbrush and then turned back to face Jen. 'If you must know, I did see him last night, but that was the first time since I came back to the village. Nothing happened, so there's nothing for you to worry about – yet. It's up to Dan now.'

That was too much for Jen and she leapt forward and slapped Emma around the cheek. Emma screamed.

Just as Jen shaped for a second strike, the door opened, and a man she recognised as Toby, the sculptor, came in.

'What on earth is going on? Stop it. They'll hear you downstairs, there might be customers,' he said, grabbing Jen's arm.

'Get off, you bastard,' she shouted and then started to cry hysterically.

'You, madam,' Toby continued, 'have lost your bloody marbles, and I'm escorting you off the premises.'

'Just remember what I said: Leave him alone,' Jen shouted at Emma as she found herself being dragged off. 'Take your hands off me, leave me, I'm going,' she protested.

Breaking free, she ran down the stairs and out of the gallery, only stopping about halfway across the village square. She momentarily thought about going into the garage to confront Dan. But decided she'd probably done enough for one day.

# Chapter Twenty-Eight
# Emma

From two thousand feet above sea level, the views were magnificent. You could see as far as the sea and, surely, that was Scotland in the distance? Two buzzards circled, riding the thermals as they searched for prey. A middle-aged couple walked their dog back to the car. It didn't take them long to load him in and drive off. Emma's old Ford was now the only car left in the windswept car park. She'd driven up to this viewpoint before. She'd even painted from here using the distant hills as inspiration. Not only was it a beautiful place to stop and take in the stunning landscape, but it was also a good place to think. She hoped the air would help clear her mind. The last twenty-four hours had certainly taken its toll, and she needed some space.

She was still shocked to the core by Jen's visit to the gallery; she still felt angry, and she still felt the slap across her cheek. She did actually have some sympathy for Jen, but what could she do? It was up to Dan - she couldn't decide who he should be with. He had to do that. There were winners and losers in love, as well as in life. If Jen lost out this time, she'd just have to pick herself up and get on with it. On reflection, the whole slapping episode might not be a bad thing. Jen would go back to Dan, there'd be a row, and it would drive him into her arms.

She was still tingling all over from Dan's visit. It had been so good to be with him again – even if it had been such a brief encounter. It had taken her totally off guard. Of course, the subsequent conversation with Toby had been awkward and unfortunate, though probably for the best in the long run. She still hadn't had a chance to talk properly with Dan. There was so much to tell him, so much planning to do, including, hopefully, their whole lives together.

She reclined the seat of her car, put on the radio, and closed her eyes. She needed time to relax. She was so tired.

This living life business - trying to get what you wanted - was exhausting. Some people just let things happen to them, they went with the flow, but Emma knew that wasn't her way. Ever since she'd been persuaded, forced, whatever, to go against her instincts and give up her baby, leave her boyfriend, leave her home – she'd wanted control. Now she wanted what *she* wanted. And if things didn't happen naturally, well, she'd have to make them happen.

She knew, too, that she could, if she chose, make certain things *happen* for Jen. After all, the woman had threatened her. Toby had said he'd heard it all through the wall. He'd been great. He'd immediately made her a cup of tea, sat her down, and inspected her cheek. He'd even taken a picture of it on his phone, though there wasn't much to see, just a slight red mark. Despite the failed dinner party, he seemed to be his usual self, covering her back, caring about her, and trying to cheer her up. He hadn't said anything about the previous evening. Perhaps, she should have done - to help clear the air - but it seemed easier to just let it pass. They both now knew where they stood, and, hopefully, he still wanted to remain her friend. She certainly needed him, needed him now more than ever.

For a start, he could help nail Jen. He was a witness. Should she go to the police? She didn't think for one minute that Jen was serious when she'd said, 'S*omething very horrible is going to happen to you.*' But that threat, plus the probability that she was responsible for the graffiti attack, would certainly be enough to put her in trouble - big time. She fished in her handbag and pulled out the calling card for Sergeant Gary Townsend. He'd said she could give him a ring if anything else happened, or if she had any thoughts on who might be responsible for the message scrawled on her window. She took out her mobile and began to dial the number. But then she stopped. No, she had to be careful. How would this play with Dan? She didn't want to do anything which would push him away. Perhaps, it would be better to cling to the moral high ground, that's where she should be. While Dan made up his mind to come back to her, she'd be brave and noble. She could picture how, when they were back together, she would tearfully reveal to Dan what Jen had done and how he would then take her into his arms and say how sorry he was and what a terrible woman Jen had become. He'd say that it had taken Emma's return to the village for him to realise what a mistake he'd made in ever setting up home with Jen. She put the phone and the officer's card back in her bag.

# Chapter Twenty-Nine
# Dan

It was a lovely warm evening as Dan climbed out of his dirty overalls at the end of the day. Asif and Deano were washing their hands at the sink.

'Fancy a drink, Dan? You look like you could do with some cheering up,' asked Asif after deliberately waiting until Deano had left for the night.

'Yeah, why not? But just the one pint, mind,' replied Dan. He had half an hour or so free before Jen got home from work.

Just as they were leaving, Emma's car pulled up. Dan's heart rate began to quicken. Asif shot him a glance.

'Hi Dan,' said Emma, brightly, after winding down her window. Then looking at Asif, she added, 'I'm afraid I can't remember your name.'

'You should, Emma, this is Asif. Remember, he was at school with us? Asif, you remember Emma?'

He shyly said that he did. And Emma returned that, of course, she remembered Asif now, adding that school had been such a long time ago. Dan hoped Asif would walk on to the pub and get the beers in, but instead he bent down to undo and then re-tie his shoelaces.

'I, err, just popped by to see if you, or the garage, whatever, whoever, could look at my car? It's not running very well. I think it needs tuning or something,' said Emma.

'Yeah, no problem. But it's best to book it in, I can't get to the diary now because the office is closed up. We'll have a new receptionist starting next week, so if you ring her on that number,' he pointed to the sign above the garage's double doors, 'then she can book you in.'

'Oh, ok, thanks,' said Emma, with a lovely smile. She started to tap the phone number into her mobile.

Asif was showing no sign of moving, he seemed to be having great problems with his shoelaces. Emma glanced at him and seemed to judge that he was preoccupied because she blew Dan a kiss. Then, she made a phone call sign with her hand, reversed up, and drove off.

But Asif saw it all. 'Blowing kisses, eh, well, well, well, Danny boy, what's that all about?'

'Nothing, leave it,' said Dan grumpily.

They arrived at the pub, and Dan bought a round of drinks. He knew Asif wouldn't let things go, and he decided, maybe rather too quickly, that actually he might like, need, someone to talk to. Could he trust Asif? He thought he could, they were pretty close, and he'd kept quiet that time when there were problems in the band that Dan had to sort.

Sure enough, as soon as they sat down, Asif began pushing him. 'Well?' was all he needed to say, with a quizzical look on his face.

Dan took a gulp of beer and came to a decision. 'Ok, I'll tell you, but I've got to trust you, for fuck's sake,' he said, looking about him to make sure no one else could hear.

Asif pulled his stool in a bit closer. 'Of course you know you can trust me. Bloody hell, what you been up to, man? You're not giving her one, are you?'

'No, nothing's happened, but it nearly did, she wants me back. I don't know what to do, that's why I need to talk. It's driving me fucking bonkers; I'm going out of my mind with it.'

'Does Jen know?'

'Know what? There's really nothing to know at the moment. But, yes, she's suspicious, just because Emma's back here in the village, really.'

'Well, I told you it was a bit odd,' said Asif. 'So, Emma's still got a thing for you after all these years. Lucky boy Danny, she's gorgeous, always was. Not that Jen isn't great too.' Asif took a sip of his pint and then added, 'You lucky bastard, I can't even get one girl, and you've got them queuing up.'

'It doesn't feel lucky,' replied Dan. I don't know what to do. I really don't.'

'Well, can you have both? That'd be my starting point.'

'Ha, yeah, thought it might be. Nah, that's not right. I need to get my head around it.'

Dan took a sip of his beer and weighed up whether to say more. He decided he would. 'I haven't really had a chance to talk to Emma properly yet. I went to her place last night after a row with Jen. She thought I was just out for a walk to cool off, and I wasn't away for long, but we - Emma and me, that is - sort of ended up having a bit of a rumble on the sofa. And then, just as things were getting interesting, that sculptor, you know, the tosser, Toby, turned up. Emma had invited him to dinner – some sort of celebration. They're just friends, she says. Anyway, that was about it, and I left.'

'Well, you've got to talk to her then, mate; that's the only answer, and the only way you're going to know what she wants, and the only way you're going to find out what you want.'

'You're right, but I keep wrestling with whether I should just walk away, ignore her, and get on with my life. I've been happy with Jen - I am happy with Jen. We're thinking of getting married, having kids, for Christ's sake. What sort of a bastard am I if I start messing around? But the trouble is, I just can't get Emma out of my head. When we were together, back then, we were bloody brilliant.'

'I remember you were pretty much a unit,' said Asif. 'But I didn't know you as well back then. Why did she fuck off from the village and school so quickly?'

'Her dad. He got a job, and they had to leave all of a sudden. She said there was no point carrying on. I wrote loads of letters and stuff to an address I got from someone, I can't even remember who now. But, to be honest, I don't know if she ever got them or whether it was the right address. I was pretty pissed off at the time that she'd just dropped me like a stone.'

They sipped their beers and Dan opened and shared a bag of cheese and onion crisps. 'The trouble is, Jen is so suspicious. I don't know how I'm going to get to talk to Emma. I don't want to be seen going around to her flat, Jen knows everyone in this village. It was a bit risky last night, but I got into a state. And now that the Toby bloke knows, and you know, well, it's all getting very dodgy.'

'Haven't you got her phone number?'

'Not a mobile, no, it's too risky to have it stored on my phone. I have her work number, but anyway, we need to do this stuff face to face.'

'You shouldn't have spent so much time on her face last night, you prick,' laughed Asif. 'I tell you what, when she brings her car in, I'll sort it so that she can meet you in that little store cupboard at the back of the garage. You can be in there already, and I'll find a way of getting her in there too. But talk, don't shag.'

Dan agreed that it was a decent plan, and they talked about the band until they finished their drinks.

Dan ambled home, hoping that Jen was back. Whatever happened with Emma, he still wanted Jen. But the question was, who did he want the most? His head said Jen, but other parts of his anatomy said, Emma.

Jen was home before him. As he walked through the door he said, 'Hi, babes,' as if he didn't have a care in the world.

# Chapter Thirty
# Jen

'Steady tiger. You've not even got your coat off yet.' Dan was all over her. He'd only just come in, and he still had that oily garage smell about him. She liked it.

'I've been thinking about this all day,' said Dan, as he buried his head into her neck.

She had a choice; she'd thought it through earlier in the day. She could either confront him with what she now knew; that he *had* been to see Emma the previous night; ask him how strands of Emma's hair had managed to get all over his shirt; ask him exactly what was going on; or she could keep quiet, and fight for him. And when she'd finally calmed down after that morning's confrontation, she'd thought about what Emma had *actually* said. Yes, she'd admitted meeting Dan, but she'd claimed nothing had happened. To be fair to Dan - and Jen wasn't entirely sure why she should be – that explanation did seem plausible because, after all, he hadn't been away from the house for very long. Emma had also said it was now up to Dan what he did next – which it was. But he could, of course, be influenced. At the end of the day, Jen concluded, all he'd done was talk to an old girlfriend – well, so what, that wasn't so bad? So, if his currently roaming hands were his way of choosing between them, well, for now, she'd give him the benefit of the doubt – and show him just how much she loved him.

Afterwards, as she lay resting her head on his chest, Jen figured that Dan couldn't possibly have heard about the confrontation with Emma at the art gallery. Hopefully, he never would. Hopefully,

Emma wouldn't tell him; but it was probably only a matter of time before she did. So, what should *she* do? Confess? This certainly wasn't the time or the place, and she'd certainly leave it for tonight. Maybe it would be a better tactic to wait for him to bring it up. After all, she hadn't done anything wrong. All she'd done was fight to keep them together. He would understand that. Maybe that was what was turning him on. It must be good for any man's ego to be wanted by two women. A part of her thought, why should I put up with this; why should I be treated like this? But the other half of her understood the reality of splitting up. It would mean being on her own, again, all her dreams shattered. This could be just a blip in the great scheme of things. If she and Dan looked back after fifty years together, they'd barely remember it at all.

'Glass of wine, sweetheart,' said Dan later on that evening as she got the dinner ready.

'Yeah, sure, don't hold back,'

'Did you have a good day at work?'

'Oh, so-so, never mind that, tell me about your day,' she said. She was eager to change the subject, because she certainly didn't want him to know she hadn't gone to work at all that day.

'Oh, nothing much, Asif and I were working out a new song at lunchtime. It's called Sunrise.'

'Sing it.'

'Sod off, it's not finished yet. You'll have to wait.' He crept up behind her and put his arms around her as she tried to turn the fish over in the pan.

'I don't like waiting for things,' she said, coquettishly wriggling her backside into his groin.

'I've noticed.'

But, after dinner, as they watched TV, Dan, who'd been quiet for a while, suddenly turned the sound down with the remote. What was coming now?

'Jen,' he said and then paused.

'Yes darling, what?'

'Jen.'

'Yes.'

'I think I should be honest with you.'

She braced herself.

'I don't want there to be any secrets or for you to worry about anything.'

Oh dear, she thought.

'So, I'm telling you that Emma has booked her car into the garage for some work. I won't personally do the job, but I guess I might see her briefly.'

That was it?!

'Right, ok, no worries,' was all she could think of to say. She got up and went to the kitchen to start washing up the dishes. Normally, he'd come to help, but he'd found some football on TV.

So much for honesty then, thought Jen. No mention of going around to Emma's place; no mention of how that woman wanted him back or what he was going to do about it. But Jen knew she must keep her anger in check and remain calm if she could. Another big row would not help her cause.

But, an hour later, as she gave him the third great time he'd had that day, she realised the battle wasn't over yet. She'd made a silly

138

threat, maybe she shouldn't have, but maybe, she should just carry it through. The thought was quickly side-lined as she lost herself in the moment. She loved Dan so much, and she must fight to keep him.

# Chapter Thirty-One
# Toby

Toby was working late. It was past ten, and he was getting tired. He was on a tight timetable if he was going to get his model finished in time for the London presentation. Interruptions, like the altercation involving Emma and Jen this morning, didn't help. But he was also finding it hard to concentrate. A lot had happened in the past couple of days. His meal with Emma, the revelation about her and Dan, followed by his own emotional declaration. And then, this morning's extraordinary catfight between Emma and Jen.

Right now, a voice in his head was trying to convince himself to just get on with his own life – but that voice wasn't having much success. Don't let Emma obsess your every waking moment, it said. You've given her your best shot, you've declared yourself, now move on. But there was another narrative that argued that there was still hope. It said there was every chance Emma and Dan's relationship wouldn't work out. Hang in there, was the message from this voice.

He returned to his work. It had been a laborious process pressing the self-drying clay into the wire and mesh frame and then building it up layer by layer until it was thick enough to start moulding into shape. The student girl, volunteer, whatever she was, Maddy, had been a help and a hindrance at the same time. She was certainly keen; he would say that for her. Over the past week, she'd been in four days. He felt he'd got to know her quite well. She'd been a help in that she'd moulded the clay so that it was soft enough for him to apply, and she'd even helped on the main model itself. But she was also a hindrance because she did talk rather a lot. Not only questions about what he was doing but about the art gallery, other people in the gallery – especially Emma for some reason – and about his life.

She was quite a flirt – and she'd got flirtier as the days passed. But she was much too young for him. And, anyway, a new romantic interest was out of the question when his head was still so full of Emma.

He'd decided that he'd try to be as normal as possible with Emma, despite the Dan thing. It had only been right that he'd helped her calm down after the shock of Jen's visit that morning. Poor Emma, it had been horrible; mad. Mind you, it was her own fault. What did she expect? She was playing with fire.

Emma had left the studio following the altercation. She'd said she wanted to clear her head. He wasn't surprised. He needed to think too. He'd hated the night before what had happened and how he'd handled it. When he'd got home, he'd sat drinking whisky until the early hours. It hadn't helped much. But despite an alcohol-disturbed night and the subsequent hangover, he was beginning to think a bit more clearly now. The reality was that it was no surprise Emma was still in love with Dan. He had to accept that. He would have to play the long game and keep things a bit cool for a time. From now on he'd keep to his own studio, stop popping around to hers for so many chats, he'd be a bit more distant. The Emma project would be scaled back.

He was also embarrassed that he'd reminded her of *that* night. That night in the cricket hut, when she'd dragged him down onto the sofa. Did she really not remember what happened, that, as usual, he'd been the perfect gentleman – well, nearly? They'd had a kiss and cuddle, and she'd seemed keen that they go further, but he'd quickly realised that she was too far gone and that he couldn't take advantage. So, he'd got her home safely, helped her turn the key in the lock, and helped her inside. By then, she'd sobered up a bit, and in a hushed voice, he assumed to avoid waking her parents, she'd said she'd be ok to get to bed.

Toby looked at the clock and began to pack up for the night, putting damp cloths over the left-over clay to keep it moist until morning. He'd had a special box made for the model, which was sitting on the side. It would enable him to take it down to London on the train for the presentation to the company's board. If they gave him the go-ahead, then working with the stone at the garage would also keep him out of Emma's hair; her beautiful hair, he could almost smell it.

He then began to wonder how she was. She must have had a hell of a day. He hoped she was alright. Maybe, she should go to the police about that Jen woman. They hadn't had time to talk, and actually, the more Toby thought about it, the more he thought she really should go to the police about Jen. What if she had also been responsible for the graffiti attack? For some reason, he hadn't put those two things together until now. And then a worse thought took root in his mind. What was it Jen had said? *'Something very horrible is going to happen to you.'* - that was it. He'd heard it clearly through the wall. They'd been shouting at each other. At the time, he'd immediately dismissed it as an idle threat. But what if Jen really was off her rocker, driven to do something desperate because she was losing Dan? What if she did *'do something very horrible?'*

He picked up his mobile and texted Emma asking if she was ok. Then he finished clearing up. Before covering his model he stood back to admire it. He was pleased with what he saw. He felt it was a real statement piece, well, it would be when it was full size. It was promising to be the best thing he'd ever done. The design, he'd discovered, had been lurking in the back of his mind for ages. It was just waiting for a commission like this.

No reply from Emma.

There was a fair amount of clay on the floor. There always was. He didn't want to waste any, so he got down and began the laborious task of scraping up all the little bits and putting them into a bowl.

Still no reply from Emma.

He'd have to go round – just to check she was alright.


When he got to her place he could see that there was a light on in the lounge - a good sign. He approached the flat's window, but then stopped in his tracks seeing movement inside. He retreated and crouched down behind Emma's car, peeking out from around the boot. After a while, he crept up to the window again and peered in. Emma was lying on the sofa reading a book. She seemed ok. That was a relief. So he crept away and jogged home.

# Chapter Thirty-Two
# Emma

It was one of those dreams from which she awoke with a start. Emma wasn't even sure if it was actually a dream rather than a distant previously lost memory buried in her subconscious. She must have dozed off lying on the sofa, her book had fallen to the floor. She sat up, rubbed her face with her hands, and tried to come round. It was half past eight, and she'd not eaten, so she investigated the fridge to see what it had to offer. Not a lot - a lump of cheese and a bit of tired salad. It would have to do. She poured herself a glass of wine. In the dream, she'd been, well, with Toby. It had felt warm and safe. He was being very gentle and tender. It had left her with an almost ethereal glow. But she was bothered by it. She sipped her wine and just stared out of the window for a while, replaying the images. Then she remembered, it was in a bedroom, the dream was in a strange bedroom with pink wallpaper – not the old cricket hut. So – and this was what was bothering her - it must have been a dream. Not a memory. That was a relief. But why had she dreamt of Toby and not Dan? The brain was odd like that. She remembered how she'd once dreamt about sex with one of the blokes in the office where she used to work. The next day she'd not been able to look him in the eye for the embarrassment.

But her unease wouldn't disappear. What if she and Toby had actually had sex that night, the night she'd got very drunk? What was it he'd said last night? She'd wanted him, she'd been all over him, and she'd not been able to get enough of him. She honestly couldn't remember any of it. The last thing she recalled was staggering into her bedroom at home. Yes, Toby had taken her home, she remembered that. But what if they had *done* it? What if, for some reason, it hadn't occurred to her before this horrifying moment? What if, what if Toby was the father of her baby? The timings would work. She and Dan had made up after their row a couple of days later. Either one of them could be the father of her baby. Oh my god. She'd always just assumed that Madeleine was Dan's child, their love child. She poured herself another glass of wine. She was slightly shaking now as the argument raged in her head. No, surely not, Maddy must be Dan's. She must be. Toby wouldn't have taken advantage of her. Not while she was inebriated. These days it would be considered rape, probably back then too. What a terrible thought. He wouldn't have done it. Madeleine had to be Dan's baby.

Emma dismissed the thought. She was over-tired. It had been some day. First, that horrible woman had attacked her, and now this new thought was attacking her as well. The house phone rang, which was rare.

'Hi dear,'

'Oh, hi, Mum.'

'Oh, you sound tired, Emma, you must make sure you get enough sleep, you know. Anyway, just a reminder that we're up on Monday. We won't stay long because we've got to try to reach a place just outside Glasgow by evening. So, what if we meet for lunch?'

'That'd be great. And after lunch, I could quickly show you around the gallery. It won't take long. Dad could see what he's helping to pay for,' said Emma.

They finished making the arrangements, and Emma put the phone down. That was all she needed with everything else kicking off. But her parents were her parents, and, at the end of the day, it was only a flying visit.

What a pity she couldn't introduce them to Dan, the new man in her life, but it was a bit premature for that – and it probably wouldn't go down too well. She smiled at the thought of it. Her parents would certainly be shocked. Anyway, right now, she didn't even know when she was going to see Dan again. That was why she'd booked the car into his garage so that she could engineer a chance to speak to him.

She picked at her food - she wasn't very hungry - and she poured herself a third glass of wine. Her mind began to think of Dan, and she swapped him for Toby in the image which still remained in her head. Here conviction strengthened that she must consummate matters with Dan as soon as possible. That's what was required to secure him – Dan - the father of her child - surely? It's only a matter of time before we're together again, she thought.

On Monday, her parents arrived exactly on time. This was typical of her father, if not for her mother; he would be running the whole thing like a military operation. After the usual hugs and complaints about traffic, they went into the smarter of the two pubs, The Royal Crown, and settled down at a table towards the back. She noticed that her father looked a bit peaky - very pale and rather tired. He was now pushing seventy, so perhaps that explained it. The break in Scotland would do him good. Her mother looked much the same as she always did. She was a very smart, well-dressed woman. Emma took after her in that they both had lovely smooth skin and those much remarked upon beautiful eyes. Only her mother, Emma thought, had always rather overdone the eye shadow.

'Not a bad pub this, hasn't changed much from what I can see,' said her father.

'Oh, it's changed quite a lot, I think.' Her mother corrected. 'Those curtains are new, and all the covers on the seats have been replaced.'

'Well, that's just window dressing, my dear. Fundamentally, it's the same place. Same bar, the same fireplace, and probably the same bloody landlord. I guess we haven't been in here for nearly twenty years.'

'Actually, it's nearly nineteen years,' corrected Emma pedantically. 'It's almost nineteen years since we left the village. But no, you're wrong,' she loved saying that to her father, 'I gather the landlord has changed several times.'

'I expect there have been lots of changes in the village,' said her mother. 'I doubt there's anyone we know living here now. It's all a very long time ago. Shall we have a look at the menu?'

'Well, there are still some people I remember,' said Emma. 'People I knew back then. People I knew very well.'

Her father glanced at her mother, looking over the top of his glasses.

Her mother quickly said, 'I quite fancy the soup. I wonder what it is today. Yes, soup and a roll will do me. So, Emma, how's it going at the gallery? Have you sold any work?'

But her father, typically, interjected before she had a chance to answer.

'Can't see why you'd come back here. I mean, it's an ok sort of village, but it's a bit out of the way, isn't it, for a budding artist, I mean, you know, a bit off the beaten track?'

'That's the way I like it, Dad. Anyway, to answer your question, Mum, I'm doing pretty well, I think. Last month I sold four paintings.'

'Four?' blustered her father. 'That doesn't sound like it'll keep the wolf from the door.'

'Well, she's only just starting out, dear,' said her mother, resting her hand on her husband's, which was beginning to drum the table.'

Emma decided to put in their food orders at the bar. She bought another round of drinks. This was going to be a very long couple of hours. The conversation didn't get any better. Her father kept sounding off about things, while her mother tried to keep the peace. His views on politics were directly opposite to Emma's. In fact, his views on almost everything were directly opposite to hers. She felt her agitation rise.

'The trouble is we can't just let anyone we like into the country. There'll be no jobs for anyone, let alone services. How's the NHS supposed to cope – what about the schools?' her father rumbled on, rather too loudly.

'That's got nothing to do with immigration, and you know it. It's because of the cuts, that's why the country is struggling,' fought back Emma.

'And why do we have to cut because your lot spent all the money?'

'That's not the case, either, is it? There was a worldwide banking crisis.'

Every now and again, her mother would remark upon something else to try to change the topic. 'Oh, look at that picture above the fireplace, isn't that lovely?' But she was fighting a losing battle.

By the end of lunch, Emma had just about had enough. She wished they'd head off straight away on their journey north. But she had promised to show them her studio.

'Well, let's see your place then, see what I'm paying for,' said her father as they stepped from the pub into the village square. It was beginning to drizzle with rain.

'You're not paying for all of it. I'm doing my best,' responded Emma, the upset coming through in her voice.

'Of course, you are dear, we understand that,' soothed her mother.

Upstairs in the gallery, Toby was busy in his room. His door was half open, and Emma smiled at him as she came up the stairs. She could see him quickly wiping his hands on an old cloth, looking a bit flustered.

'Mr and Mrs Taylor, err, how, um, delightful to meet you again,' he said, stepping out of his room.

'Again, why do you say again, what's your name?' said her father abruptly.

'Toby, sir, I used to be a friend of Emma's in the sixth form at school.'

'Hello, Toby,' said her mother shaking his hand but then looking as though she wished she hadn't as she brushed bits of clay from her glove. 'We remember you, of course we do, Toby. Emma has told us all about how much you've helped her since she came back here. How marvellous that you two are in the same line of business. I hear that you're doing really, really, well.'

Toby explained a little about his new commission before Emma showed her parents into her studio.

'Thought he was that bloody wastrel Dan for a moment there,' said her father. 'I knew I recognised the face.'

Emma quickly closed the door. 'Dan isn't a wastrel.' She wasn't going to let the comment go. 'He has a very good job.'

Immediately, she knew she'd made a mistake, she could see the alarm in both her parents' eyes. She should have kept quiet, but her father was getting to her, and she just couldn't help herself. Her mother looked at her father as if, Emma thought later, she knew of the gathering storm.

'How do you know? Is he here? Is the little toe rag still here in this village? That's not why you've come back here, Emma, is it? Tell me it isn't? I feared as much as soon as you wanted to move back to this village. I should have questioned you, but as you didn't mention him I thought he must have moved on. Tell me, girl, what's going on?'

'Nothing is going on, not yet anyway. And my name is Emma, by the way, not "girl." Hello, I'm your daughter, how do you do. Anyway, even if he was the reason I came back here, it's none of your bloody business. Now keep your voice down, these walls are pretty thin.'

'Listen,' he waved a finger at her. 'That boy, that Dan, is bad news, Emma. He got you pregnant; with child, up the duff, expecting a baby. Remember? You were just a schoolgirl,'

'Shush, shush, not here, Dad. Keep your voice down,' said Emma, she was beginning to panic.

'Yes, quiet at once,' said her mother. Emma had never heard her so stern. 'It's all water under the bridge. Time has healed, Things have moved on. Emma is a grown woman, and she must lead her own life.'

'Well, she can lead it without my help if that scoundrel is in the picture,' said her father. 'I'll leave it there, Emma, out of respect for your mother. But I think you need to do a lot of thinking. We should talk again about this when we get back from Scotland.' He opened the studio door, steadied himself, as he seemed a bit wobbly on his feet, and then left.

'Oh dear,' said her mother. 'Why does it always have to end like this?'

'Because he's a jerk, Mother,' Emma replied. 'You know he is.'

'He's your father, Emma, and he's done a lot for you.'

'What, like he did eighteen years ago? That was for me, was it? I'd say that was pretty much against me. You have no idea what damage that decision has done.'

'We did what we thought best. And you agreed.'

Emma spoke in a controlled but angry whisper so her voice wouldn't travel through the walls – though she thought it was probably too late for such a precaution.

'Only because I felt I had no choice, only because *he* bullied me. Now I'm thirty-six with no man, no husband, and no baby - no child.' Emma paused for a moment, trying to collect herself. 'She must be eighteen now, Mum. Do you realise that? Your granddaughter. A grown woman herself.' She felt the tears prick her eyes.

'Yes, I know, I know, don't upset yourself, I'm sure she'll have been well looked after.'

'How are we sure? How do we know she's happy?'

'Oh, Emma,' said her mother putting her arms round her. 'There's no good getting all worked up. You need to move on. That's what we've always said. Are you sure coming back here is a good thing, all these old memories?'

But before Emma could answer, her father was back at the door. Behind him, she saw Toby coming up the stairs. Thank god, she thought, hopefully, he wouldn't have heard what was said.

'Are you coming, Susan? We need to get on our way,' spluttered her father. He ushered her mother out of the door before adding: 'Thanks for lunch, Emma, the studio looks very nice.' As if that made everything alright.

# Chapter Thirty-Three
# Maddy

As she approached the rather shabby old garage, which was begging for a coat of paint, a small shudder passed across her shoulders. A car repair company wasn't the sort of place Maddy had ever expected to start her working life. But, if it was a means to an end, then she'd bear it. She was nothing if she wasn't tenacious. She'd started this project, and she was going to finish it.

'Right, Madeleine,' said Tom, who was looking about as shabby as his business. 'Can I call you Madeleine?'

'I'd rather you called me Maddy, everyone else does.'

'Right, Maddy, this is your desk, why don't you put your things down and get straightened out? Then you can make us both a cup of coffee and after that, I'll run through your duties in detail.'

Tom left her and went into the smaller connecting office where the interviews had taken place. Maddy settled herself in. From her handbag, she took out a small notebook, a pen, a pencil, a calculator, and her mobile phone and laid them out neatly on the desk. Then she fired up her computer screen. No password was required. That was something she'd need to change. As the computer completed its start-up, she re-filled and turned on a rather filthy old red kettle.

At least Tom seemed nice, thought Maddy. Old fashioned, rather patronising, maybe, but probably just paternalistic. It made her feel instantly guilty that she was going to have to let him down in a few weeks' time and disappear back home. How was she going to handle that? For that matter, how was she going to handle everything?

After about half an hour, when they'd both finished their drinks, Tom re-emerged and took Maddy out into the workshop. He introduced her to all the staff, calling her Madeleine each time, and each time she corrected him, saying they should call her Maddy. Asif, Laser, Deano, the apprentice, and Dan. They were all very friendly - apart from Dan, who just grunted.

'I'm sorry Dan seemed a bit stand-offish,' said Tom when they returned to the office. 'Perhaps, I should explain,' he continued. 'You see Dan's girlfriend, or perhaps these days I should say partner, also applied for this role.'

'Yes, I met her - Jen. Remember, we both had to wait in here for a while before our interview.

'Oh right, yes. Anyway, I gather Jen took the disappointment badly, and Dan hasn't really spoken more than three words to me since. I'm sure he'll get over it. I'll certainly have a word with him if he takes it out on you. I'm not having that.' He paused for a moment and blew his nose into an oily, filthy-looking handkerchief. 'If I were you, I'd just let a little water go under the bridge and see what happens. I'll give you a tip. Dan likes hot chocolate to drink. Maybe you could make him the odd hot chocolate, and then things will get better.'

Maddy was beginning to think this job was more about making hot drinks than anything else. And she didn't think Tom should be tiptoeing around an employee just because he was in a state about something which had been legitimately sorted by fair selection? She put that thought to one side and concentrated on deciphering a handwritten briefing document Tom had prepared detailing the tasks she was expected to perform. It all looked fairly straightforward and she felt she could easily handle the job. No problem. That was a big relief, but she still felt incredibly anxious about her subterfuge and her plan. Before, when she'd been thinking things through, it had all seemed so far off - stuff that would probably never happen - but now she was in the middle of it, living it, lying, pretending she wasn't who she really was, it was all rather different. Everything was becoming a bit too real. She knew she was in way over her head, but there was no turning back. Not now. She began to sweat a little as the thoughts raced through her mind.

She decided to make herself busy. She'd make that hot chocolate for Dan. When she'd met Jen for coffee, she'd gone on and on about what a fantastic bloke Dan was. Well, there'd been little evidence so far.

And before she'd had a chance to make the drinks, Dan came through the door. He chucked down an order form on her desk and barked out, 'Can you get that lot in – make sure that the head gasket is a hundred mill?'

Maddy didn't know what a head gasket was, but she wasn't going to ask him and show her ignorance. She'd just have to get to grips with everything.

'Yeah, sure, no problem,' she replied. He didn't say anything back to her and simply marched out of the office.

'No *problemo* at all, you rude bastard,' Maddy said under her breath.

She inspected Dan's note. Tom had given her details of their main parts supplier, so she simply copied Dan's form and e-mailed it across, piece of cake.

The rest of the morning passed slowly but fairly smoothly. The other guys were friendly enough when they popped into the office to submit their worksheets, especially Deano, who she'd met in the pub at Dan's concert and who still seemed to be quite interested in her. He was just a boy, though, and when he'd returned to the workshop, Maddy quickly switched her thoughts to the one man in the village who had, so far, really interested her. The same man who was taking her out for lunch today, Toby.

Her original idea had been to just use Toby to find out more about her mother. She'd extracted a few interesting titbits but nothing very revealing. Toby had simply said what a great artist she was and then quickly changed the subject. For most of the time she'd spent with Toby at the gallery, they'd just talked about sculpture. She'd watched him run his hands around the full curves of a large piece of clay, gently pressing it, needing it, smoothing it – and she'd found it all rather erotic. To her mind, she and Toby just seemed to click. So, as the lunch, which had been his idea, approached, she was getting butterflies in her stomach accompanied by that *I'm meeting someone I like* feeling. She'd texted her friend Amy about it and told her that Toby had texted *her* that he had a surprise. What could it be?

Deano came into the office again. Obviously, feeling more confident. 'So, Mads, can I call you Mads?' he asked, with a cheeky grin on his face.

'No, definitely not, I may well be mad, but who the hell would want to be called Mads?' she said good-humouredly.

'All Scots are mad if you ask me.'

'I didn't.'

'Where exactly are you from, anyway?' persevered Deano.

'Haven't you got work to do?' she said. She didn't want to get caught in personal conversations involving more lies or half-truths.

Deano carried on trying to extract information from her for a while and teasing her about this and that. Eventually, Tom shouted for help from the workshop, and he left. She typed some letters and sorted some invoices. Then, when she couldn't think of anything else to do, she took out a clean sheet of paper and wrote on the top: *Things to Find Out.* Under a subheading of *Lunch with Toby,* she wrote the following: Try to find out more about E. Is she nice? Is she kind? Is she married? If so, to whom, and is *he* my father? Were

155

they together when E was eighteen? Has she any (other) children? What are they like? How old are they? And so on.

The clock ticked around slowly to one o'clock, and at last, it was time for lunch. Tom had returned to his office and was eating sandwiches out of a Tupperware box.

'I'm off to lunch, Tom,' she said through his open doorway.

'Ok, Madeleine. How did you get on this morning?'

'It's Maddy, please call me Maddy,' she said again. 'Alright, I think, yes, I've enjoyed it,' she lied.

Toby had suggested they meet in the White Swan. There weren't many people in there. They took a table at the back of the bar and ordered something to eat and a drink.

Maddy started the conversation brightly, asking what sort of a morning he'd had. He seemed a bit distracted and a bit flustered.

'Interesting, I'll say that.'

'Tell me more.'

'Nothing really, just a bit of a kerfuffle with a customer, nothing at all really.'

'What just you, or did it involve anyone else, that artist next door to you, err, Emma?

Toby looked uncomfortable again and wriggled in his seat. Maddy realised she was obviously pushing too hard – especially bringing her mother into it. She'd better back off. Take her time, be careful.

'Err, no, no, not really, it was nothing. How's your morning been?' asked Toby, closing down her inquiry.

Maddy ran through everything in as humorous a way as possible, and Toby occasionally laughed at the way she put things. But she wasn't sure she had his full attention. She decided not to tell him about Dan. But she did tell him how Tom had put the wrong leg into his overalls and nearly fallen over. It wasn't true, but Toby gave her a big cute smile. Then Maddy remembered what he'd said earlier.

'Oh yes, so tell me, what's my surprise?' she asked.

'Right, um, yes, no, err, right,' began Toby, who suddenly seemed unable to get his words out. 'Well, I have to go to London to, um, talk through my drawings for the, err, commission. It'll be a two-day stop. I'd go down on the train Thursday afternoon, ready for the presentation the next day. Soooo, I could err do with an assistant. And I just wondered, though I'm sure you won't be able to get the time off so soon or anything, I mean, you've only just started, and I know we barely know each other, so it's all stupid, really, but I wondered if, maybe, you could be my assistant and come too.'

Well, that was indeed a surprise!

'Oh, well, I do have Fridays off, I'm only working four days a week, so it should be ok. But I don't think I'd be able to afford the, err, train fare, though.'

'I'd pay for everything, hotel, and stuff,' Toby interjected.

This was all moving rather quicker than Maddy expected. She became flushed.

Toby seemed to spot her train of thought, 'Of course, I'll pay for your room out of the project's business expenses,' he said.

She was relieved and a bit disappointed at the same time. This trip would be a chance to get to know Toby much better, and, well, one never knew how things might develop. She was tingling all over at the prospect, not to mention the fact that she'd have lots of time to find out more about her mother.

'What exactly would you want me to assist with?' she asked, trying to look serious and business-like but with a tease playing on her lips.

'Well, really, just someone to hold my drawings, help display them on a desk, set up the clay miniature, operate a laptop while I chat to them. To be honest, it's just to make me look more, err, important. It's, um, all bollocks, really, I just think it will help impress them. You'd impress anyone.'

She flushed again.

'I mean, because you have an obvious interest and aptitude for sculpture, and you're obviously someone who is very intelligent,' he said hurriedly. Maddy said she'd love to help if she could. She'd just have to double-check with Tom that he'd let her get away early on Thursday afternoon.

It took until they were drinking coffee at the end of the lunch for her to work her mother back into the conversation. 'So when you're away from the gallery, who deals with any business enquiries for you - does Emma help?

'Ha, to be honest,' said Toby. 'I don't err, have all that many business inquiries. I don't think it's likely to be a problem. Most of them come in by e-mail anyway, and I can deal with them on my phone or tablet.'

'Oh right, but you do have a good relationship with other people in the gallery, I guess, all helping each other and that kind of thing. I like that. Has Emma been there long?' she tried to sound as relaxed as possible. She already knew the answer to her question, but Toby did reveal some new information.

'No, not long. Emma came back recently. I think her marriage broke down, and she, err, returned to the village to find her roots.'

'Oh, so, she lived elsewhere then?'

'Yes, she left the village when she was about eighteen, a bit suddenly actually, something to do with her dad and a new job, I think.'

'Did you know her husband, her ex-husband, and does she have any children or anything?' asked Maddy, pushing things along and wondering, with a jump of her heart, if this ex-husband could be her dad.

Toby paused for a while before answering, 'No I never met him and there were no children. Why are you so interested?'

Maddy didn't say anything, she just shrugged but didn't say anything more. She wanted to look casual as if it didn't matter, and she'd also read somewhere that people would often carry on talking because they would be embarrassed by silence. It worked.

'She's a very talented artist,' continued Toby. 'We went to school together, you know, in the same year, and she was good at art back then. But I think she gave it all up when she got married. Anyway, I'm gossiping, which, err, I shouldn't.

So, Toby did know her at school. That meant he must be older than he looked. She'd have to enquire more when they were together in London. She liked the sound of that - together - in London.

'Oh, don't worry then, that's ok,' she said. 'I just wondered what sort of a place your gallery was and what it's like to work with a bunch of artists? It's something I might like to do someday.'

'You mean rather than work in a garage.' said Toby. 'Why have you taken that job anyway?' he asked.

Now the ball was on the other foot, and Maddy felt a bit awkward. 'Oh, it's just a fill-in job,' she said, immediately wishing she hadn't said that. 'Not that I've told them that, of course.'

'Don't worry, I won't say anything,' laughed Toby. Then, looking as if a thought had just occurred to him, he said, 'How old are you, by the way, if, err, you don't mind me asking?'

It was a clumsy question, and he immediately looked embarrassed in that way that he often did. She briefly considered whether she should tell him to f-off, but before she knew it, she'd replied, 'Twenty-three, why?'

'Oh, no reason, I just wondered,' he replied.

# Chapter Thirty-Four
# Toby

Later that afternoon, Toby tried to work, but he couldn't, his concentration had gone, and he kept making mistakes. He decided to reply to Maddy's recent e-mail. She'd sent it within an hour of their lunch together, and it said she'd managed to clear the necessary time off for his London trip. She was certainly keen.

*Re: London Trip*

*Toby <toby.sculptures@gmail.com>*

*Hi Maddy, great to meet up for lunch today and hear that you can help with my project. This is just to let you know I've booked for us to travel down on the three o'clock London train this Thursday afternoon. So, yes, you'll be able to work at the garage in the morning. We should have plenty of time to get to the hotel and maybe have some dinner. It'd be great to spend the evening with you chatting and stuff, but obviously, if you have friends to go and see, I totally understand. Our meeting/presentation is at ten the next day, so we shouldn't stay up too late. Not that I can tell you what to do, or anything!*

He then decided to make himself yet another cup of tea. He stepped out of his room to fetch some more milk from the café downstairs. Just as he did so, Emma came out of her room, and he manoeuvred around her awkwardly in the corridor without saying anything. Back in his room, Maddy had already sent a reply.

*Re: London Trip*

*Maddy <Maddy@Tom's Garage.co.uk>*

*Hi Tobes, yes, I'm really looking forward to spending some time with you – oh, and your interesting project! I shall look forward to our stay at the hotel! I shall be available for dinner - and chatting - in the evening – and for "stuff," whatever "stuff" might be!! I agree it would be terrible if we were to stay up too late!! By the way, you can <u>try</u> to tell me what to do, but I'll never take any notice!! Hope you're having a good afternoon. Maddy.*

Toby read it several times. He was no expert on this kind of thing, but he was pretty sure she was flirting with him, if only by over-use of the exclamation mark. It gave him a bit of a rush - after all, his self-esteem had taken a beating lately. He wrote back:

*My afternoon has been a bit dreary, to be honest. But the day was considerably brightened by our lunch together. The model sculpture should be ready in time. I'm really confident they'll like what I'm proposing.*

She clearly wasn't too busy at the garage, as she again replied within minutes.

*Well, that's what I'm here for – to brighten your day. Is the sculpture all nice and curvy? I like the way you work on curves(!!) - and I can't imagine anyone not being interested in anything you propose!*

Now, he definitely knew she was flirting. He felt a bit hot. He decided it might be better not to send a further reply. While it was fun to flirt, it didn't feel right. Emma filled his mind, and, anyway, even if Maddy was twenty-three, she was still too young for him.

Just then, Emma knocked on his door. He quickly closed down the screen on his laptop.

'Hey,'

'Hey,'

'Err, sorry if things got a bit heated earlier with my mum and dad. I wasn't sure if you heard anything or not. I saw that you'd been downstairs.' Emma said, looking very uneasy.

'No, no, I didn't really notice anything, I mean hear anything, well not much. I sort of thought I'd make myself scarce, so I went downstairs to talk to Sally for a bit. I hope you sorted things out.'

'Oh right, ok then, yes, just the usual spat with my father,' she looked relieved. 'So, how's it going with the commission?'

'Yeah, great. I've now fixed the London trip for Thursday. I'll have a small transportable model and some other drawings. I'm really, err, well, you know me, but yes, confident, I think, for once- ish.'

She laughed, and her eyes shone, that was nice. He hadn't seen this Emma for a few days. 'You sound it,' she said.

'I'm, err, going to take that young student with me. Well, she's not really a student - she's actually got a job at the garage - but I think she'd like to be a student. She's very keen on sculpture.'

'Oh right. So, you're taking a young apprentice - are we, um, overnighting at all?' Emma was teasing him, and he quickly blushed, which made things worse.

'Yes, well, I'll need a bit of help with things, and it seemed a good idea.'

'I could have gone with you,' she said.

Toby was surprised, the thought hadn't occurred to him. 'Oh, I assumed you'd be far too busy, but that's really kind. I, err, just didn't think of it, sorry, Em, I should have thought more about it, you might have liked a trip to London,' he spluttered.

'Don't worry, Tobes, I *am* only teasing. I am far too busy. But I'm sure you, and your young assistant, will have a wonderful time together,' she said with a big smile on her face.

'Oh, it's all, err, above board and everything. Two hotel rooms and all that,'

'You don't need to explain to me. I don't want to know about your sordid plans,' said Emma as she closed the door behind her.

Toby knew exactly why he'd told her about Maddy. He wanted her to see him as steadfast and loyal – but it wouldn't do any harm for her to know that he couldn't be taken for granted either

He also knew that what Emma had really been inquiring about was whether he'd overheard the row with her parents. He'd left her with the impression that he hadn't, that he'd missed it all after going downstairs. But the truth was Toby *had* heard every word of what her father said. It had rocked him to his boots. That was why he was distracted at lunch and why he couldn't get on with his work this afternoon. Emma, his Emma, had been pregnant back when she was just eighteen. It was astonishing news. He now realised that was why she'd left the village in such a hurry. It explained so much.

He'd known straight away that he couldn't tell Emma he'd overheard. It was her secret. Her secret to keep or tell when she chose. His heart ached. Poor Emma, carrying a burden like that for all these years. The thoughts were racing around his head. He had

164

so many questions. Did she have the baby? He assumed not. How utterly awful if she'd had an abortion. Did Dan know? Surely, she would have told him at the time? But she can't have done. Otherwise, he'd have stood by her, wouldn't he? Toby knew what he would have done. He'd have married her. He'd have done the decent thing.

# Chapter Thirty-Five
# Dan

Dan looked through the big plastic crate again. He was checking new parts sent by the supply company against his written list. There was only one conclusion to reach. That soppy girl had only gone and screwed it up, just as he'd predicted. He'd have to have a word. She had to learn very quickly, or quit, allowing Tom to give the job to someone who knew what they were doing.

He was annoyed, what a shame; he'd come into work that morning feeling really chilled after a great weekend. He and Jen had been *at it* almost the whole time. He couldn't believe it; suddenly, it was like she'd been injected with some kind of sex drug. She just wanted him all the time, and he was happy to oblige - well, as much as his body could take. What a fantastic woman she was. He knew he was lucky to be with Jen and that he really ought to shake Emma out of his mind. But he was struggling. It was like a curse.

'Maddy, look, sorry, but this order is totally wrong,' he said after barging into the office. He showed her the paperwork. 'These are the parts I wanted, and this is what they've sent, you've screwed up. I know you're new and all that, but you've got to get your act together. We can't have crap work here.' He wasn't holding back – why should he?

Tom emerged from his office. 'Cool it, Dan, what's the problem? I'm sure we can sort it out,' he said. Typical Tom, thought Dan.

'Well, I'm sure we can, Tom, but in the meantime, I can't get on with my job this morning. So, someone's going to have to phone Mrs Harris and tell her that her car won't be ready today because we've screwed up? Or rather, Maddy has screwed up.'

Tom held his hand out. 'Give me the order sheet, I'll ring her. We'll just have to get the parts for tomorrow. I'm sure Maddy will soon learn the ropes - a few teething problems are inevitable.'

'Actually,' interjected Maddy, who'd been busily tapping keys on her computer, 'I've just checked the e-mail I sent the supply company and, as you can see, Dan, I simply copied and pasted the list you gave me word for word. It's their fault, not ours, not yours, and certainly not mine.'

Dan bent over the screen. Bollocks. Sure enough, she was right, her order was correct. It was the supply company's mistake. Humble pie wasn't his favourite dish, but he had little choice. 'Ok, well, sorry,' he said, grudgingly.

'Perhaps you should have asked Maddy to check the order first before sounding off, Dan?' said Tom, rubbing the salt in. He wasn't usually so pompous, thought Dan, he was probably just playing up to the new member of staff.

Dan swallowed his anger and turned to go, but then he remembered something. 'Oh, by the way, has an Emma Taylor booked her car in? She told me last week that she wanted us to look at it.'

Maddy checked the appointment book as she blew her nose into a handkerchief. 'Yes, she rang this morning, as a matter of fact,' she said. 'She's coming in at nine-thirty tomorrow morning. Is *that* ok?'

'Yep, fine, all the same to me,' replied Dan, casually leaving the office and closing the door quietly behind him, trying to give the impression that the angry exchange had just been part of a normal day's ups and downs. But, as he walked back to his work bay he cursed, acknowledging the embarrassment he felt.

Asif was in the corner of the workshop, inflating a tyre. 'Asif, man, are you still on for sorting out that chat with Emma?' said Dan.

In his awkwardness, he swallowed Emma's name at the end of the sentence and had to repeat it.

'Oh, yeah, no problem, if I can. I mean, she might not want to,' replied Asif.

'Oh, I think she will. Anyway, she's dropping the car off on Thursday at nine-thirty. So, if I'm in the storeroom, perhaps you can persuade her to join me. Then we can talk, or at least set up another meeting.'

He owed it to Jen to talk to Emma and get things straightened out between them. It was just that he didn't quite know what *straightened out* meant.

# Chapter Thirty-Six
# Maddy

The little bell tinkled above the tea-shop door as Maddy rather timidly pushed it open. She quickly surveyed the small but cosy room. It was busy, but there was a table for two in the far corner. A waitress, who looked more harassed than welcoming, gestured towards it. Maddy was glad Jen hadn't arrived yet; it meant she had a few moments to text her friend Amy. She'd kept Amy fully informed of all developments – especially her growing admiration for Toby – and, of course, his work. Amy loved it all, and her replies were full of exclamation marks and all kinds of emojis.

But before Amy had time to reply, the bell above the door sprang into life, and in walked Jen, wearing a pair of ripped jeans - fashionable rips, but not something Maddy would have worn - and a bright, rather horrid, orange top.

'Oh, hi, Maddy, y'alright, brilliant to see you again, how's it going? Have you ordered?' gushed Jen.

Maddy said she hadn't and waved at the waitress who moodily sauntered over. They asked for two cappuccinos and cakes. Maddy was surprised that Jen had texted her wanting to meet up again, was she short of friends or something?

'Well, how are you finding things at the garage then?' Jen began.

Maddy knew this simple but incredibly difficult question was coming, and she'd debated how best to answer it. If she was honest and said that, so far, the job had been rather boring and easy, that might annoy and insult Jen. Such a remark could also get back to Tom. But, if she made out it was incredibly hard work, Jen might tell Tom that she was obviously struggling, which could play into her and Dan's hands. She'd already assumed they were jointly plotting to get her out. She was very much on her guard.

'Oh fine, early days, but I'm settling in ok and gradually learning what needs to be done,' she said, hoping she'd pitched it about right.

After ten minutes of incessant chat from Jen, Maddy thought that perhaps she needn't have worried. Jen didn't seem to be very interested in her career prospects, she'd mainly been talking about Dan and the band.

But then she changed tack slightly. 'I don't know if running that band isn't all too much for Dan, he's been a bit funny lately. One day he's all over me, and I mean all over me, night and day, if you get what I mean?' she touched Maddy's forearm. Maddy just smiled and raised her eyebrows toward the ceiling. 'The next day he's a bit moody and uncomunica…incom…,' she gave up. 'You know, he won't talk to me. Have you noticed anything at work?'

'Well, actually,' began Maddy, sensing her chance. 'Now you come to mention it; he has been rather bad-tempered and, err, difficult with me.' She paused slightly, looking solemnly down at the table for effect. 'I don't think he likes me. He seems to blame me because you didn't get the job.'

'Oh no, that's not nice, not nice at all,' said Jen, touching her arm again. Maddy wished she was rather less tactile. 'I'm sure he doesn't mean anything. I've told him I don't care about Tom's rotten job. I'm quite happy where I am. They're very good to me there. I mean, take last Friday when I was sick, and today when I've got the dentist, no problems at all.'

'Oh right, well, I was wondering,' ventured Maddy, 'If you, um, might have a word with Dan then? Tell him just that, you know, that you're happy with me being there or something, then he might lay off a bit.'

'Yes, of course, Maddy. I'll tell him tonight,' said Jen, and again she patted her arm. 'That's not good at all. It's not like him – he's normally the sweetest of men. But do you know what? He's not been himself ever since an old girlfriend of his turned up in the village. Her name's Emma Taylor, an artist at the gallery; a right bitch by all accounts.'

'Emma Taylor? I know her. She's just booked her car in for a service tomorrow,' replied Maddy, as casually as she could.

'Not that I'm worried about Dan or anything," continued Jen. "He's always been rock solid for me. Tomorrow, you say. Right, yes, Dan told me about it. Anyway, we're totally together, Dan and I, and I've got no concerns in that direction, no worries at all. It's just that she seems to have messed with his head a bit. Have you seen anything going on between them?'

'Err, no, like what?'

'Well, I suppose I wondered if you might have seen if she comes into the garage often when she's not booking services, for example. Or, whether Dan goes over to see her at lunchtimes or anything? I thought maybe you could tell me if you do see something.'

So that was why Jen wanted the coffee. She wanted information about Dan. She wanted to use her as a spy. But more importantly for Maddy, this was definite confirmation that there had been a *thing* in the past between Emma and Dan. She thought she'd seen a connection at the concert when her mother had blushed up when Dan sang that song. Her intuition was right, there *was* something there. She tried a question of her own.

'So did Dan and this Emma go out together before you came on the scene, so to speak? Not that it's any of my business, sorry if I shouldn't ask.'

'No, No, don't worry, Maddy, we're friends,' said Jen, touching her arm once more. Maddy pulled it away and tucked it under the table. 'No, yes, this was way back when they were at school in the sixth form, I think,' Jen continued. 'They were only about eighteen. I gather they were boyfriend and girlfriend for a couple of years, you know, in the way you are at that age. Well, of course you do, you *are* that age.'

'I'm a bit older than that, actually,' put in Maddy quickly.

'Of course you are. Well, anyway, they had a fling, and then I think it ended all of a sudden when her family had to move away. But now she's back, causing trouble.'

'Right,' said Maddy. It all fitted.

As Maddy walked back to the garage, her head was a jumble of thoughts. She felt anxious, happy, and fearful, all at the same time. This was a life-changing moment. Dan, who seemed to dislike her, who'd certainly been horrible to her so far, could be, was most likely to be, almost certainly was, her father. If Dan had been Emma's boyfriend at the time she disappeared from the village, she must have been pregnant, and that was why the family had left in a hurry. What was also clear was that either Dan had not told Jen that he and Emma had had a baby together, or – and this would be amazing – he didn't know himself. After all, his name wasn't on her birth certificate.

So, thought Maddy, when she entered the office and sat back down at her desk, it looked possible that her mother had simply gone off, left the village, given away her baby for adoption, and not told the baby's father. She'd not told Dan. How utterly terrible. Maddy sat there in a daze. So much had happened in such a short space of time. She'd discovered who her mother was; she'd seen her mother; she'd even bumped into her mother and been called a bitch by her mother; and now she almost certainly knew who her father was. She worked with him. They were colleagues. A part of her was excited by what she'd found out, but a part of her felt more alone than ever. It was all a bit of a mess. Maybe the idea of finding out about one's parents in this undercover way hadn't been such a good idea. She let that thought sink in for a bit. But then she concluded that, on the other hand, this was the very reason why she had come up with her plan in the first place. She'd wanted to know what her mother was like before deciding whether to reveal herself. It was just that, so far, neither her mother and now her father appeared to be quite what she'd hoped for.

# Chapter Thirty-Seven
# Jen

Jen liked cooking what she called "proper" dinners. They didn't eat ready meals, and they didn't even own a microwave. Tonight was chicken stir-fried with some mushrooms, olives, chopped runner beans, and a tomato-based sauce. Rice or potatoes? She decided on rice. Dan came home at his normal time. That was good, thought Jen. He certainly seemed happier and more settled after their exertions over the past few days. In fact, he seemed to be running out of steam a bit. Perhaps he needed a rest, poor lamb.

'Did you have a good day?' she asked. 'Was it busy?'

'Yeah, we're pretty much fully booked at the moment, which is good, I suppose.'

'And, um, did that, err, Emma woman bring her car in, you said you might have to see her this week?'

The question seemed to stop Dan in his tracks as he headed for the hook which held Barney's lead. After a long pause, he said, 'No, I think she's coming in tomorrow morning. Asif is handling it.'

'Oh right.'

Dan put the lead on Barney, who was following him around the kitchen, his tail wagging madly.

'I'll just take the dog out for a spin. How long's dinner?'

'Oh, about four and a half inches, I think,'

'Very funny…you know what I mean.' Dan gave her a slap on the backside, and she let out a little squeal.

'That's sexual harassment, you know,' she said playfully. 'Dinner will be about fifteen minutes, so just take him around the block. I'll give him another walk later on.'

There, they could actually mention the Emma woman and recover from it and be normal, thought Jen. She was feeling more optimistic. Dan still hadn't said anything about her visit to Emma's studio the other day. So, if he didn't know about it yet, it suggested that he and Emma hadn't met up again. She was sure he wasn't texting Emma because she'd checked his phone. So, that was another good sign. Maybe her *chat* with the Emma woman had done the trick. The test would come tomorrow when she brought her car in for its service, and that left Jen with a dilemma. They'd had a great few days, and she didn't want to rock the boat. But, if he was eventually going to hear about her visit to the art gallery, it would be better if it came from her lips rather than from Emma's. So, should she tell him? Should she confess? First, she'd do a little more probing.

When they'd finished their dinner, and Dan had put the kettle on, she decided it was a good time to talk. 'So, what will you say to this Emma if you come face to face with her tomorrow? Because, as far as I can gather from what you've told me you've had one brief conversation in the pub with her, and that's it.'

'Best kept that way, I'd say,' he replied, grumpily, after what seemed another long pause. 'Anyway, she'll just come in the office, drop her keys off, and that'll be that. So, there's no reason why I should see her. I just thought, given that you're so insecure about it all, that I'd warn you she was coming to the garage. Now can we just forget it?'

'So, that's definitely the only time you've spoken to her, then?'

'Yes. Jen, please, we've had a lovely few days, let's not ruin it,' said Dan, who was now standing with his back to the work surface while Jen remained seated at the table. The kettle was building up a head of steam, and all of a sudden, so was Jen.

'The thing is, Dan, you're a bloody liar,' she said, managing to keep her voice quite calm. Dan put his hand to his forehead and dragged it slowly down across his eyes.

'You see, I went round to see the lovely Emma at her studio.'

'You did what?'

'Yes, I went round there.'

'What the hell for?'

'Because, lover boy, I found three of her lovely long auburn hairs on your shirt that night you went out for a walk. It was to cool off, you said, but I don't think you did much cooling off at her place, did you?'

Dan didn't reply. He just stared at her.

'Anyway, we had a bit of a chat. And she admitted you'd gone to hers and that she'd told you to make a choice – between me and her. She says you've always been hers, apparently, so God knows what the last six years have been about because I thought we were a couple, and despite this little problem period, I think we've been good together. I really do.' Her voice began to break as she came to the end of the sentence, and her eyes filled with tears.

'We *are* good together, Jen,' said Dan.

'So why did you go to see her?'

'I just wanted to talk to her to find out why she was back here. To find out how she was. We were very close once, and she went off very quickly. But that was it. Nothing else.'

'I hit her,' said Jen.

'You did what?'

'I hit her. I slapped her. I'd have given her another if that Toby bloke hadn't come in the room and stopped me. I hate her, Dan. What's she doing here? Getting in the way of what we are, trying to break us up. I want her out of this village.'

'Calm down, Jen,' said Dan, coming over and putting an arm around her shoulders. She shrugged him off.

'I suppose I could talk to her and ask her to go,' he said. 'But what right have I got to do that? She's all set up at the gallery, and she's hardly likely to just give it all up,' he added, not very helpfully.

'She can just fuck off, that's what she can do,' said Jen, who was sobbing hysterically now. 'I threatened her too, and I meant it,' she said through the sobs.

'Jen, for Christ's sake. What did you do that for? What on earth did you say?'

'I told her that something terrible was going to happen to her.'

'Fucking hell. It's a wonder she hasn't called the police.'

'And do you know what else I did?'

Dan had opened himself a beer from the fridge and poured Jen a glass of wine.

'Jen, for Christ's sake, calm down,' he said again.

'I scrawled a message on the window of her flat.'

'When did you do that, for fuck's sake?'

'A couple of weeks ago.'

'Jesus.'

Dan took in a big gulp of air, then a big gulp of beer, and then he sat down and took her hand. 'Look, I'm going to say it again. Nothing has happened with Emma. It was a long time ago. Get a grip. I'll talk to her. Now, no more of this, you'll end up in big trouble.'

Jen dried her eyes and tried a smile. She felt better for having told him. And he was being really nice about it. Well, sort of. Perhaps she had overreacted, and there was nothing in it. Oh God, what a mess.

'It's just that I love you, Dan Cartridge. I love what we've got here, and I'm so scared of losing it, of losing you.'

Dan squeezed her hand and got up from the table. But he didn't say the words Jen wanted to hear. He didn't say he loved her.

'Look, I'll take Barney out for another bit of a walk, and you go and have a nice bath or something and calm yourself down.'

He put his shoes on and a light jacket. It was quite chilly for a summer's evening. Barney was again in a state of frenzy at the thought of a walk, and before Jen could finish blowing her nose, they were gone.

At first, she felt reassured, but then the doubts started creeping in again. Was he really going to just take Barney for a walk? Or was he going to nip around to her place again? Would he really talk to her and "put her straight," or was he lying while he dithered and made his mind up about what to do? Would he leave her for this bitch, Emma? She was glad she'd told him what had happened; at least he now knew the score and knew how much she cared. But what wasn't clear, not clear enough, was exactly how much Dan cared and for who.

# Chapter Thirty-Eight
# Emma

She was nervous, nervous about the possibility of meeting Dan, and nervous about the possibility of not meeting Dan. The whole idea of this check, which the bloody car didn't really need, was to make contact with Dan. Since the night around her place, which was nearly a week ago now, she'd not heard from him. How could that be, after they'd re-connected – literally? Maybe, she should tell him about Jen's visit and make him realise what a horrible woman she was? But that was high risk.

She had to deliver the car to the garage by nine-thirty. She gulped down the remains of her mug of tea, which was tepid at best, picked up her bag, and checked that her car keys were in there. They weren't.

'Where are the bloody car keys?' she said out loud, the stress was building.

A quick search around located them in her coat pocket. She put it on, it was threatening to rain. Ok, she was ready for the short journey around to the garage. It was nine twenty-eight. She hated being late, but she should be ok. Deep breaths.

When she arrived at the garage, Asif was standing outside the entrance to the workshop, almost as though he was waiting for her.

'Hi, Emma,' he said after she rolled down the window. 'Just drive into the back of the workshop, and I can sort the car from there. Laser will be carrying out the checks.'

She drove in slowly. No sign of Dan. Damn.

'How are you on this not-so-glorious morning?' asked Asif, holding the door open for her as she climbed out of the car.

'I'm ok, I guess, do you need this?' she said, detaching the car key from the rest of the bunch.

'Yes, err, thanks.' Asif was suddenly looking at her in a rather shifty way.

'What time will it be ready?' asked Emma.

'Well, it should be about five-ish, but it's best to ring us to check that there aren't any problems. Ring the office. Um, Emma, look, err, Dan wanted to have a word. I think he's in that store cupboard over there. Up to you, of course, but I said I'd ask.'

'I'm not sure why he has to hide away in there, but ok.' said Emma, her heart suddenly racing. She walked over to the store cupboard. The door was half open, and she pushed it the rest of the way.

Dan was standing near the back looking at, or pretending to look at, some boxes. He turned to face her, but before he could say anything she rushed forward and into his arms.

'Oh Dan, why haven't you rung me? I've been waiting for your call all week.'

'It's been difficult, Em,' he said. He seemed to be gently trying to push her back. But she wasn't having that, she needed to take her chance and she knew how. She began kissing him.

'I think we need to t…' Dan began to speak but had to break off as she kissed him again. He responded, and they were locked together for what seemed ages. She had him. She pressed herself into him, and she could feel him begin to respond.

'Em, no,' he said.

'You won't be saying that in a minute,' she replied breathlessly, kneeling down in front of him and reaching for his belt.

Behind her, she heard the door open and then a female voice.

'Oh, sorry, um, Dan, Tom wants you. Sorry,' it said, and the door closed again. Emma stood up; the moment was lost again. 'Get out,' she screamed at the girl. Jesus, what did she have to do? Dan looked like thunder. Emma quickly recovered her composure. She had to.

'Who was that?' she laughed, telling herself to keep things light.

'The new girl in the office," said Dan. "Bloody Asif was supposed to watch the door. Bollocks. Jen has been for a coffee with her. She'd better not say anything. Look, Em, you can't keep doing this, leaping on me.'

'Ha, me leaping on you. I think it was the other way around the other night,' she teased.

'Yeah, well, ok, but anyway, we need to talk, but not here, it's not going to work. I could see you tomorrow night for a while. Jen's out. It'll have to be somewhere discreet, though, at least until we've talked and sorted things.'

'I tell you what, as you seem so nervous about everything,' she touched the tip of his chin with her first finger, 'Meet me tomorrow night in the car park at Lakey Hill. Let's say six o'clock. There's not usually anyone up there, we could, um, get up to whatever we want. Do you know it?'

'Yeah, ok. Em, I'm sorry, you're very sweet, my fault, I'm sure, but I think this is probably not the time or place. And we do need to talk.'

'No worries. I'm good.'

She was holding both his hands as she said this. He didn't look cross, just a bit agitated. She gave him a quick kiss on the lips and walked towards the door. Then she turned, looked over her shoulder, and with her big eyes wide open and a playful smile on her lips, she said, 'Tomorrow night then.'

On her way out, Emma went into the garage's office. The red-haired girl, the same girl she'd seen at the gallery, the same girl who'd presumably walked in on her and Dan just now, was head down at her desk, a thick pair of glasses in her hand. She looked up.

Emma's breath was taken away. It was like looking in a mirror, the same eyes, the same chin. The girl hurriedly put her glasses back on.

'Hi, can I help you,' she said, looking flustered herself.

'I just wanted to say, what you thought you saw just now, you didn't see it,' said Emma, still somewhat stunned.

'Oh right, ok, no problem,' said the girl.

Emma left. She walked out of the garage into the bright sunshine which had emerged behind a grey cloud. It dazzled her, and she was certainly in a daze. Surely not, it couldn't be, but she had the right name and the way she'd just looked at her. 'Oh, my fucking god,' said Emma out loud.

# Chapter Thirty-Nine
# Maddy

'Quick, or we'll miss it,' Maddy shouted through the doorway. Why was he taking so long? The train was actually pulling into the station by the time Toby ambled out of the toilet, still tucking his shirt in.

'Where's the sculpture?' she asked in a panic. The train came to a halt, and the doors began to open.

'Oh, crikey,' Toby dashed back into the toilet and retrieved the suitcase on wheels, which contained the box, which contained the bubble-wrapped model sculpture. Fortunately, there were a few people boarding ahead of them, so they made it onto the train in good time.

'What were you doing in there?' Maddy laughed.

'I err, couldn't get the hand drier to work,' said Toby, looking just a little more flustered and dishevelled than usual.

They sat facing each other, either side of a table. An elderly couple – at least Maddy assumed they were a couple – occupied the other two seats. It was obvious she and Toby weren't going to be able to chat easily, so she got out her phone to look for messages. There was a text from Amy and one from Jen. Jen's text was a bit cryptic – it was simply three question marks and two exclamation marks. Maddy knew why. In the heat of the moment, after her mother had shouted at her, she'd sent Jen a text saying. "I have an update" What her mother and father got up to in a garage store cupboard was, of course, up to them. She'd been quite shocked to catch them, she didn't approve of secrecy. She smiled at the irony of that thought. But then, her situation was different, there was a moral justification, wasn't there? But there was certainly no morality in deceiving someone when it came to love. And in any case, she didn't like the way her mother had spoken to her. Who did she think she was?

She texted back: *Bad news, I'm afraid. I caught them kissing and stuff in the store cupboard. Would you believe it? I didn't!! Sorry to have to tell you that. On a train now, so phone probably won't work.*

She then turned her phone off, knowing that Jen would immediately reply, wanting to know more. At first, she quite enjoyed the thought of dropping such a bombshell – even a toned-down version of what she thought was really going on between them. But then, a new thought took hold, and Maddy was surprised and disturbed by it. By passing on what she'd seen, she might help bring her real mother and father back together. It might hasten a split between Dan and Jen. Despite the shock and a surprisingly prudish reaction to witnessing her parent's duplicity, she'd only just realised, and it surprised her. Actually, she did desperately want her parents back together.

She began to feel rather hot, wishing she hadn't sent Jen that text. She'd try to forget it. She turned to a magazine that she'd bought in the railway station shop and began leafing through the celebrity stories. She wasn't interested in any of them, but it ought to distract her. It didn't.

So, did her mother recognise her? It had been a mistake to take her glasses off, to be caught out in that way. She thought she'd noticed the surprise on Emma's face. Oh god, had she recognised her? She wasn't ready. She wasn't ready to reveal herself. Maddy had wanted to be in control and decide the timing of any *proper* meeting herself, or if there'd be one at all. And now, by being careless, she might have lost that control. She was annoyed with herself, but she was absolutely furious with her mother. Back to the magazine, read, read, read, she repeated to herself, lose yourself. After a while, she glanced up and looked at Toby. He'd turned his scarf into a pillow and was dozing against the train's window. The discovery that Toby was at school with her mother and older than she thought – thirty-five or thirty-six — needed further contemplation. An age gap of up to eighteen years - a man as old as her real mother and father - was that too weird – even if *she* was pretending to be older? She was, of course, jumping the gun somewhat. But that's what a daydream was for. So far, all that had happened was that they'd spent a bit of time together, and she'd been a bit flirty. He hadn't objected to the flirting – and he seemed to really like her, laugh at her jokes and everything. But the truth was, he hadn't given her any great clue that he was thinking of taking their 'relationship' any further. She resolved to just wait and see what happened. After all, sophisticated modern women had flings all over the place; they didn't always have to mean something or lead somewhere. She'd always said to herself that she'd want to be experienced when she met Mr Right. She certainly wasn't going to be a virgin on her wedding night. That wasn't what women did these days. She felt she was on a big adult adventure, and if some adult behaviour was required, well, she'd go for it. She opened her handbag and looked inside the chemist's paper bag. She'd come prepared.

# Chapter Forty
# Emma

Could that red-haired girl in the garage really be her Maddy? How come she was here - in the village? How had she tracked her down? It couldn't possibly be a coincidence. Thoughts danced through Emma's head; she was in a terrible state. If this Maddy was her Maddy, why hadn't she said anything? In that moment, she thought back to the time she'd spilt her paints in the art gallery, and this morning when she'd shouted at her; oh god she'd not been very friendly to Maddy at all.

That morning Emma had decided to start a new painting to take her mind off things, but it wasn't working. It was impossible to concentrate. 'Fuck it,' she said out loud, picking up her brush and scribbling all over the canvas. More questions filled her head. Why hadn't Maddy made contact through the normal channels? What was she planning to do if, of course, it was actually her? Emma was clinging onto that qualifying statement for now, yet deep down, she knew the truth. And she wanted it to be true. She wanted this girl to be Maddy, even though the thought of it terrified her. On the one hand, she was filled with a fantastic feeling of sheer joy; on the other, she was scared, more scared than she'd ever been, of rejection. Maddy might be her daughter, but she wasn't a baby or a child anymore, she was a grown woman who could make her own decisions.

And what about Dan? She knew his name wasn't on the birth certificate, and she was convinced her own father wouldn't have mentioned him to the adoptive parents, whoever they might be. So, Dan and Maddy couldn't know about each other? Could they? If Dan *had* somehow discovered the truth, he'd have said something, wouldn't he? Now Dan and Maddy were working in the same place, just yards apart, how weird was that? And, after this morning when she'd caught them together, Maddy would put two and two together for sure. If she didn't know Dan was her father before, she would guess now. Now that she'd seen them in a compromising position she was bound to work out that Dan was her father, especially if she talked to other people in the village and found out about their past. Emma knew, more than ever, that she had to be the first to tell Dan about Maddy. She should have done it already, now it might be too late and that would be a disaster.

Emma decided to make some tea and sit down calmly at her computer. She needed to slow things down. Slow down her mind. First, she'd try to find something out about Maddy. She still didn't know Maddy's surname, so a *Google* or *Facebook* search would be of little use. In any case, none of the hundreds of photographs of Maddies or Madeleines she'd trawled through before had the striking family resemblance she'd seen earlier that morning. Perhaps Toby knew her surname. She could ask him.

Then she suddenly had another thought - nearly dropping her mug of tea - as a new horror hit home. Toby might be off for a sordid night of passion with Maddy in London. Bad enough that Maddy might be her daughter. But worse than that, what if something *had* happened on that drunken night when they were teenagers, she could be Toby's daughter.

What a mess, what a terrible mess. It'd be incest. Toby could end up committing incest without knowing it. Surely not, there couldn't be anything between them - could there? The age difference, for one thing. Yes, she'd teased him, but he wouldn't, would he? He wouldn't do something stupid on the rebound from her. Maddy was too young. But she decided she'd better get in touch with Toby to warn him.

She took out her mobile but paused before dialling. Rationality was now wrestling with panic and just about winning. She decided it would be pointless trying to talk to Toby while he was on the train. The signal was never reliable, and there'd be nothing worse than getting halfway through a conversation of that nature. Also, he'd be sitting opposite, or next to, Maddy. So, instead, she decided to send Toby a text saying it was important he rang her as soon as he got to the hotel.

Then she returned to the substantive issue, establishing if Maddy really was her daughter. She remembered the rules about making contact, but surely, they went out of the window in circumstances like these. Anyway, Maddy was now over eighteen. Did those rules still apply?

If this Maddy was *her* Maddy, then it was totally implausible she'd arrived in the same village by chance. So, Maddy must know about *her*, and for whatever reason, she'd so far decided not to make herself known. By befriending Toby and lurking around the gallery, it was pretty obvious what she was up to. She'd come to spy, to find out about her. Emma recoiled in horror again at the memory of how bad-tempered and foul-mouthed she'd been that day in the gallery when she'd knocked her easel over. And how she'd shouted at her when Maddy caught her and Dan in the store cupboard.

She paced around her room and eventually decided that an old-fashioned letter was best. It had worked with Dan. She opened up a new page on her computer and began to type. It took her about an hour. She carefully sealed the envelope and, after deciding that it would be too risky to deliver by hand, addressed it to Maddy at the garage and stuck on a stamp. She only had a second class one – but she thought it wouldn't matter if it took a few days to arrive, as Maddy wouldn't be back in the office until Monday. With that, she decided she'd had enough of work for today. She'd go home early, post the letter, and pick up her car from the garage later. Just then, her phone rang. It was a local number, so not Toby.

'Hi, Emma,' said Asif. 'I'm afraid we're not going to be able to finish your car tonight. It needs some parts, and they won't be here until the morning. Is that ok, I'm really sorry?'

'Yeah, no problem, I'll collect it tomorrow,' she replied.

Perfect, that was a relief. It meant she could go home after posting her letter, have a nice long soak in the bath, and try to calm down. Mind you, she'd have to think through what she was going to say to Toby.

He rang at about six-thirty.

'Tobes, how's it going? How was the journey?' said Emma, trying to keep it light.

'Um, yeah, not bad, actually, the taxi to the hotel was expensive, though.'

'It always is in London. Still, you've got plenty of money,' replied Emma,

'Yeah, right.'

'Um, Toby,' Emma began. 'The reason I'm ringing is because I need to have a rather awkward chat with you. Are you alone?'

'Yes, I'm in my room. What's up? You're frightening me? Are you ok?'

'Yes, yes, fine. It's nothing to worry about. At least, I'm hoping there won't be once we've had this conversation. Do you remember that night we talked about when you came around for dinner? That night when I was very drunk back when we were at school. You said I was, um, all over you, so to speak?'

'Err, yes, I'll never forget it.'

'Well, as I said, it seems I'll never remember it.'

'Em, why are you bringing this up now?' asked Toby.

'Oh, it's just been bothering me, that's all. The thing is, Toby, did we, well, you know, did we, on that night? Did we, well, do anything, you know, it?'

There was a pause on the other end of the line.

'Emma, you're asking me if I took advantage of a totally drunk girl, the girl that I loved, the girl that I loved back then, just as I do now?'

'Well, err, yes, I suppose I am. You didn't, did you, Toby? You're too nice, aren't you?' said Emma, who was beginning to wish she hadn't started this conversation.

'No, Emma, I did not. I walked you home, helped you open the front door, and said goodnight.'

'Right, of course, you did. I knew you did. I knew you would have done. Toby, you're a lovely, lovely man,' she said, relieved.

'Ok, well, I'm glad you, um, appreciate that. And, by the way, you don't have to worry about anything on this trip either. It's all totally professional. Nothing will happen between Maddy and me,' volunteered Toby.

'Oh, I never thought it would, Toby. Obviously, it's entirely up to you what you do in your private life, but she is very young. I don't know for sure, of course, but I don't think from the look of her that she can be much over eighteen.'

'No, um, maybe not, but she told me she was twenty-three.'

'Oh, did she? Well, I'd say she's having you on there, Toby, definitely not twenty-three. Not that I know, as I said,' she added hastily. 'Anyway, good luck with the presentation. I hope it goes well. Sorry to have bothered you. Love you. Bye.'

Toby said goodbye but sounded rather puzzled.

# Chapter Forty-One
# Dan

Jen launched a verbal assault as soon as he walked through the door. 'What have you been up to now, you lying, cheating bastard,' she shouted at him.

'Oh, for Christ's sake, what now?' said Dan, completely taken aback.

'You and that Emma seen together in the cupboard at work. Kissing and stuff, and who knows what else. What the fuck's going on, Daniel?'

'Who told you that?'

'Maddy.'

'Oh great, thought so. Well, whatever she's said, she's got it wrong.'

He squeezed past Jen, who was resolutely stationed in the hall, her shoulder propping up one wall, and he made his way into the kitchen.

'How can she have got it wrong? She saw what she saw, and I see no reason for her to make it up. Tell me the truth, Dan,' said Jen, following him into the kitchen.

Dan slowly put his bag down on the table and turned to look at her, mascara was smeared down her cheeks. It was important for him to stay calm.

'Look, I was in the store cupboard. Asif must have told her I was in there. She comes in, I try to talk to her, she literally throws herself at me, I didn't want her to, but I'm trapped in there, Maddy pops her head round the door and gets the wrong end of the stick. That's it,' said Dan. It was close to the truth, just not the whole truth.

'She threw herself at you, and, of course, you managed to catch her, how very good of you. I can't believe you expect me to believe that. But let's say I do - and I don't - she's got to be stopped, Dan. She's a total fucking menace. She's tearing us apart; she's tearing me apart. She's got to be stopped, and if you won't do it, then I will.'

'I will sort it, Jen. Like I said, I just need the chance to talk to her properly like grown-up human beings. I've arranged to meet her tomorrow night in a car park, which seems a pretty safe and neutral place to me.'

'Right, well, see that you tell her to stop bothering us, or we'll call the police.'

'I don't think that's a good idea, Jen, not after what you've done.'

'I've not even started yet. That bitch is going to have to suffer she really is. Now let me get on with some dinner. And I want you to come back tomorrow night and tell me everything is sorted; everything is back to normal. I love you, Dan fucking Cartridge, you do know that.' She was tearful again.

Dan took her in his arms and put her head against his chest.

'I know you do, Jen, I know you do.'

She broke away from him, drying her eyes as she went to the sink and began peeling the potatoes. Dan decided it would be prudent to keep out of the way, and he took himself off to watch the news. He told himself she'd appreciate a bit of space. He'd just about gotten away with that conversation, he thought. No thanks to Maddy. But he still didn't know what he was going to do next.

They got through their dinner, just about saying only a few neutral things to each other. The conversation was stilted and tense. Afterwards, Jen said she'd walk Barney. Dan offered to do it instead, but only half-heartedly. Jen had a determined look in her eye, she seemed desperate to get out.

'I've taken your keys,' she shouted back at him as she opened the front door. 'I'll take him for a long walk, so I might be an hour or so.'

'Ok, take care,' replied Dan. It would still be light until ten, so he wasn't worried about her safety, just her state of mind. Hopefully, some fresh air would help.

# Chapter Forty-Two
# Maddy

As she unpacked her bag in the hotel room, Maddy was struggling to remember the name of the company commissioning Toby's work. That wasn't good. But, no doubt, they'd talk about the presentation later, and all the details would sink in. She hoped there wouldn't be too much shop talk over dinner. She wanted time to push him for more information about her mother, and also, well, flirt, and possibly more…she smiled to herself. The thought of the - possibly more - suddenly made her very nervous.

She had a bath, and then she carefully applied her make-up, not too much - just the right amount. She brushed and brushed her hair until it shone, and on one side, she put a clip shaped like a rose. Then, as she stared in the mirror, she picked up her phoney glasses. On or off? She was sick of wearing them, but was it a risk? She could see the family resemblance, Amy could see it, but would Toby? Men didn't always notice these things. Anyway, if things developed with Toby, she'd have to take the glasses off at some point. In fact, if things really got going with Toby, she'd have to tell him her whole story – however weird that might seem to him. Bloody hell, he was going to have a shock. Would he freak out? She didn't know. Anyway, she decided not to put the glasses on, she looked so much better without them.

Toby seemed somewhat stunned as she walked down the stairs to meet him in the lobby. She must look great, she thought.

'You've taken your glasses off,' he said, stating the obvious.

'Yes, I'm as blind as a bat,' she laughed. 'Actually, I can see ok up to about ten feet, so as long as you guide me to the table we'll be alright.'

'Well, would you, err, like a drink, err, first, or, um, dinner? I mean, obviously, you can have both, and you will have both, but what I mean is, shall we go to the bar first and then have dinner, or go straight in and see if they've got a table, which of course they will have, because that's what restaurants have – um, tables?'

She laughed at him, or with him, she wasn't sure.

'Let's have a drink first. Mine's a white wine – a large one. I think you need one, too,' she said.

'Right, we mustn't have too much, though, not with tomorrow being tomorrow and all that.'

'You sound like my dad,'

'Oh, I hope you don't think I'm old enough to be your dad,'

'Ha, no, not at all, I think you're mature and experienced, and I like that,' she gave him her most wonderful smile.

Maddy wasn't used to hotels, she'd previously only stayed a couple of times at a budget hotel with her mum and dad. It was all a bit posh here. Waiters flicked napkins, ice buckets were delivered, and guests were called "sir" and "madam." She tried to look as sophisticated as possible, but when she was first addressed as "Madam," she didn't even realise the waiter was speaking to her.

'Oh, you mean me?' she said. Toby just laughed. She hoped he didn't guess that she was out of her depth. It was pretty obvious.

The first part of the meal was spent talking about the presentation, how it might go, what Toby would say, what she needed to do. It was all very business-like, really. Then she managed to move the conversation onto the gallery and whether he saw his future there, and that, ultimately, gave her the opportunity to introduce the subject of her mother.

'I did bump into Emma when I was at a concert in the pub a couple of weeks ago. I don't think you were there,' she began.

'No, I, um, gave that concert a wide berth.'

'Oh, why do you say that?'

He reddened. 'Nothing really.'

'Go on, tell me. Half the village was there and you weren't, I'm intrigued.' She was playing him.

'Ok, if you must know, I don't really like Dan very much, so I didn't particularly want to see his band.'

'Well, now you are going to have to tell me more. To be honest, I've not been too impressed with him, either,'

'Oh right, now you're going to have to, err, tell *me* more,' Toby fired back.

'You first,' insisted Maddy, cupping her chin in her hands and leaning on the table, ready to listen.

'Well, Dan, was always a bit flash at school. He had a band back then too. He was good-looking, good at sport, and he got the girls. It used to, well, get on my nerves a bit.'

'When you say he got the girls, you mean Emma?'

'Yes, how do you know about that?'

'Oh, just something Dan's other half, Jen, dropped into the conversation.

'Jen, don't get me started on her. Bloody mad woman she is,'

'Oh my God, now you're going to have to tell me more - again,' said Maddy gleefully, as though she was catching up on an episode of some TV soap opera. 'So, Emma and Dan, what happened there then?'

'Well, they went out with each other for probably a couple of years in the sixth form. Then her family left, and it broke up. That's all there was to it, really,'

Well, thought Maddy, there was actually a lot more *to it*. But Toby just didn't seem to know, or if he did, he wasn't saying. She looked into his face for a moment and then asked, 'Did you also like her back then?'

He blushed. There was an awkward silence.

Maddy realised at that point that her evening wasn't going to go quite the way she'd hoped. After a short pause, she said quietly, 'And you still love her now, don't you?'

Toby paused, took a sip of wine, shrugged, and looked just a little crestfallen. 'I can't help it. But she still wants Dan. That's why she's back here, so, no hope for me. I'm stuck. Stuck up there on the shelf with all the sad people.'

Maddy felt her heart sink, for herself more than him. But she didn't like self-pity in anyone, and she quickly moved the conversation on. 'What is it about her, this Emma, then? What's she like? I've got to be honest when I bumped into her at that concert, she was rather rude.'

'Oh, she's nothing like that. I think, maybe, she's been under a lot of pressure lately. But the real Emma is one of the sweetest people I know. She'd do anything to help. She's funny, she's clever, she's talented, and she's beautiful. She just lights up the room.'

'Bloody hell, you've got it bad, Toby,' was all Maddy could think of in response. Toby looked a bit awkward, and they were silent for a time as they finished their meals.

After that, they talked some more about the next day's presentation as they enjoyed a dessert course and some coffee. Maddy had never seen a pudding menu like it. It took her ages to decide what to have.

'It's time we were calling it a day, well for me anyway,' Toby eventually declared. 'We need to meet down here for breakfast about seven-thirty, I reckon.'

'Yes, fine. Thanks for a lovely meal, Toby, and our very interesting conversation, let's really go for it tomorrow,' said Maddy, getting up from the table and giving him a high-five, accompanied by another lovely smile. She wanted the evening to end well, if not in quite the way she'd imagined and hoped for.

There was no awkwardness as the lift stopped at her floor. She just gave Toby a quick kiss on the cheek and said goodnight before sauntering off sleepily to her room - alone.

# Chapter Forty-Three
# Dan

Sitting on the bed in just his boxer shorts after a long hot bath, Dan was leafing through a small notebook that Jen kept on a side table. There was nothing much in it, just a couple of innocuous things-to-do lists. He felt rather guilty spying on her while she was out of the house, but he was worried about what she was thinking and what the stress was doing to her. He knew he could make things a whole lot better. But he didn't yet know, for sure, what he wanted to do himself. It was tearing him up.

Jen was taking longer on that walk than he expected, he thought. Then his foot bashed against something under the bed. He looked down to see what it was; an old tin box. He pulled it out and inside there was a very old beaten-up-looking book. He carefully opened it - it seemed to be a diary. Emma's diary! Where the hell had that come from? His pulse quickened. He read the first few pages and quickly realised exactly when it must have been written and about what. How on earth had Jen got hold of it? She must have stolen it? The list of potential crimes she was clocking up was becoming really, really, scary. He dipped into a few pages, and then his impatience took the better of him, and he went straight to the back to see what Emma had said about leaving the village and leaving him.

*Dan must never know. Nobody must know. This will be my shame, my burden. I have come to a terrible decision. It's not a decision I want to make, but I can see that it is a decision I have to make.*

*I hate my father. He has forced me to make this decision. I can see why he says what he says. I can see the logic. Maybe he's right, and as time passes, I will see that it is - as he keeps saying - "for the best."*

*But as I write this diary entry, sitting in our hut where we have spent so many happy times, blissful times, ecstatic times, I cannot help but feel I am betraying our love, betraying Dan, and, ultimately, I will betray our baby.*

Our baby! Dan's mind was racing. Our baby! As he tried to get a grip on what this meant. His first thought was for Jen. She must have read this. How could she have kept quiet knowing this astonishing information? No wonder she was going out of her mind. Why hadn't she confronted him? She wasn't one to hold back. Did she assume *he* knew about a baby, that he'd been keeping it a secret all this time? She must love him very much to cope with that.

And what of the baby? Did Emma have it? Is he or she alive? What would they be – eighteen years old by now? It was incredible. It was at this point that a feeling of anger began to grow within him. Why the hell hadn't Emma told him? Why hadn't she told him back then, and why hadn't she told him now? It was his baby, too, whether it existed, whether it was born or not. He could be a father, for Christ's sake. What had she been playing at? And then he thought, how the hell did it happen? We were always so careful. Well, apart from maybe that one time. He read on:

*This is my last entry. I will leave this diary in this hut – the hut where I have been so happy. Our love is locked into this place. It is a part of what we have been to each other. If you are reading this diary now, perhaps many, many, years after I wrote it – maybe a hundred years or more – you will now know of our story, our love, and how it ended, like a Shakespearian tale – so tragically.*

She always was a terrible romantic, thought Dan. He'd have smiled to himself if he hadn't been shaking all over. Typical of her to leave the diary behind, hoping it would be found by some future generation. It was likely, he surmised, that Jen must have found it in the old cricket hut that time she found his old coat. Why did she go there in the first place? How did she know it was their special place?

*Everything is sorted. We leave the village tomorrow. I have told Dan, my lovely Dan, that our time together is over. But it will never be over in my heart. My father is wrong there. I will not get over him. I will always love him. But I will have to bear this pain and try to rebuild my life. I <u>will</u> go to university, I <u>will</u> get a degree, and I <u>will</u> fulfil my destiny to do my parents proud and strive for a good career. As our school motto says: "I will be the best I can be."*

*But I <u>will</u> have our baby first. My father has not won that battle. Our baby will be adopted. He or she will live a good life with a couple who can bring him or her up. This is so painful. Half of me knows the decision is right. Half of me knows the decision is totally wrong. I love Dan, I want to be with Dan. I want our baby. I want to live here with Dan and our baby. But I also want to be the successful professional I've always dreamed of being. I hate my father, but I also hate myself. I am weak. I hope Dan will forgive me. I love him.*

And that was it. After that, there were two rows of kisses on the page. Then nothing. It felt incomplete. Yes, there was an explanation, but it didn't seem enough for Dan. He had so many questions. She should have told him. He'd had a right to say something about the baby being adopted.

My god, the reality struck home now, so he was a father. He'd been a father for those eighteen years. His son, or daughter, would perhaps be about to go to university, or out to work. All of these thoughts just made him angrier and angrier. Emma should have told him. How could she have treated him as though it didn't matter? As though he didn't matter. They'd made this baby together, and yet he'd been kept out of everything - then and now. He was convinced her father would have played a big part in the decision-making. He'd always hated him. He was a pompous arse and a bully.

He heard the door go. It was Jen. He quickly put the diary back in the box and pushed it back under the bed. What would he say? Jen had not said anything, so he'd leave it that way, at least for now.

'Hi Jen, I'm turning in early,' he called down. 'I'm knackered.'

'I bet you are,' he heard Jen say.

'What?'

'Nothing.'

He had to talk to Emma first. My god, did he need to talk to Emma fucking Taylor.

# Chapter Forty-Four
# Emma

In that state between sleep and wakefulness, Emma was trying to hang onto the memory of an erotic dream. They were in the hut, and they'd drunk some wine. She'd tried to pour a glass out of an empty bottle, and Dan had laughed. She'd been taking her clothes off, and she'd just unclipped her bra. Then, annoyingly, the dream had jumped, Emma had found herself in a hospital where she was telling a nurse that the baby had been conceived that night in the hut. The nurse had said she'd have to tell Dan, and in the dream, Emma had screamed. Now, as she came around, it was a relief to know that it *was* just a dream. But the truth was, the time had come to tell Dan. She would have to tell him tonight when they met at Lakey Hill.

She got up and went to the bathroom, returning with a drink of water. It was early, about six o'clock, one of those brilliant summer mornings with a perfect blue sky. The birds had long since finished their initial chorus, but they were still noisily chirping outside her window. She thought there must be a family of house martins nesting in the eaves.

What would she say to Dan? It was crunch time for her plan; the plan to claim Dan, to tell him about their baby; and then, together, try to find her. Only, of course, it seemed the baby had already found them. There couldn't really be any doubt about it. Maddy's face was burnt into her mind. Those eyes, as she'd raised her head from the desk, would live with Emma forever. It was a startled look, as though she knew she'd made a mistake taking her glasses off. Were they supposed to be a disguise, or did she need them?

Maddy might be her daughter, but Emma didn't feel she knew her at all. She didn't know what she was thinking. What was she doing in the village? What was *her* plan? Why the secrecy? It petrified her. Everything petrified her, and she clung to the duvet.

Later, as she sat in the bath, rehearsing a number of conversations, she came to the conclusion that she couldn't predict Dan's reaction. She didn't, after all, know what he already knew. Until now, it had been *her* secret, her secret to keep, and her secret to tell. But now she'd lost control of it. So, she'd just have to wear her heart on her sleeve and see what happened. It was time for the truth. The thought of losing the burden, the burden of deception, filled her with relief but also dread in equal measure.

Emma decided she'd go to the garage straight after breakfast to pick up her car. Then, as she poured some cereal into a bowl, her phone rang. It was her mother:

'Hi Mum, what's up?'

'It's Dad.' It was immediately obvious that her mother was upset. Oh God, what now? Her mother continued with sobs between every word, 'He's in hospital. He's not well, Emma, he's not well.'

'Oh, mum, what's happened? Take a deep breath, tell me all about it.'

'He'd had bleeding, Emma, lots of bleeding. I called 999. They say he has a perforated bowel. We're in hospital. They're doing some tests. They say he might have,' she stopped as the sobs took over, 'he might have leukaemia. He's been so tired lately, so pale, that's why we went on holiday.'

'Oh Mum, that's awful, that's terrible. Oh god, what a shock. I noticed he didn't look well when you came on Monday. Where are you? Where is he?'

'We're in Glasgow. They've managed to stop the bleeding now, and he's ok but very weak. He's lost quite a lot of blood. I think they're going to give him a transfusion. They say his white blood cells are very down.'

They talked for some time and with Emma's help her mother gradually calmed down. Emma asked her when she'd hear about the results of the tests but she didn't know. It was agreed that as soon as she'd picked up her car, Emma would make her way up to Glasgow. Then she remembered the meeting with Dan. That would have to wait for now. She'd re-arrange it. Whatever she felt about her father, an emergency was an emergency.

Emma packed a bag. She wasn't sure if she'd have to stay over in Glasgow, so she packed enough clothes for three days – that should do it. Hopefully, her mother would be able to cope on her own if his stay in the hospital was any longer. She didn't know a lot about leukaemia – if that's what it turned out to be. It was cancer, and the big "C" was scary as hell, even if they were curing a lot more people these days. She guessed her father could be looking at chemo-therapy, maybe a bone marrow transplant. Maybe her bone marrow, she didn't know. She wouldn't hesitate to offer, despite everything.

At the garage, Laser talked her through the bill for the car. Considering she didn't really think she needed anything done, it was expensive. Apparently, they'd replaced the alternator and given it a health check, whatever that was. Emma wrote a cheque and then asked Laser, as casually as she could, how Maddy was getting on. Laser wasn't the chattiest of blokes, but he said she seemed nice, was obviously bright, and seemed to be settling in quickly.

'Deano gets on with her the best,' he said. He then explained that she was in London and that she didn't work on Fridays anyway.

'I think Tom can only afford four days,' he grinned.

Emma took the keys with a smile. She was managing to hold herself together. 'Is Dan about, I need to tell him something?'

Just at that moment, Dan emerged from the store cupboard, and Emma walked over. 'Look, I'm really sorry, but I can't meet you tonight. My father has been taken ill, and he's in hospital in Glasgow. I'm going to have to go and help my mum. But we'll get together as soon as I'm back,' she touched his arm.

'Oh right, ok, sorry to hear that. Not that I ever liked him much,' said Dan, unsympathetically.

She grimaced. 'He's sick, Dan. What can I do? They think it might be serious.' She turned to go.

'The thing is Em. The thing is, we do need to talk like pretty bloody urgently,' said Dan. She turned back. He looked strange, het up. He was standing with his arms by his sides, his fists clenched. 'I know about the baby, Emma, I know about the baby,' he blurted out. Her heart leapt, and she couldn't help putting her hand over her mouth.

'When were you going to drop that little surprise on me?' he continued. He was very angry now. It took her breath away, and she took a few moments to recover. Oh God, not now, not now, she thought. She couldn't have this discussion now. Surely, he could see that. This was not the time or the place. This wasn't part of her *plan*.

'Oh Dan, I was going to tell you tonight. I've been going to tell you ever since I got back here,' she said, her voice quiet and shaky.

'And what about the last eighteen years, Emma? What about telling me at the time? I am the father? At least I assume I am the father.'

'Dan , I really, really can't do this, not now. I know I owe you an explanation, and you'll get one. I love you, I will explain everything, but I must go,' said Emma, turning towards her car.

'Like you did before because your father said so. Yes, I understand, Emma, as I had too then. Go, go and do what your father wants.'

She didn't react. This wasn't going to get them anywhere. As she climbed into her car, she noticed Laser and Asif just standing there with their mouths open – probably not believing what they were hearing. She didn't either. As she began to reverse the car out of the garage, she heard Dan shout, 'I had a right to know, Emma, a right to know.'

Emma sped off, her mind in a whirl. She was dizzied by it. She felt she couldn't take any more physically, or emotionally. Everything had gone wrong. She'd mishandled it all, and everything had conspired against her plans. She felt her life was spiralling out of control. And Dan – the man she believed she loved – how could he do that when she'd just had the terrible news about her father? Her mind was a complete mess. Tears rolled down her face. She was shaking as she sped up Lakey Hill, the quickest way to the M6, the route she'd take to Glasgow. The road twisted upwards. She took a bend too fast, *slow down.* She tried to correct the steering, but the car wasn't responding. Something was wrong, she wasn't going to hold it. She hit the brakes, but the rear of the car had lurched sideways, and it was already spinning out of control. She crashed through a fence, she saw a wheel bounce past her at speed – then, oh my God, a tree.

# Chapter Forty-Five
# Toby

'This is Maddy, my, err, assistant,' said Toby as they were greeted in the plush reception area of Miller and Highfield.

'Pleased to meet you,' said a secretary, who introduced herself simply as Julie. She shook their hands and gave them a big, wide, rather false smile - almost certainly, thought Toby, aimed at showing them her perfect white teeth. They didn't look real.

'If you'd like to follow me, I'll take you up to the boardroom,' she continued. Then she bowed ever so slightly and pirouetted on her stiletto heels. She was very thin, and she sort of sashayed down the corridor. Maddy pulled a face behind her back.

Everything around them screamed money; the reception desk was deep mahogany; the floors were tiled with Welsh slate; the walls boasted expensive-looking artwork, most of it abstract. Toby wondered if he could get Emma a commission. It would pay her serious money.

'This is where the sculpture will go when I've, well, finished it,' Toby whispered to Maddy, pointing to a plinth opposite the lift, which currently carried a table supporting an enormous flower arrangement.

'Well, I didn't expect you to bring it *before* you'd finished it,' Maddy said, also in a hushed voice. The whole place had that effect, the opulence imposing its own rules on etiquette.

On the seventh floor, they were led down a wide corridor, their feet sinking into a thick pile carpet. The large oak doors of the boardroom were directly ahead. Toby could feel his heart beating faster than usual – he was suddenly very nervous. He licked his lips.

Maddy must have noticed, she squeezed his hand and then quickly let go again.

'It's going to be great,' she whispered.

They were shown to a small waiting area, set off to the right, just outside the boardroom, and offered tea or coffee. Toby asked for two glasses of water, and the secretary sashayed off to fetch some.

'Bloody hell,' said Maddy, 'They're not short of money, are they? Are you sure you're asking enough?'

'Ha, yes, I reckon I am. It'll be the biggest deal I've ever done – if it comes off,' Toby replied, touching the wood of a small table. 'You'd better get the laptop fired up, Maddy, and then you can just link it to their overhead projector. It's all been arranged.'

Toby leafed through his notes. But then his phone, which he'd set to silent, vibrated in his pocket. It was a text from his mother wishing him good luck. That was sweet of her to remember. He texted her back, saying they were going into the "lion's den" in a few minutes.

Only it wasn't a few minutes. They'd already waited for twenty when the sashaying, sauntering, and now simpering, secretary, came over to apologise for the delay. 'I think they must be over-running on the main business,' she said. 'You're the last item on the agenda – a bit of light relief for them to finish on, I think.' A keyboard of teeth flashed in front of them.

Thanks very much, thought Toby. He didn't feel "light" at all. In fact, he felt rather heavy and rather sick.

'Oh, that's fine; we're ready when they are. Hot to go, in fact,' he replied, instantly wishing he'd chosen a different expression. Out of the corner of his eye, he could see Maddy cringed.

Eventually, the boardroom door opened, and a man Toby recognised as Tim Harmison, the MD of the company, came over.

'Toby, my man, great to see you again, so sorry to have kept you,' he said, each word spoken in a mannered, rather drawn out, way. He exuded confidence and power in a way that Toby admired and abhorred at the same time. Tim looked inquiringly at Maddy.

'Oh, this is Maddy, my assistant,' said Toby, slightly flustered. 'She's going to help set up our model, our maquette.' He pointed to the suitcase on wheels. 'And also, with the, um, power-point thingy.'

'Well, do come through. We're just having a short comfort break for five, and then we'll be ready to hear your pitch,' rattled back Tim, turning on his heels.

'Tickety-boo,' replied Toby. Maddy gave him another strange sideways look. 'Tickety-boo, where did that come from?' she whispered.

Calm, calm, get a grip, thought Toby.

Despite all his fears and reservations, the presentation went extremely well. The Miller & Highfield executives didn't know a lot about art, but they seemed to know what they liked, and they liked his proposal. Maddy was very efficient with the power-point, setting up the projector and then clicking through the slides exactly as he'd required. Toby was pleased with her, and himself, and how it had gone. Now all he had to do was get on and finish the job.

'Is there a deadline?' asked Maddy, as they walked away from the office.

'Not a firm one. I've said it should be finished in two to three months. That's probably a bit ambitious, but I don't want it to take very much longer, as I'll want to start other stuff ready for Christmas.'

'I suppose the longer you take, the less you make,' replied Maddy. 'Unless it's a fake,' she added, obviously amused by the rhyme.

'Very funny,' he said, sticking his tongue out. 'Shall we go and grab a coffee over there?' Toby was parched.

They picked up a couple of cappuccinos and then settled into some leather-effect armchairs at the back of the coffee bar. Toby felt his phone vibrate again. This time it was a call from Sally at the gallery.

# Chapter Forty-Six
# PC Reynolds

The flashing blue lights disappeared around the bend in the road. PC Pauline Reynolds hoped that the ambulance would get to the hospital in time. She turned to look again at the scene in front of her eyes. A broken fence, deep cuts in the ground, a gouge out of a tree, and a smashed-up car resting in a field. Thirty yards away the car's missing wheel had come to rest. It seemed pretty obvious what had happened.

'Ok, pick-up on its way,' said her colleague, Dave, as he walked over. 'What a bloody mess, do any of the witnesses know who she might be?'

'No, but I spotted her handbag and a suitcase in the car. Have a look through while I start mapping the scene and taking measurements.'

PC Reynolds loved being a police officer, but she was having a difficult time. She'd been in the traffic division for about six months now, and she'd attended a succession of fatal accidents, each more horrible than the one before. Four times she'd had to break the worst news and help console next of kin. It was a horrible task. Some coppers could brush it off - they were much harder than she was. She'd lost sleep over it, and even when she did sleep, she had nightmares. She didn't pray often, but today she was praying inside that the young woman currently speeding towards the hospital would pull through. She made a mental note to herself to put in for that transfer to cybercrime.

It would take a couple of hours before everything was cleared from the site. The damaged car would be put on a loader and taken back to the station, ready for the vehicle inspectors. Their report would take a few days. They'd then have to appeal for eyewitnesses. The driver who'd reported the crash said he'd arrived after it happened.

Dave came back across the field with a handbag tucked under his arm. He was holding a business card. 'I'm assuming this is her - there's half a dozen of them in her bag - she's called Emma Taylor. She's an artist in the gallery down in the village, we can start there. I can't find any info on her next of kin. Here's her phone, but it's got a lock on it.' He pulled out some folded papers from the bag. 'There's also this receipt for a car service with today's date.'

'Ok, well, we'll need to talk to the garage then,' said PC Reynolds. She took the receipt and mechanics report from Dave. 'Look at the time on this. I'd say she'd only just picked the car up. It looks like the garage have some questions to answer. We'll talk to them tomorrow after we've sorted out the next of kin.' She placed the paperwork in a plastic evidence bag.

'It suits you, by the way,' she added, looking at Dave.

'What?'

'The handbag.'


PC Reynolds had been to the gallery a few times on days off, just for coffee and a cake. She wasn't much interested in the art; it was just a nice relaxing place with a great community feel. But for today, at least, she was about to change all that.

She asked for the manager, and a flustered, arty, flamboyantly dressed woman, with an excess of dangly jewellery, came out of a small office.

'Can we talk in private?' said PC Reynolds, already aware that the arrival of two police officers had caused a bit of a stir among the customers. They sat down in the manager's office and established that her name was Sally Graham.

'Now, I believe you may have an artist working here, an Emma Taylor?' PC Reynolds began.

'Yes, Emma, why, what's happened? What's happened to Emma? Has someone attacked her?'

'No, but she's been in a car accident. The wheel of her car came off, and I'm sorry to say the car hit a tree,' replied PC Reynolds, touching Sally's arm in a vain attempt to keep her calm. 'She's been badly injured and is now in hospital.'

Sally Graham clasped her hand to her mouth and gasped. PC Reynolds was glad it wasn't too loud, or the people outside in the gallery might have heard. The least fuss, the better, was her general rule.

'Now the important thing at this stage, Ms Graham, is contacting her next of kin. Can you help us with that at all? Dave, why don't you go and get Ms Graham a cup of tea?'

Sally avoided the question and just began rambling. 'The thing is, I could have believed an attack, an assault, or something, not a car crash because there was a very peculiar event here just over a week ago. This young woman came in, I think her name is Jennifer or Jen, and she went upstairs to see Emma. There was a bit of a commotion, and the word from her studio neighbour, Toby, was that Jen had hit Emma around the face.

PC Reynolds was surprised and irritated by all this detail. Things were going off on a tangent somewhat. 'Maybe we can deal with that later if it's relevant,' she said. 'But first of all I need to get in touch with her next of kin.'

Eventually, Sally pulled herself together. She looked through her computer and came up with the names of Emma's parents and a mobile phone number.

'I suppose we ought to tell Toby too,' she said.

'Who is Toby?' asked PC Reynolds. 'Is he Emma's boyfriend?'

'No, I don't think so. She told me they were just good friends. They are very close, mind. He'll be very, very, upset. He's in London, you see, he had to go to a presentation about his sculpture.'

PC Reynolds explained that she would phone Emma's parents straight away and after that Sally could phone Toby. 'The next of kin need to hear from us, the police, first, so they don't get the news from another source, which might prove unreliable,' she explained, as Dave returned with a cup of tea.

Later, back in the patrol car, after they'd left the gallery, PC Reynolds made a quick note in her notebook about the alleged incident involving the woman called Jen - just in case it became relevant.

# Chapter Forty-Seven
# Maddy

For the third time, Maddy mouthed the word 'who?' All she'd heard so far from Toby was an 'Oh my God,' an 'is she alright?' and another 'oh my God.' It sounded serious. Maddy was already shaking.

Toby finished the call and told her everything.

Maddy was both shocked and surprised by the emotions which swept over her in the moments that followed. When she looked back, she realised her first thought was an overwhelming sense of guilt. She'd spent weeks messing about, pretending to be someone else, lying to people, making up stories, almost enjoying her secret, and now she might never have a proper conversation with her mother, who was now in hospital, critical, unconscious, and possibly dying.

Toby just kept muttering, 'Oh my god,' even after the call ended.

He was in a right state, shaking all over, and Maddy could see he was on the verge of tears. She reached over and held his hands.

'She's very strong, I'm sure she'll pull through,' was all she could think of to say, without any supporting evidence. Tears were welling up in her eyes.

The other emotion Maddy felt caught her equally off guard. She'd come to the village hoping to discover she was wrong about her mother. To learn that she wasn't a cold unfeeling person who'd given her child away. She'd wanted her maternal "real" mother to fulfil her childhood fantasies of a family life. But, so far, nothing she'd seen or heard, limited though it was, had changed her original opinion. So, the distress she now felt on hearing this terrible news surprised her. She felt like her insides had been ripped out. *Her* mother was critical in intensive care. It was awful. She could die. But she mustn't die. Not now. Their story wasn't over - it hadn't even begun. She was deeply upset - because, at the end of the day, Emma was family.

There was another hour or so of their train journey to go, and Maddy's thoughts turned to whether she should now tell Toby the truth about herself. She knew that when they arrived back in Cumbria, she'd want to go to the hospital to be with her mother, and, well, that might need explaining. Toby wouldn't understand.

But she quickly decided that a crowded train wasn't the right place to reveal secrets of such magnitude. It would come as another terrific shock for Toby. More than he could take in one day. She did resolve, however, that the lies and the deception had to end. She'd wait for the right opportunity to tell Toby and, after that, everyone else - including her adoptive parents. It felt odd that she didn't really know what to call them anymore. They'd always simply been her mum and dad. But now those names seemed wrong. Perhaps she'd just have to have two of each from now on. Anyway, they'd be back from Italy in a few days' time, and they'd expect to hear from her. The prospect of that conversation was daunting, to say the least.

Just then, the refreshment trolley lurched into the carriage. It slowly made its way to where she and Toby were sitting. She ordered two teas and two chocolate bars. Toby was looking pale and toying with his phone, like he wanted to call someone or text someone but didn't know who. She took out her own phone and decided to text her friend Amy. She'd feel better if she could tell someone.


At last, the train arrived at their station about twenty minutes late. Toby had been flapping about whether they should go to see Emma straight away, or stop off back home. He rang the hospital to try to get an update.

'She's still unconscious, that's not good,' he said to Maddy.

'No, but I've read that they do sometimes deliberately put people into a coma after they've suffered trauma. It helps them recover.' Maddy felt it was important for her to hold it together and try to counterbalance his panic and pessimism. It also made *her* feel better. She needed her real mum to recover so that she could do what she now had to do.

After further discussion, Toby decided they should take a taxi home first. 'Thinking about it,' he said. 'You don't really know Emma, so I guess you might not want to come.'

'I do want to come,' she replied, in a voice that sounded, even to her, surprisingly determined.

'Well, you don't need to worry about me. I mean, don't come for my sake, I'll be ok,' said Toby, not understanding where she was coming from. 'I expect Emma's parents will be there by now, although, come to think of it, they were on holiday in Scotland. I wonder if they know? Anyway, no, you don't need to come.'

'I *want* to come,' Maddy insisted. Right now, she didn't want to explain why, but she said it firmly enough to stop Toby from fussing.

An hour and a half later, the taxi waited while they both sorted themselves out at their respective homes or, in Maddy's case, lodgings. They only took about five minutes each, and then they were on their way to the hospital. Toby had rung through to the ward, again, for a condition check – but there was still no change.

The traffic was heavy, and Maddy stared out of the window. As the taxi crept through town, she watched people going about their business. It was now late afternoon, so some were getting last-minute shopping. With it being a Friday, there were also plenty of people who had simply finished work early and were on their way home. How many of them had ongoing trauma in their lives, thought Maddy? They probably all had problems, maybe money troubles or love affairs that weren't working out. But there wouldn't be many who'd deliberately lied to a whole bunch of people, including friends and relations, and who'd been sneaking around in disguise, spying on their own mothers. Just how awful was that? As she sat silently in the taxi, Maddy was in total despair. She couldn't hold it back any longer – tears streamed down her cheeks.

# Chapter Forty-Eight
# PC Reynolds

Tom Burrows at the garage seemed an honest sort of bloke, PC Reynolds could tell by his face and his unselfconscious manner. He looked like he hadn't slept much, and he probably hadn't. PC Reynolds gathered that he'd heard about Emma's accident the previous evening when the news spread around the village.

'We'll need to speak to the mechanic who carried out the service on her car, Mr Burrows. I'm not saying there was a mistake, and I'm not saying that it was deliberate.'

'Deliberate, of course it wasn't,' interjected Tom. 'I don't see how we could have made a mistake with the wheel anyway, all my guys are well-trained and know their jobs.'

'I'm sure they do, but, nevertheless, it's one possible cause of the crash we're looking at. A wheel appears to have come off Ms Taylor's car within a few miles of leaving the garage. But I emphasise, at this stage, we have to keep an open mind.'

'It's awful, just awful,' muttered Tom. 'How is she? Do we know any more?' he asked.

'Well, the hospital said this morning that she's no longer critical, but still serious, and in an induced coma. She was lucky the airbag took most of the impact.'

Tom took his glasses off and ran his gnarled hand down his deeply furrowed brow and across his bloodshot eyes. He began slowly shaking his head. PC Reynolds knew she needed to take her time, partly for Tom Burrow's sake, but also because she didn't want him or others at the garage to get too defensive. If that happened, she knew she wouldn't get anywhere. Eventually, he looked up.

'I think I ought to tell you something,' he said.

'Please do,' she replied.

'When Emma came to pick up her car yesterday, I gather there was a bit of a commotion.'

'What sort of a commotion?' she asked, intrigued.

Tom paused as if reluctant to say anything. 'It's complicated, and I've only got this second hand, but I suppose it might have contributed to her state of mind, the way she drove, and it's best you know.'

'Go on.'

'Well, she and one of my mechanics, Dan Cartridge, used to be a thing, you know, together, boyfriend and girlfriend, many years ago when they were at school. Well, Emma recently came back to the village, and there's been, well, shall we say, a bit of tension. It seems she wants Dan back, but he has a new partner now, a lovely lady called Jen.'

There was that name, Jen, again, thought PC Reynolds, writing it down in her notebook. This Emma seems to have ruffled feathers.

'I hate gossip,' continued Tom. 'But there we are, better you know than not, anyway, according to one of my other mechanics who overheard an argument, or discussion, between Dan and Emma, Emma had a baby, a child, back when she was eighteen. But - and this is the thing - she didn't tell Dan about the baby, or that he was the father. You see, Emma's family left the village suddenly before the baby was born. Dan has only just learnt all this and is mad about not being told. Well, you would be, wouldn't you?'

'Do you know how heated this argument was, Mr Burrows?'

'Just raised voices, I gather. In fact, I popped my head out of the office and heard the tail end of it. There's another thing too,' continued Tom, 'which makes it all the more awful. Emma had, apparently, only just heard that her father has leukaemia.'

PC Reynolds took all this down, making copious notes. Then she thanked Tom for the information and decided that she ought to take statements from all the mechanics. She left Tom and spoke to the secretary in the outer office. She was a young, red-haired girl with glasses who looked like she'd been crying. She'd obviously not slept much either, evidenced by the dark rings under her eyes. PC Reynolds introduced herself and discovered the girl's name was Madeleine McCarthy.

'I'm going to need a room to have a chat with a few people. Is there anywhere suitable?' PC Reynolds asked.

'You can use this office,' said Maddy, 'I can make myself scarce.'

'Thanks, that'll be fine,' said PC Reynolds, sitting down on a rickety old chair in front of the girl's desk. 'Look, are you ok,' she added. 'I know it must have been a big shock for everyone? I presume you knew Emma.'

'Yes, I was at the hospital last night, she's my ...' Maddy broke off what she was saying and seemed to collect herself. 'Anyway, they're saying she's not critical anymore. But she's still in a coma, and we still don't know if she'll be alright.'

'She's your what?' asked PC Reynolds, quickly picking up on Maddy's unfinished sentence.

Maddy paused again for a moment, or two, before answering in a hushed voice, 'Look, oh god, I can't tell you yet, I haven't even told my real dad, if he is my real dad, I mean, Dan yet.'

PC Reynolds' mind was razor sharp, and she quickly put two and two together. 'Oh, you mean…Emma is your mother?'

'Shush, keep your voice down, please, no one knows,' said Maddy looking nervously around her. 'But, yes, well, I'm ninety-nine per cent sure she is. How do you know?'

'Oh, I just worked it out,' replied PC Reynolds, hoping the answer would suffice and not wanting to drop Tom in it. She couldn't believe how things were unfolding. What kind of a mess had these people got themselves into?

The girl started to cry, 'It all fits if even you, who doesn't know me, can work it out,' she blubbed. 'They are my parents.'

When she'd recovered herself a little, Maddy went on to explain why she'd come to the village, and PC Reynolds quickly decided she wasn't going to make much more progress today. 'Right, look darling, this is what we do. I'll ask Dan to come in here. I need to see him anyway to tell him I'm going to take statements from everyone. Then I'll leave, and you two can talk. I'll come back on Monday and get statements from everyone then. Is that ok?'

Maddy, who was drying her eyes, said that it was.

# Chapter Forty-Nine
# Toby

The stone spoke to him, challenged him. All the time, it said *take me on if you dare*. Each piece was combative in this way, a battle to the end. The rock with its strength and integrity against the artist with his vision and skill. In his workshop, which was no more than a converted garage, Toby was in the early stages of this titanic struggle. Sometimes he worked standing up, sometimes, perched on a small step-ladder. Sometimes he just stared at it, and the stone stared back, defiant, yet ultimately compliant. One sculptor had likened it to breaking in a horse. The initial prep work had been rather brutal. Toby had achieved an outline of the basic shape before starting all the fine work, and all the time, with each tap, hammer against chisel, knowing he couldn't afford any splits or cracks. It was slow progress, but nevertheless, it was progress.

He stopped for a cup of coffee. He had a kettle and a tiny fridge in the corner of the garage, next to a beaten-up old armchair. This was solitary work, but he quite liked being away from his studio in the art gallery. In this shabby space, it felt raw and real, like he was suffering for his art. He thought about how he'd brought Emma here once to show her the set-up. She hadn't been at all impressed, she hadn't got it, and she'd just taken the Mickey.

'Emma, Emma, Emma,' he said to himself, looking upwards, hoping, praying - and that was something he never did - that she would be alright. The hospital last night had been very, very scary. He'd only been allowed to see her through a window, lying there, unconscious, not moving, machines flashing, nurses coming and going. Her mother, because she was family, was allowed by her bedside, but even she was asked to leave from time to time while they wired in some new piece of kit.

He and Maddy had taken Emma's mother for a coffee, all of them struggling to hold back tears. Emma's mother said a doctor had been quite optimistic. He'd looked at some scans, and they'd shown only minor bruising to the brain, and he thought Emma had a good chance of a full recovery. But, as with all trauma victims, the next forty-eight hours would be crucial, that was when complications could often emerge. Apart from the head injury, it seemed Emma had some broken ribs and a multitude of cuts and bruises. She'd been lucky, though; the airbag had saved her. The doctor told her mother it was their intention to keep Emma in the induced coma for the time being to allow her body time to recover from the shock and the injuries.

As they drank their coffee, Emma's mother also told them about Emma's father and the terrible news that it looked as though he had a type of leukaemia. She said she'd spoken to Emma about it on the morning of the accident. That was another big shock. And Maddy appeared to be badly shaken by it too. Toby thought of poor Emma having to digest the news, and he wondered if it contributed to the accident. It must have done, that was the only logical conclusion.

He planned to return to the hospital for visiting time that afternoon. Maddy was going to get time off work and come along as well. It was odd that she seemed so upset when she hardly knew Emma. Maybe she was upset just because he was.

Toby resumed his work and made good progress over the next hour or so. He glanced at his watch. He'd arranged to pick Maddy up at two. He was determined to be at the hospital for as much time as possible. He wanted to be *there* for Emma when she woke up. Or, if she remained in a coma, he could at least talk to her. He knew people did that when patients were unconscious for a long time. He hoped the doctor was correct and that they would just be able to bring her back when they judged she was ready. He loved her so much. This couldn't be happening. It was all a gigantic nightmare.

Then, another thought struck him - where was Dan? He hadn't been there last night, but perhaps he hadn't known by that stage. Toby had to assume that if Dan and Emma were supposed to be back together, or nearly together, then he'd also be hanging around the hospital from now on. He had to assume Dan would be just as distraught and just as keen to be by her bedside in case she came around. Of course, visiting Emma might be more complicated for Dan, given he had a partner, the crazy Jen woman. This was going to bring things to a head, Toby thought. If only, please God – there he was praying again - she came around and recovered, and he had the old Emma back again. That would be enough.

# Chapter Fifty
# Maddy

The clock ticked. She sat still and quiet - waiting. It was an old-fashioned wooden wall clock, probably as old as Tom himself. Maddy could hear the muffled sounds of her boss talking on the phone next door; she could hear clanking noises breaking through from the garage floor; very faintly, she could hear a radio playing on the far side of the workshop. By just listening to her surroundings, probably in a way that few of her friends would appreciate, with their surgically implanted ear-phones, it helped Maddy collect her thoughts.

Maddy had no idea how the forthcoming conversation with Dan would pan out. She was trying to work out what to say. She'd previously rehearsed conversations she might have with her mother, but not with her father. PC Reynolds had rather hurried her along, and she wasn't as prepared as she would have liked. She put her hand to her brow, she was sweating a little, and she could feel her heart, its rhythm in time with the ticking clock.

It was time; time to tell the truth - or at least what she believed to be the truth. She couldn't be one hundred per cent sure of anything until she'd completed the conversations she now had to have. The time for procrastination was over, she said to herself, remembering her sixth-form Hamlet with a smile. Maddy had expected the circumstances of this meeting, this moment, to be rather different. She hadn't envisaged declaring herself to her real father in a shabby office, in a shabby garage, with shabby old Tom next door. Certainly not while her real mother lay in a coma in intensive care.

The door opened. 'Hi,' said Maddy, smiling up at her father.

'What do you want?' Dan inquired, grumpily, as he entered the office.

'I, um, would like to talk to you if you've got a minute.'

Dan stood holding onto the door, reluctant to come in.

'You could sit down for a bit,' said Maddy, gesturing towards the wobbly wooden chair in front of her desk.

Dan came over and roughly pulled the chair towards him, Maddy thought it might break. He sat on the edge of it as though he wanted to escape at the first opportunity. 'You'd better be quick,' he said. 'I've work to do.'

Maddy licked her dry lips, took a sip of water from the bottle on her desk, and began. 'This isn't really the time, or the place, for this conversation, but it really can't wait any longer, too many things are happening too quickly,' she began.

'Well, spit it out. Have you messed up again?' he demanded.

Maddy tried to excuse his demeanour. He, too, must have been badly affected by what had happened.

'Have you heard any more about Emma this morning?' she asked. 'You must be really upset.' She paused for a brief moment before adding, 'I, err, couldn't help seeing you two together the other day.'

'No, I haven't heard anymore,' replied Dan, sulkily.

'Well, I gather, from the police, that she's improved a bit this morning. She's still in an induced coma, but she's off the critical list. I'm going to see her later with Toby - you know, her friend at the gallery - would you like to come?'

After a short, rather awkward pause, Dan said, 'I don't think I can.'

'I'm sure Jen would understand,' said Maddy. Dan just shrugged, so she continued, 'So, I know it's none of my business, but are you and Emma, you know, getting together?'

'You're right,' said Dan firmly, 'It *is* none of your business. Look, where are you going with this? I've got to get back to work.' He shaped to stand up.

Maddy gestured for him to hold on, 'Well, actually, it kind of might be my business, in a way,' she said.

At this point, she took off her glasses. She tried to do it casually as though it was a perfectly natural thing to do. She wanted to see if he would react. It seemed ridiculous that this action, rather like Superman and Clark Kent, could matter. But she knew the thick-rimmed glasses did help disguise her familiarity with her mother. And Dan did react. Not much, but it was there. There was no turning back now.

'You, um, might not know what I'm about to tell you, and it might come as a shock,' she began. Her heart was racing now, and she felt fresh beads of sweat form on her brow. She hoped that Tom would stay in his office, at least for the next few minutes.

'Go on then, I'm not going to know if you don't tell me,' said Dan, still sounding impatient and annoyed, but he was now looking at her quizzically.

She took the plunge. 'Well, did you know Emma had a baby about eighteen years ago?'

Maddy wasn't sure what she expected from Dan; how he would react to this statement. She assumed, from what she'd learnt from Jen, that he didn't know about a baby, so she'd expected considerable shock and surprise. But he just sat there, as still as a rock. All he did was slowly pucker his lips and grimace slightly.

Eventually, he said, 'I suppose everyone knows now after I sounded off at Emma in the workshop. Was it Asif or Laser who told you? Not only does Laser screw up her car and nearly kill her, he's blabbing all my business.'

'Oh, no, neither of them told me,' said Maddy quickly. She knew nothing about this apparent "sounding off," and she didn't want Laser to get the blame. Before she could continue, Dan spoke again, and it took her by surprise.

'If you must know, and it *is* none of your business, yes, as you might have heard, Emma and I were together when we were at school. And, no, I didn't know about a baby, not until the other day. I had a go at her about it, about not telling me, just before she drove off. I told her I couldn't ever forgive her for not telling me.' His voice suddenly broke a little. 'I wish I hadn't, well, I wish I hadn't lost my temper with her. Maybe the …well, anyway.' He paused but then seemed to gather himself. 'Anyway, I won't start up with her again now, whatever she wants, assuming…. not when I was kept in the dark like that.'

Maddy understood why he wanted to unburden himself. He felt guilty, guilty about the accident. But he was also angry and defiant. And she couldn't help but feel disappointed at the news that her mother and father might be permanently estranged because of her existence.

She must press on. Her eyes were also watering now. 'The thing is,' she began. 'I'm not really who you think I am. I came here to the village and applied for this job for a reason. I wanted to find out about someone. Someone who I thought was my mother, who is my mother. I wanted to know what sort of a person she was, to find out how she could possibly have just given me away,' she paused. Dan was staring at her open-mouthed. 'It's Emma. She's my mother, I'm her daughter,' finished Maddy in a rush.

Dan visibly wobbled on his chair, which really did now look on the verge of collapse. Then he got up, turned a full circle in the middle of the room, and held his hand over his mouth. He pulled it away. 'You're my daughter?' It was half a question, half a statement.

'Yeah, well, yes, I think I am. I am if you say I am,' Maddy was half laughing and half crying.

'You're my daughter?' repeated Dan.

'Yes, I am – can't you see the resemblance without these stupid false glasses?'

'I knew there was something about you today, but for some reason I couldn't see it. I can now, you've got the same eyes. And you've got my ears. In fact, you're practically a copy of Emma, just with red hair, bloody hell.'

Dan now stood facing Maddy, who had also got to her feet and was crying and shaking from head to foot.

She didn't really know what to do next. Part of her wanted to come around the desk and give him a hug. But the other half of her still wasn't sure what she felt about him. He'd been horrible to her since she'd arrived, inexcusable, whatever the circumstances. This was all going to take time.

Dan obviously felt the same. 'I need to get my head around this,' he said. 'It's all too much.'

He stood and looked at her for a few moments – as though he was appraising her. 'Look, I'm sorry, Maddy, I don't know what you expected from this, but I'm going to have to have some time to get my stuff together.' And with that, he turned on his heels and left the office.

Within half an hour he was back. 'You do know I knew nothing about you, don't you?' he said, after shutting the office door.

'Yes, you said. But I'd already guessed that might be the case. You see, there was no father named on my birth certificate.'

'Not named on the birth certificate. Well, that shows what she thought of me,' said Dan. He looked like he was struggling to keep his temper. 'Mind you, it was her father who manipulated the whole thing. She says that in a diary I found.'

'A diary?'

'Yes, she kept a diary all the time we were going out, not that I knew anything about it. I, um, found it.'

'I'd love to read that,' said Maddy.

'It's full of stuff you're never going to see,' said Dan, with a hint of a smile on his face. She hadn't seen that before, it changed him. And in a softer tone, he continued, 'Look, Maddy, don't blame your mother for having you adopted. She loves you; she says so in the diary. She let herself be manipulated. Her father, your grandfather, is the one to blame.'

Maddy wanted to believe him. 'You know he's got leukaemia, my grandfather?' she said.

'Well, yes,' replied Dan. 'Emma told me yesterday morning. He doesn't deserve that. But he was, and probably still is, an awful man. He tried to dominate her life. Her relationship with me was the only way she could rebel. He tried and tried to split us up. It looks like he's got his wish now, once and for all.'

# Chapter Fifty-One
# PC Reynolds

Back at the station there were two messages and a crime report for PC Reynolds to see; one via a phone call, taken by the desk sergeant, the other from the one-zero-one service. She made herself a cup of tea and called Dave over. He'd spent part of the morning writing up details of the accident scene and the rest of his time with the vehicle inspectors.

'Any news from the shed?' she asked.

'It's a bit preliminary, but they say some of the wheel nuts sheared off. They weren't able to find them at the scene, which suggests separation during her journey. They're carrying out a thorough check on everything else,' he explained.

'So, on the face of it,' she replied, 'It looks like incompetence on the part of the garage, which is strange because all the guys down there seem to have a lot of experience.'

'What have you got there?' Dave replied, pointing to the messages.

'Oh, I don't know,' Dave waited patiently while she studied the notes.

'Well?' he asked.

'There's that name again,'

'What name?'

'Jen.'

Dave looked puzzled.

'It's a name I've heard three times now,' said PC Reynolds. 'Right, well, someone in the village claims she saw Jennifer Clark enter the garage at around eight-thirty on the night before the accident. This woman reports seeing her unlock the side door and enter the building. She thought it a bit strange at the time, but assumed because she seemed to have a key it must be alright.'

'What made her ring us, though? She's quickly put two and two together.'

'Well, our caller went on to say that Jen's hatred of Emma is the talk of the village. So, she thought we ought to know in case there's a connection.'

'A regular Miss Marple, then,' said Dave. 'I'm assuming she doesn't work at the garage, this Jen?'

'No, but her partner Dan does. This is where it gets complicated. You see, Dan used to be Emma's boyfriend when they were teenagers, eighteen years ago. And Emma got pregnant. But it seems she moved away from the village with her family, pretty sharpish, without telling Dan. So, he's only just learnt about this baby, who's now grown up - a girl called Maddy. I hope you're still with me.' Dave rolled his eyes. PC Reynolds took a deep breath and continued, 'Well, this Maddy is now, believe it or not, working in the office at the garage. Only, neither Emma, it seems, nor Dan knows who she is - yet. Well, having said that, Dan might by now.'

'Blimey, run all that past me again,' said Dave, looking incredulous. 'It sounds like an episode of Coronation Street.'

'That's what I thought. The mess people make of their lives. Anyway, after we've finished interviewing all the mechanics, I think we had better have a chat with Jen Clark. Let's bring her in.

'What, arrest her?'

'Well, I'll have to run it past the Inspector, but my approach would be to bring her in voluntarily at first. For one thing, it keeps CID out of it until we know a bit more. I think coming into the station might just make Jen sweat a bit, don't you?'

'You're the boss,' said Dave, non-committal as always.

Next, PC Reynolds read the crime report. 'Well, well, well, the plot thickens. This is from a few weeks back, and the case is still open. Someone wrote graffiti with lipstick saying, *"Go Bitch Go"* on the window of Emma Taylor's flat. Could that be Jen again?'

Then she opened the last note and had to laugh: 'And, you really won't believe this one,' she said. 'This is from someone else - what a village, talk about peeping bloody toms? A woman, living next door to Emma Taylor says she saw a man she believes to be a sculptor at the gallery.' She checked her notebook. 'That would be a Toby Forbes. She saw this Forbes chap lurking around Emma's car, crouching down behind the back wheel. She thought he looked suspicious. Eventually, she says, he ran off.'

'So, we'd better have a chat with him too. It's all hotting up nicely,' said PC Reynolds, snapping shut her notebook.

# Chapter Fifty-Two
# Toby

Maddy had hardly spoken since they got in the car. Toby noticed how agitated she was, and he could see her hand shaking slightly. She wasn't wearing her glasses again, and that disturbed him, though he wasn't quite sure why.

'Toby, do you think we could pull over somewhere before we get to the hospital? There's something rather important I've got to tell you?' she asked.

'Yeah, sure, um, err, would you like to stop at a café, or something?' he replied. 'We've got a bit of time in hand before visiting hours.'

'No, it may sound odd, but if you don't mind I think we're better off in the car; it's a private thing,' said Maddy, adding even greater mystery.

Toby pulled over into a large lay-by. It was separated from the main carriageway by a bunch of scruffy-looking trees. There was a burger van making a decent trade, with half a dozen truck drivers standing outside holding polystyrene mugs of tea. Toby drove twenty metres beyond the burger van and turned off the engine. He twisted in his seat so that he was sideways onto Maddy, who stared straight ahead.

'Toby?'

'Yes?'

'This is going to sound very weird and may come as a big surprise.'

'Right, ok.'

'I'm going to just come out with it,' she said, turning towards him.

'Ok, out with what exactly?' He hoped she wasn't going to declare her undying love for him. He knew he was guilty, early on, of not discouraging her flirting, but he thought his business-like behaviour in the hotel would have quashed all that.

'I'm Emma's daughter,' said Maddy.

It took his breath away. He just sat there with his mouth open, looking at her. But the more he looked at her, the more he could see it and believe it. He could see Emma. Why hadn't he noticed before?

'That's why Emma, my mother, left the village in a hurry all those years ago. She was expecting *me*. That's why I'm here.'

Suddenly, thought Toby, it all made sense. Emma had had the baby. He managed to make a few incredulous grunts but little other sense for quite a few minutes. Then he asked Maddy to tell him everything.

Maddy explained how she'd found her birth certificate; traced her mother's name to the village; and obtained a job in the garage - all so she could, in effect, spy on Emma. She admitted that she'd at first befriended him to find out more about Emma, but she said that now she did really, genuinely, like him; and that she hadn't just been using him. Good of her, he thought. She added that he was now a dear friend and that she really admired his work and even wanted to be a sculptor one day.

To say Toby was stunned was an understatement. After overhearing Emma and her parents and the shocking news that Emma had been pregnant, he convinced himself that she would have had an abortion. She'd never said anything about a child. He had no idea. But it made more sense. Emma wasn't the type of girl to abort a baby.

He couldn't believe that such momentous life events had happened to the woman he loved without him knowing anything about it. And he realised that, although he thought he really *knew* Emma, he obviously didn't know her at all. He didn't doubt Maddy's story for one moment. Apart from anything else, she looked so much like Emma. He could see it clearly now. There couldn't be any doubt. But how could Emma have held on to such a secret for so long?

Maddy continued to explain that she thought Emma's father, her grandfather, had persuaded Emma, indeed forced her, to have her baby adopted. Maddy said she didn't think Emma knew who she was. They'd only met for a few brief moments.

Toby managed to splutter out how shocked he was, and he told Maddy that Emma had never spoken about a child. Then two rather obvious, as yet unanswered, questions came into his mind.

'But you're the wrong age. You're twenty-three,' he said.

'I'm afraid I lied to you about that. I'm actually only eighteen.'

Toby took a few seconds to absorb this, and then he asked his second question. 'Do you, err, know who your father is?'

'Well, it has to be Dan,' said Maddy, in a matter-of-fact way, as though she'd deduced it like Sherlock Holmes.

Of course it has, thought Toby bitterly.

'*He* thinks it must be him, too,' Maddy went on. 'There's no father named on my birth certificate, you see, it's just blank, so, God willing, when Emma, mum, mother, whatever, gets better, I'll be able to triple check with her. But you can see how much we look alike, don't we,' finished Maddy, turning towards him again. 'This isn't my real hair colour, by the way, it's normally the same as hers.'

Maddy flashed an embarrassed smile. Toby smiled back at her, taking her in, fully appreciating that she *was* just like her mother. Without the thick-rimmed glasses, the resemblance was haunting.

'Maddy are you absolutely sure about all this?' said Toby.

'Yes, I was ninety-nine per cent sure, as I told PC Reynolds, the police officer who came to the garage today. But then Dan confirmed it. He said that on the day of the car crash, he'd had a big row with Emma. He was angry that she hadn't told him that she was up the, you know, pregnant. Either back then, or since she'd returned to the village. He only found out, it seems, because he discovered an old diary of Emma's,' she paused for breath. 'So, Toby, what do you make of all that? A bit of a surprise?'

His head was reeling. 'Maddy, it's all amazing, stunning, and extraordinary, I don't know what to say. You're Emma's daughter, and she kept it a secret all these years. And then you, her daughter, you came to find her, but you also kept it a secret.'

'Well, yes, sorry about that. But I had to find out about her. What she was like. At first, I wasn't sure I wanted her to *know* me.'

'And what changed your mind, assuming you have changed your mind, and that's why you're telling me now?'

'Well, yes, I have. I do want to have a proper relationship with her. Mother and daughter. And I do want to properly know my grandparents. The accident has changed everything. I suddenly know what I truly feel about her, about this family. Well, it is my family, isn't it? And I've not had one before, not a proper one.'

'Well, I can see how the accident would change things, blood thicker than water and all that,' said Toby, trying to show her his support.

'You see, Toby, ever since I knew I was adopted at the age of twelve, I've felt isolated, rootless, despairing sometimes, so much so you just wouldn't believe it. I couldn't understand, or believe, that my mother, any mother, would give away a tiny, helpless baby - her baby. But I've come to realise that I shouldn't judge, at least not until I know everything. These past few days have made me think it doesn't matter what happened in the past; it's what happens in the future that counts now. Emma, Mum, must live, make a full recovery hopefully, and I must be a part of her life, and she mine.'

Toby was quiet for a bit. He was thinking what an impressive, mature daughter Emma had.

Maddy continued, 'It was Dan who told me about her father being the one who gave me away, not Emma. Dan says her father, my grandfather, bullied her and dominated her. She's written about it all in a diary.

'Well, that wouldn't surprise me at all,' agreed Toby. 'He's stuck in the Victorian era, that man. From what I know about him, and that includes a recent encounter, he'd have been angry, and more importantly for him, ashamed, about Emma being pregnant - even though we were approaching the year two thousand back then. He's a proud pompous man, to be frank. Sorry, I know he's your grandfather, but there it is. It looks as though he behaved in just the way I'd have predicted. He shipped the family out and kept it all hush-hush. The only thing I can't explain is why Emma didn't defy him in more recent years? She's her own person now - especially since she split from that Roger.'

'Roger? You didn't get to tell me about him when we were at the hotel,' said Maddy. 'She's been married before?'

'Well, yes, she still is, just about. I expect she was bounced into it by her father. Now I know why. She's told me she wasn't a real person during the time with Roger, that she was living in stasis, that's how she described it. Maybe that explains a lot about the way she's behaved. I don't know why she hasn't told Dan, though, after coming back to the village. You can see why he'd be mad,' he added, after a short pause.

Toby was, actually, considerably heartened by the news of the argument between Emma and Dan. Perhaps the emergence of their child, of Maddy, would break them up for good, even if it ought to have the opposite effect. And then, rather belatedly, it occurred to him that the row with Dan might have been a major factor in Emma's traffic accident. Not only did the garage screw up the wheel, or rather not screw up the wheel, but Dan had upset her and probably made her drive faster, or more erratically.

He and Maddy decided they'd better get to the hospital, and as they drove on, they discussed what to say to Emma's parents and to Emma herself if she was awake. Toby advised that if Emma was conscious, Maddy shouldn't say anything at all. A big revelation would be too much of a shock. In fact, they thought it best - if Emma had come around - that Maddy shouldn't even come into the room. But, if she was unchanged and Emma's mother, and possibly her father, were both there, they could all go off somewhere quiet and have that big conversation. My goodness thought Toby, that was going to be one hell of a surprise.

Like most people, he hated hospitals. It was partly the smell, that vague whiff of disinfectant; partly the lighting, always too bright; but mostly the fact that, not surprisingly, hospitals were full of so many ill, scared, or dying people. The soulless magnolia-painted corridors were busy with a motorway of trolleys mostly carrying elderly patients hooked up to drips or oxygen tanks. Some were unconscious, others distressed or confused, and most just stared vacantly ahead, looking depressed or past caring. Even when there were attempts at humour, or cheerfulness, with a nurse or porter, it all sounded rather desperate – like gallows humour. There was always plenty of activity in a hospital, but most people weren't moving fast enough to where they really wanted to be – home.

He and Maddy made their way to intensive care. Toby was scared witless. He was worried about how Emma would be. And now, well, there was the added pressure of Maddy's revelation and how that would pan out. He longed to see Emma, but he also longed to be back in the quiet of his shed with his chisel and a simple lump of stone. He and Maddy didn't speak as they traversed the endless corridors, accompanied by other equally worried looking folk, all arriving for visiting time.

They turned the corner. The intensive care ward was straight ahead and they were able to see Emma in the first bed next to the window. It was quickly obvious she was still unconscious. Her mother was sitting by her bedside, holding her hand. No sign of her father yet. He must still be in a hospital bed himself. Toby noticed there seemed to be a little less equipment around Emma than last night. A nurse was changing a drip and fiddling around with the cannula injected into Emma's arm. Toby waved to her mother, who acknowledged him and then came out.

'Hello Toby,' she said. Then looking at Maddy, she added, 'I'm sorry dear, I've forgotten your name.'

'I'm Maddy,'

Emma's mother seemed to check herself. 'Do I know you from somewhere? You look incredibly familiar? Are you a friend of Emma's? I forgot to ask last night.'

'Well, yes, you do know me, sort of,' Maddy replied very quietly. Toby wasn't sure Emma's mother heard. Anyway, he quickly changed the subject and asked her for an update. She explained that the doctors were as pleased as they could be with her daughter's progress. Her vital signs, heart rate, blood pressure, and temperature had stabilised, and there was no indication of any significant internal bleeding. One always had to be cautious with head injuries, the doctor had said, but there was every hope of a full, if slow, recovery. They didn't know how long they'd keep her in a coma – at least another day or two.

'How's, err, Mr Taylor?' Toby asked.

'Oh, he's better than he was, thank you for asking, Toby. They gave him a transfusion which boosted his blood count. The doctors have suggested that he's now well enough to transfer down to this hospital. We'll have to pay for a private ambulance, but that's ok. It would certainly make things easier in terms of visiting. Once he's stabilised, they'll put him on chemo, we think. Longer term he may need a bone marrow transplant.' She paused, and then in a very soft voice, with watering eyes, she said, 'There is hope – hope for both of them.'

'Oh, Mrs Taylor, what a few days you've had. It must be so difficult,' said Toby, reaching out to touch her shoulder.

Emma's mother patted his arm; she seemed to like him. She said she'd go and ask the nurse if Toby and Maddy might be allowed by the bedside to say a few encouraging words to Emma. She went back inside the ward.

'Toby, you know, I think it'll be too much for Emma's mum, just at the moment, if I start going into who I am and everything,' said Maddy. 'Let's leave it for today, at least.'

Toby thought that was sensible. She really was a very sensible girl. Mrs Taylor re-appeared, apologised, but said bedside visiting was still restricted to immediate close family. Toby couldn't help glancing across at Maddy, for that's exactly what she was – close family. But he said they'd visit again tomorrow. 'I want her to know I've been here for her,' he said.

Emma's mother squeezed his hand. 'If she wakes up, I'll make sure she knows.'

# Chapter Fifty-Three
# PC Reynolds

PC Pauline Reynolds and her colleague, PC Dave Lewis, arrived at the hospital reception area just as Maddy and a man - whom she assumed to be Toby Forbes - were leaving. PC Reynolds had already decided it would be better to talk to Forbes sooner rather than later. And that was why they'd come to the hospital, in the hope of finding him.

It seemed unlikely to PC Reynolds that Toby Forbes could have done anything to Emma Taylor's car a whole two weeks before it crashed, which was when he'd been spotted by the neighbour lurking outside her flat. But it was just possible.

He could have deliberately tampered with the nuts, which then worked lose over time. Anyway, she wanted to know why he'd be skulking around Emma's flat. Maybe an interview could formally eliminate him from inquiries. On the other hand, perhaps his suspicious behaviour would lead their investigation somewhere else.

'Hi, Maddy,' said PC Reynolds, using her friendliest tone. 'How did your conversation go, the one I left you to have at the garage?' But then she quickly realised she may have spoken out of turn, and after throwing a quick glance at Forbes, she added. 'If you don't mind me asking.'

'Oh, don't worry, it's fine. Toby knows,' said Maddy, picking up on her meaning. 'Better than I expected, to be honest,' she added.

'And how's the patient today?' asked PC Reynolds.

Maddy and Forbes looked at each other, seemingly waiting for the other to speak first. PC Reynolds decided to break the awkwardness by introducing herself. 'You must be Toby Forbes,' she said.

Forbes looked a little taken aback. 'Yes, um, I am. Pleased to meet you.' He offered his hand, but PC Reynolds didn't take it, and it was withdrawn.

'We're investigating the circumstances of Emma Taylor's accident,' said PC Reynolds, keeping her tone formal.

'Oh, right,' said Forbes.

PC Reynolds immediately thought he looked rather shifty.

Maddy stepped in to answer the earlier question. 'Emma is about the same, really, still in the induced coma,' she said. 'But the doctors seem happy with her progress. Her mum is with her, she can tell you the latest if you're going to the ward. Oh, but she doesn't know about me, who I really am. I haven't had a chance to speak to her yet.'

'Right, good, yes, I understand,' said PC Reynolds. She noticed her colleague, Dave, shuffling from foot to foot, no doubt wishing she'd get to the point. He had no patience and none of her people skills. 'Actually, we're not going to the ward. Mr Forbes, we'd like to ask you a few questions, if we may?' she said.

'Oh, ok, I'll help in whatever way I can, but I'm not sure how,' he replied.

'Well, if you could follow us in your car to the police station in town, we'll just run through a few things. Turning to Maddy, she said, 'My colleague can then take you home from there, Maddy, or back to your work.'

At the police station, PC Reynolds left Toby Forbes to stew in the interview room until Dave returned from dropping Maddy off. This was to be a voluntary interview, and when they eventually got underway, she explained to Forbes that, at this stage, he wasn't under arrest; he was simply helping with inquiries.

Forbes laughed, a little falsely she thought, and said he didn't like that phrase very much. They never did. He looked very nervous. PC Reynolds liked them that way.

'Well, let's start with establishing how you'd describe your relationship with Emma Taylor?' she said. Dave was yawning. He was sitting to her left, supposedly ready to make notes if he could stay awake for long enough. She kicked him under the table, and he jolted upright.

'She's a friend,' said Forbes. 'She has been since we were at school together.'

'Just a friend?'

'Well, yes, um, just a friend.'

Forbes was shifting in his seat. PC Reynolds had already been given a hint about his designs on Emma from her chat with the gallery manager Sally Graham. She guessed that the complicated soap opera unfolding before her was about to take another twist.

'I've always been, err, very fond of Emma,' disclosed Forbes. 'That's why I could never do her any harm.'

PC Reynolds thought him strangely defensive because, so far; they hadn't accused him of anything.

'Fond of her. Is that all?' she probed? Forbes flushed, which answered her question, and she continued. 'So, let's be clear when Emma Taylor came back to the village, you discovered that she still had the hots for her old flame Dan Cartridge. How did that make you feel?'

'Sad, I guess.'

'Sad? Not jealous? Angry? Angry with her?'

'I could never be angry with Emma.' Toby Forbes was getting more and more agitated. 'Where exactly are we, err, going with this?' he asked. 'I, um, came here to help you. Now you seem to be trying to, well, blame me for something.'

'I'm simply asking the questions I have to ask Mr Forbes. You just concentrate on answering them truthfully. I repeat, were you angry with Emma Taylor?'

'No, I was not angry. I've never been angry with Emma,' Forbes insisted.

PC Reynolds decided to get to the main point. 'Can you account for your movements on the seventeenth of this month?'

'Err, no, not off the top of my, um, head, hat, no, err, no, I can't. What day of the week was that?' Forbes replied, flustered, taken aback.

'It was a Friday, two weeks ago. What were you doing at about nineteen- thirty hours?'

Forbes sat for some time, thinking of an answer. But in the end, he just shrugged. 'I don't remember to be honest. You've, um, obviously got something in mind.'

'Well, let me help you. You were seen outside Emma Taylor's flat.'

'Oh, right, yes, that must have been the day I went to check she was ok.'

'You went to check she was ok?' repeated PC Reynolds, making a note. 'So, why did that involve crouching down behind her car, in what's been described to us, as a suspicious manner, before being seen to run off? What were you up to, Mr Forbes? That was a very funny way to check on someone. Why didn't you just knock on the door? In any case, why were you checking on her in the first place?'

Toby Forbes was looking more and more uncomfortable, but seemed to be winning the battle to keep control of himself. PC Reynolds was actually quite impressed.

'I was checking she was ok because she'd had a bit of an argument, a sort of fight in fact, with someone who, err, came into the gallery,' he said.

'A fight? And did you know this person she had a fight with?' asked PC Reynolds, guessing that this must be the incident the gallery manager had described involving the woman, Jen Clark.

Forbes didn't answer straight away. He took a sip of water and stared into the top corner of the room. His mouth was making a strange chewing motion. PC Reynolds watched with interest. This Toby fellow was definitely a bit odd. But this part of his story had been corroborated, and overall, he struck her as being just a rather eccentric, vague, artistic type, rather than anyone bad. PC Reynolds prided herself on being a good judge of character. But he wasn't off the hook yet.

'Well, Mr Forbes?'

'I'm going to have to tell you the ins and outs of everything, aren't I?' He collected himself, swallowed hard and eventually said, 'She had a fight with a woman called Jen Clark. It was over a man called Dan Cartridge. Emma and Dan used to be an item when they were at school. But Jen is Dan's partner now, and she came into Emma's studio in one hell of a temper asking Emma to leave Dan alone. You see, Emma returned here to get back with Dan for some reason.'

'How serious was this fight?'

'Well, Jen, Miss Clark, slapped Emma around the face.'

'Was it a hard slap, was she injured?'

'I wasn't in the room when it happened, but no, I don't think so. Emma just had a red mark for a while.'

'And where were you when this alleged assault happened?'

'I was in my room next door when I heard the commotion. I came into Emma's room, and I told Jen to leave, which, thankfully, she did. After that, Emma was upset, so she said she was going to drive up to Lakey Hill to get some fresh air. Then, at the end of the day, I sent her a text message to see how she was. When I didn't get a reply I was worried about her and I went around to her house. But I didn't want her to see me, you know, to see that I was fussing. She doesn't like fuss. When I saw her walk into her front room, through the net curtain, I quickly hid behind her car. After that, I peeked in to see that she was ok. She was reading a book, lying on the sofa, so I just jogged away.'

'And you didn't interfere with her car?'

'Good god, no,' said Forbes, looking affronted before adding, 'you do know the car had been in for some work at the garage, don't you? That's obviously where the mistake was made, why the wheel fell off. It's the garage you need to be talking to.'

Got him, thought PC Reynolds. 'Yes, and obviously we are,' she said patiently. 'But how do you know the wheel fell off, Mr Forbes? We haven't told you that?'

'Oh, Sally at the gallery told me,' he replied calmly.

Damn, thought PC Reynolds. Her mistake. She must have said too much to the manager at the gallery. Always a potential pitfall when conducting an investigation.

She sat back in her chair. 'You have to understand, Mr Forbes, that we need to follow up all lines of inquiry. Is there anyone who can corroborate your story?'

Forbes thought for a moment. 'Well, Emma could, I suppose. I think I told her the next day that I'd come around to check on her. At the time, she seemed pleased that I cared. She can confirm my story.'

'If she survives,' said Dave, helpfully.

'Is there anything else you want to tell us, Mr Forbes?' asked PC Reynolds.

He thought for a further moment, shifted in his seat, and then obviously came to a decision.

'Well, you should have an incident on file from a few weeks before the one I've described when Emma's flat was vandalised,'

'Yes, we know about that,' said PC Reynolds.

'Well, Emma suspected Jen of doing that. It seems obvious that it must have been her.'

'But she didn't say anything at the time,' said PC Reynolds.

'She didn't want to stir things up at that stage.' Forbes paused for a moment. 'There's something else I should tell you. When Jen was in Emma's room before the slap, she threatened her. I could hear it clearly through the wall, her voice was raised, almost shouting.'

'What did she say?' asked PC Reynolds.

Forbes swallowed hard. 'She said, and I'm sure she didn't really mean it, but she said, something very horrible is going to happen to you.'

# Chapter Fifty-Four
# Maddy

Thankfully, Mrs Stewart, her landlady, was out. So, after she was dropped off by the police officer at her digs, Maddy shut herself away in her room, avoiding the usual small talk. It was often difficult to turn down tea, a cake and a chat, especially the cake. Mrs Stewart had really taken to her these past few weeks, which was nice, but today she wasn't in the mood for being sociable. She kicked off her shoes and lay on the bed with her arms behind her head. At last, some time to think.

What could the police want with Toby? It must simply be routine to question everyone who knew Emma? Yet, *she* hadn't been questioned. It seemed a bit unnecessary if it was just an accident. Did they suspect otherwise? On the face of it, as Toby had told her, it was pretty obvious what had happened; Laser carried out the service, and he failed to properly re-fit the wheels. So, it was nothing to do with Toby. Laser and the garage were at fault.

Maddy decided to contact Toby in a few hours' time to find out how things had gone. In the meantime, she had another big phone call to make - to her adoptive parents – her other mum and dad. They were now back home from Italy, and Maddy had already replied to a brief text asking how she was. That had been her first contact with them in nearly a month because neither of her parents really liked mobile phones, and they were scared of foreign tariffs, despite Maddy explaining, at length, that there weren't any. Maybe, it was living in a Scottish village which made them so old-fashioned about things. Anyway, it had actually worked out well for Maddy, as she'd been able to fully concentrate on her *project*. Her head had been so full of everything over the past few weeks it hadn't seemed that any time had passed at all.

She was dreading the call, how much should she tell them? She decided to keep it brief and try to lie as little as possible - there'd been enough of that going on already. She'd already decided she'd go home in a couple of days, as soon as she had a better idea of how her real mother was doing. And then she could explain everything face to face, which would be much better.

But first, she phoned Amy to make sure she was up to speed with what she was doing, and to warn her not to be seen by her parents for just a few more days.

'What am I supposed to do, walk about in a Harry Potter invisibility cloak?' asked an exasperated Amy.

'Just be careful. If you leave the house go out the back way,' suggested Maddy. Advice which wasn't much appreciated, and they wrapped up the call soon afterwards.

And then she couldn't put it off any longer. It was time to make the call home. The conversation started pretty well. She asked how their holiday had gone, and Mum talked and talked about what they'd seen and done. She could hear her dad in the background chipping in with anecdotes. They'd obviously had a good time, and, Maddy surmised, it seemed they hadn't missed her at all.

'And what have you been up to?' asked her mother, eventually.

'Oh, this and that,' she replied. 'Yes, Amy and I have been having a really good time.'

'Right, so, what sort of things have you been doing?' her mother pressed.

'Oh, going for walks, chatting, that sort of stuff.'

She hoped her adoptive mother knew her well enough to accept she wasn't going to extract much more from this conversation, and Maddy turned the subject back to Italy and their trip. Eventually,

Maddy explained that she'd be home in a few days - she got away with keeping it vague - and said she'd fill her mother in with all the details then.

But her mother said, 'Oh right, well, you'd better leave it for at least another three days if Amy's uncle is ok about it, because we've got to go and visit a friend in hospital.' Her mother sounded slightly flustered. That was fine with Maddy; it gave her a bit more time. Her mum said she loved her and that she looked forward to seeing her. It brought a lump to Maddy's throat, and she, again, had that feeling of deep regret that she had deceived so many people. Her plan had seemed like a good idea, but now that it was all unravelling, it just meant lots of awkward conversations and, in the case of her adoptive parents, almost certainly hurt feelings. She didn't know how they'd react to news of her quest to find her biological parents. She hoped they'd be sympathetic, but she doubted they'd understand, or support her, given the way she'd gone about it. The secrecy, the lies, she didn't really comprehend it herself.

Maddy decided to go for a short walk before she made her next phone call to Toby. She wanted to get some fresh air to clear her head. It was a mild but cloudy afternoon, and in this light the greens of the hedgerows really stood out. The birds were talking to her all the way, and she spoke back, making little chirping noises and whistles. She hadn't gone far when she saw a familiar figure walking a dog. It was Jen. That was all she needed. Had Dan had a chance to talk to her yet? Should she say anything? She couldn't be the one to break the news that she was Dan's daughter. That was up to Dan. She regretted leaving her digs now. She'd lectured Amy about keeping out of the way, and then she'd gone and exposed herself to a potentially horrendous situation.

'Oh, hi, Maddy,' said Jen.

Maddy said hello and then began making a fuss over the dog, just to avoid saying anything else. Eventually, Jen said, 'What a terrible thing it was about Emma.'

'Yes, said Maddy. 'But I think she's progressing. They don't seem quite so worried about her at the hospital.'

'Oh right, well that's good,' said Jen. Maddy couldn't tell whether she meant it or not. She knew Jen hated Emma, but she couldn't believe she would wish her any serious harm. So far, nothing was said about Dan. Good, thought Maddy. So, she patted the dog some more and then said that she must be getting on – thankfully, that was that. A lucky escape.

When she arrived back at her digs, Mrs Stewart had returned home. Maddy had a brief chat with her, refused tea and cake, made her excuses and retired to her room again - from where she called Toby.

'I'm sure the police think I'm involved, somehow,' he said. He sounded very anxious. 'They kept asking me questions about an evening two weeks ago. It was when I went to check that Emma was ok. I didn't want her to think I was fussing, so I just waited outside until I saw her through the window. Some busy-body reported me, saying I was looking suspicious around her car, it's mad. I wouldn't know what to do to sabotage a car, even if I wanted to.'

Maddy sympathised and tried to calm him down. 'I'm sure it's just routine,' she said.

'They put so much pressure on me, I said something I probably shouldn't have,' revealed Toby. 'I told them about Jen slapping Emma and issuing that threat I told you about.'

'Well, I suppose it might now make them want to question Jen as well. But, at the end of the day, the accident was caused by the wheel not being put on properly at the garage. It's obvious.'

'Do you think the garage see it that way?'

'Well, Tom is being very cautious. I guess he has to be; his business's reputation is at stake. But I think he must fear that Laser is at fault. And that means the garage is at fault. Good that I don't want my job long term; it's going to get messy.'

That led them into a discussion about what she was going to do next, and Maddy explained about going home.

'You ought to have that conversation with Emma's mother tomorrow, then. And her father, if he's been transferred down and is up to it,' said Toby.

Maddy agreed, and after ending the call, she thought of something else she needed to say. She would say it to her grandfather when she eventually met him.

# Chapter Fifty-Five
# PC Reynolds

The door closed, and the mechanic, who went by the name of Laser, left the garage's office. PC Reynolds looked at Dave and raised her eyebrows.

'Well, I didn't believe a word of that, he sounded very shifty, like he was protecting someone,' she said. 'Why did he say he couldn't remember if he'd taken the wheels off or not? Ridiculous. He must know.'

Pc Reynolds looked again at the preliminary accident report on the car. 'This is pretty clear; the evidence shows the most likely occurrence was a failure to tighten the wheel nuts. It's possible, but less likely, that they were over-tightened. The mechanics would expect a failure to have taken much longer if that had been the case.'

'So, what do we do? Get Laser down the station for a more intensive grilling,' asked Dave, with a smirk on his face. He liked a good grilling.

'Well, I think we need to talk to Dan and his tempestuous other half, Jen, to see if they had anything to do with it. Maybe they conspired together. Let's get a statement from Dan Cartridge while we're here, and then we'll ask Jennifer Clark down to the station. If it's not the garage's fault, and they don't seem to know if it is or not, then fingers are pointing at her. And talking of fingers, we'd better arrange for prints of everyone and see if there are any on all the relevant tools.'

PC Reynolds left Dave to make a call to the scenes-of-crime team, and she walked out into the garage workshop. Laser was talking to a young lad; she assumed he was the apprentice, Dean Marshall. She'd need to talk to him as well - along with the garage's other mechanic, Asif Sidana. When Laser and Dean saw her approach, they quickly broke apart, looking highly conspiratorial. She made a mental note. Dan Cartridge was on the far side of the garage, with his head buried under a car's bonnet.

'We'd like to talk to you now, Mr Cartridge,' she said, then waited while he cleaned his hands at the sink. At more than six feet, he was a big guy. He certainly towered over her five-foot-six. But he wouldn't intimidate her for a moment, and she'd get to the truth.

The interview began by establishing Dan's movements while the work was being carried out on Emma's car. He didn't seem to like the questions, and PC Reynolds noted that his demeanour was very sullen throughout their conversation. He said he'd been servicing another car on the day in question, and he insisted that at no point did he have the opportunity to work on Emma's vehicle. He pointed out that there were always other mechanics in the garage, and they would certainly have noticed if he'd switched cars.

'Anyway, it was an accident, just an accident,' said Dan.

'The wheel came off the car, Mr Cartridge,' said Dave. 'How do you explain that?'

'I don't have to; it's nothing to do with me,' replied Dan, unhelpfully.

'So, what about this row you had with Emma?' asked PC Reynolds, changing tack.

If Dan was surprised that they knew about the argument, he didn't show it. 'It was nothing really,' was all he said.

'Nothing? You'd discovered, after eighteen years, that Emma Taylor had had a child, your child. She'd not told you at the time or since. I don't think anyone would describe that as *nothing*, Mr Cartridge. You were mad at her, weren't you? You were livid?'

Dan looked down at his feet. Eventually, he replied: 'Well, yes, I was mad, and I had a right go at her. I shouldn't have done and, maybe, she'd have driven off more carefully. Do you not think I know that?' he said, his voice breaking. 'But that doesn't mean I'd do anything to her car. I, I, well, Emma has meant a lot to me. We were once very close.'

PC Reynolds knew she was pushing him quite hard – especially as this was supposed to be a witness statement, voluntarily given.

'What about your girlfriend, Jen? What did she feel about Emma?' she continued.

'Well, these past weeks have been difficult for her, what with Emma coming back to the village. But she's, err, fine.'

'Back for you, wasn't she, Emma? She came back to the village to win you?'

'Maybe.'

'And was Jen upset about that?'

Dan paused before answering, first with a shrug of the shoulders and then by saying, 'Well, she wasn't very happy about it.'

'She was jealous?'

'I suppose. I told her there was nothing to worry about.'

'But did she have anything to worry about, Mr Cartridge?'

'I don't think that's any of your business,' he fired back.

'It is our business if we say it is, and it's relevant to our inquiries, mate, so just answer the question,' interjected Dave, with all his usual charm.

'Has Maddy been talking to you by any chance?' asked Dan.

'Just answer the question. Was there anything going on between you and Emma Taylor?'

'Not really. We talked to each other a bit, but it wasn't going anywhere.'

'Yes, but did Jen think it was going somewhere?' said PC Reynolds.

'Why do you keep asking me about Jen? What does she have to do with it?'

'Well, do you think she was upset enough to vandalise Miss Taylor's flat? Do you know anything about that?'

This time Dan was taken aback. He insisted he knew nothing about it and that he was sure Jen had nothing to do with any vandalism. PC Reynolds glanced across at a note Dave had written – it said: "*He's lying.*"

'Do you normally take the keys to the garage home with you, Mr Cartridge?' asked PC Reynolds, changing tack.

Dan looked surprised by the question. 'Yes, I guess so, they're on my key ring.'

'And where do you keep those keys when you're at home?'

'I usually leave them in my coat pocket,'

'Could anyone have taken them at any point?'

Dan looked extremely flustered at this question. PC Reynolds made another note. 'No, I don't think that's at all likely,' he said unconvincingly.

# Chapter Fifty-Six
# Dan

Dan knew he was innocent, but he wasn't sure the police would believe his story. Would they suspect he hadn't been honest about Jen taking his keys or the vandalism of Emma's flat? He'd lied because he'd wanted to protect Jen. If the police suspected he was not telling the truth about those two issues, why should they believe him on everything else?

Could Jen really have done something to Emma's car? The thought horrified him, and yet it wouldn't go away. It didn't seem possible. He thought back to the night Jen had gone for that long walk on her own. She'd told him she was taking his keys out of his coat pocket. He'd assumed it was for the front door key, but the bunch also included a key clearly marked "garage." He also thought of when they were mugging up for her job interview; he'd shown her how to remove and put on a wheel and the correct torque specifications. Surely not. She may be a bit impulsive and headstrong. But, no, she wouldn't do anything that stupid.

He was home slightly early, and he made himself a cup of coffee. There was a pile of washing on the floor, and he shoved it into the machine. Jen could put it on later – he didn't understand how much powder was required. He didn't even know where to put it. But he did wash up the dishes. Jen wouldn't be home for another half an hour, and he had some time to think. He decided to make another phone call to the hospital to check on Emma's condition. He got through to the ward sister, who said that her condition was stable and unchanged.

'What, she's still unconscious?' he asked.

'Yes, but it's an induced coma to help her recovery. She *has* been seriously hurt,' the nurse seemed to be ticking him off. She asked him if he'd like his call logged, so Emma could see a list of callers when she came around.

'No, no, it's fine, don't bother,' he replied.

He was still angry about Emma's deception over the baby, and it had finally persuaded him, well, ninety-nine per cent, that he didn't want to get back with her, that he wanted to stay with Jen. He told himself that his feelings for Emma were just a mixture of curiosity, nostalgia and lust. But the conversation with the police officer had rattled him and made him doubt his decision. What had Jen been up to?

First, there was the vandalism, then the assault in Emma's studio - that's how the police would see it. And now what? Could she have done something to Emma's car? Surely not. The thoughts kept going around and around in his head. He couldn't remember Jen ever taking his keys before when she'd taken Barney out for a walk. Why had she done it that one time? What if she had then gone to the garage? Could Jen have tried to kill Emma? Was she driven to it after reading about the baby in Emma's diary? Did she think he knew all along that there was a child? No wonder she was so worried about him leaving her.

'Hi love, how's things?' said Jen brightly as she came through the door. 'Hello, Barney, Barney, Barney,' she said as the dog ran circles around her legs.

Dan poured her a cup of tea. 'I was interviewed by the police today,' he said, in a matter-of-fact way.

'Whatever for?' replied Jen. 'Surely, that accident had nothing to with you. It was Laser.'

'Well, yes, but the policewoman said she had to talk to all of us as a matter of routine.' He paused and then said, as casually as he could, 'you were out walking Barney in the village the night before Emma had the accident. Did you, err, see anything suspicious?'

'What do you mean suspicious, like what? You're sounding like a policeman now. No, nothing. Don't be ridiculous, Dan, there *was* nothing suspicious, Laser made a mistake, that's all there is to it. Forget it, and it's time you forgot her too, bloody woman. Not that I want any harm to come to her, you understand.'

'They say she's stable, but she's still out of it, you know, unconscious. They call it an induced coma.'

'You phoned the hospital then,' said Jen, archly.

'Well, I thought I'd better. After all, it is our garage which worked on her bloody car.'

Jen said no more and started busying herself around the kitchen. She got the washing underway, fed Barney, and then put away the dishes which Dan had washed. All the time, he watched her intently and tried to imagine what was going on in her head. They'd charge her with attempted murder, possibly murder, if Emma didn't survive.

Then suddenly, Jen brought him back to the here and now with a thud. 'And where are we now, Dan? We seemed to have gotten over our little crisis, but what's going on in that lovely head of yours now that your ex, Emma, is lying in a hospital bed? Do you want to be with her?'

Dan looked at her and then down at the table. He was going to have to discuss things sometime. Now was as good a time as ever.

'I found that diary under your bed, you know,' he said.

'Oh, right, you did,' she replied, obviously taken aback.

'I assume you've read it all,' he asked.

'Actually, no, not all of it, too nauseating, I got about halfway through. But it seems you both had a good time back then. Very lively.'

Jen was leaning against the worktop, her arms folded. She had *that* look on. The one he hated. The one she had when he was in the doghouse. So far, she was calm, but he knew that could change at any time. Still, there was no escape. As usual, Barney seemed to sense that something was brewing, and he was hunkered down in his basket.

'So, you haven't read to the end of it?' said Dan.

'No.'

That changed things somewhat, he thought. He decided to prepare the ground. 'Right, well, it told me something I didn't know. I'll tell you what that was in a minute. But basically, it told me that she'd lied to me big time, back then and now. I can never forgive her.'

'Well, that's something, I suppose, if you're seeing her for what I always knew she was and is,' said Jen. Dan fought back an urge to defend Emma. 'But it doesn't answer the question; of whether you actually want her or me? I need to know Dan. I need to know where I stand. What's going on?' Jen added, folding her arms still tighter.

This wasn't easy for Dan. He wasn't good at saying how he felt. In recent weeks, he hadn't even been sure. But he knew now what he wanted to say. 'Jen, we're good together. I want us to stay together. I want all this other stuff to go away. I want us to get back to the way we were. Get back to normal.'

But then he checked himself. Things weren't ever going to be exactly the way they used to be. Normal had changed. He had to tell her. 'The thing is Jen, if you *had* read to the end of that diary, you'd have discovered something, a big secret that Emma kept all to herself. Well, to herself and her horrible family.'

'What, spit it out, you're frightening me?' said Jen.

'Back when we were together when we were at school, she, um, well, got pregnant.' It was out.

Jen clasped a hand over her mouth, and a small noise came out from behind it, a cross between a cry and a moan.

'She got pregnant, she went off, left the village - at her father's insistence - and then she had a baby. She had a baby girl, who she then adopted, again at her father's insistence. So, she lost all contact with her baby, our baby. It's all in that diary. He always was a right bastard. Her father. He had a real hold over her.'

'What's happened to the baby? She'd be about eighteen now,' asked Jen, still clutching her face.

'Yes, well, that's when this whole thing gets truly fucking bonkers. You'd better sit down.

Jen pulled out a chair.

'That baby, that eighteen-year-old child, is Maddy. Maddy, who works in the garage, Maddy, who got the job you went for.'

'Maddy! What the fuck! Oh my god.' Jen blurted out.

'I spoke to Maddy today,' continued Dan. 'She told me I was her father. I didn't have a clue until then. It was really, really strange. I'm still totally shocked. I can't get my head around it at all. He paused and took a sip of coffee. Jen just continued standing with her hand clasped over her mouth.

'You see, Maddy decided to come to the village, get the job at the garage, so that she could, basically, well, spy on Emma and find out if she was a good person. She said her plan was to then decide whether or not to meet her properly. I think it was only recently she also sort of worked out that I could be her father.'

Jen interrupted, 'Oh right, well, that was me; I told Maddy about you and Emma being boyfriend and girlfriend at school. So, she would have worked that out fairly easily.'

Dan thought that explanation seemed plausible.

'I think the car accident has brought everything to a head, and Maddy's decided to come out, so to speak,' he added. 'But, she's pretty certain that Emma doesn't know, hasn't guessed that she's here.'

'The little bitch,' said Jen. 'And to think she's been all friendly to me. She was just using me for information. Thinking about it, she did keep asking questions about you and Emma. Now I know why. I can't take it all in, Dan. Maddy is *your* daughter. If we were to get married, she'd be my stepdaughter. The other day I was telling her all sorts of stuff at the café. Bloody hell.'

'That's about it, yes, bloody hell. Oh, and by the way, I wasn't named on her birth certificate - which shows exactly what Emma thought of me. So, with that and her keeping things a secret for all this time, you can see why I can't forgive her,'

Jen looked up from the table. Her eyes were held wide open. She was clearly shocked by what she'd heard.

Dan continued, 'Anyway, I don't want you thinking that's the only reason why I've turned against Emma. Nothing was ever going to happen anyway. I was just thrown off balance for a bit.'

'Is that what you call it?'

Dan continued, 'You see, we're not the same people any more, Emma and me. That was then, and this is now. She's an artist. I'm just a mechanic. And anyway, more importantly, I'm with you. I love you.' There, he'd said it.

'You're not just a mechanic; you're also a bloody good talented musician, not that I'm trying to change your mind,' laughed Jen. 'Anyway, it doesn't matter what you do for a living. I'm sure that's got nothing to do with anything. It's more to do with who you are. People change, Dan; I could have told you that. God, if I met some of my old boyfriends, I'd have a right old shock, and so would they.'

Then Jen came over to where Dan was sitting and put her arms around his neck. Bending down, she said, 'So, you're mine then, Dan Cartridge. And now we have a daughter – even if we didn't know it.' And then she kissed him. And Dan kissed her back. Dan felt she was amazing to just accept his momentous news just like that. He was very lucky to have her. But he still couldn't prevent the thought from flashing through his head - yes, but are you actually a killer?

# Chapter Fifty-Seven
# Emma

She was swimming, swimming upwards towards the light. It felt like glue holding her down, holding her back. She could hear voices. She thought she could hear her name. Was that him? She knew he'd be there. But the glue, the glue was holding her back, pulling her down again, back to the land of dreams.

Holding hands in a field, a little girl running around their legs, laughing. She had a pretty ribbon in her hair, and she was holding a beaten-up-looking teddy. It looked like her own teddy from when she was a little girl. Was the little girl hers? She couldn't tell? He was there.

Someone was holding her hand she squeezed it. She tried, but she couldn't open her eyes, and she couldn't speak. Her eyes were so heavy, stuck with the glue, and it was pulling her down again, pulling her away. He was there; he was there, she was sure he was. He'd look after her.

# Chapter Fifty-Eight
# Maddy

Maddy was about to leave for the hospital when Mrs Stewart knocked on her door.

'There's a letter here for you, dear,' she said. 'It's just arrived in the post. I'm afraid our post is delivered rather late in the day.'

Maddy thanked her and studied the envelope. She didn't recognise the handwriting. But the postmark was local. Strange. She opened it and, after reading the first line, sat back down on her bed with a thud.

*Dear Maddy,*

*This is your mother, your real mum. My name is Emma Taylor. I think we met briefly the other day in the garage – and you've also been to the gallery to see Toby. You were there when I knocked my easel over. I'm not usually that bad-tempered!! But I suspect you know all this, as I must assume you know who I am.*

*I have only just realised who you are...my lovely, lovely daughter. You look so much like me, and your name is the one I gave you when you were born. Forgive me for discovering your secret, but I'm in no doubt as to who you are.*

*I totally understand why you might want to come to the village and find out about me before revealing yourself. It must be very strange for you. I think you are incredibly brave to come to find me. I have been looking for you for a long, long time. And it's beyond my wildest dreams to discover that you are here.*

*I have decided to write to you explaining what happened eighteen years ago and how I feel about you. You can then decide if you want us to meet. I love you, Maddy. I love you as I always have, all through the long years of aching to know where you were and how you were growing up. That's maybe hard for you to understand because I suspect you have repeatedly asked yourself the question: why did my mother give me away?*

There was a knock on the door. It was Mrs Stewart.

'Hi dear, sorry to intrude, but I wondered if you'd like a mug of tea now. I've brought one up, just in case. Oh, and some cake.'

'Actually, Mrs Stewart, do you know what, I'd absolutely love one.' said Maddy, walking over to the door to take the tea and cake from her hands. Her own hands were shaking.

'Is your letter from home?' asked Mrs Stewart, looking a bit concerned.

'Well, in a way, yes,' said Maddy.

'Oh right.' Mrs Stewart looked puzzled. But Maddy wasn't telling her anymore, so she quietly closed the door. Maddy put the mug of tea and cake down on her bedside table and turned the letter over.

*I was eighteen when I became pregnant with you - the same age that you are now. However, I suspect you are a lot more mature than I was then. I was a bit scared of the situation I found myself in. I'm ashamed to say I wasn't strong enough to cope with all the pressures. I made the wrong decision. It has haunted me ever since.*

Maddy read the line again - *'It has haunted me ever since.'* She wiped a tear from her eye and continued.

*What can I say, Maddy? I am sorry if you feel I abandoned you. I should have listened to my heart and not the voices around me. I have never stopped thinking about you. I have never stopped loving you. If I had been able to come and get you over the years, I would have done. But you'll be aware that there are rules and procedures around adoption. In any case, I didn't know where you were. And also, as far as I was aware, you were, and still are, happy with your new family. I sincerely hope you have been. From what I can tell, and from what I've heard from Toby (who doesn't know, by the way), you are a very intelligent, funny, talented girl with so much promise, so you must have been well brought up.*

*I long for the moment when we can get together and talk properly. But I think you might need some time to think through my explanation, such as it is. I hope you can forgive me, although I will never forgive myself, and that this letter will help you decide that we can start a new future – together.*

*With all my love,*

*Emma (your mother)*

The tears were now streaming down Maddy's face. She took a sip of tea and blew her nose. This was what she'd wanted to hear, longed to hear, for years - ever since she'd first been told that she was adopted. Her real mother loved her, and she regretted giving her away. It sounded as though she hadn't wanted to give her away in the first place. That she'd been pressured to do so, it all squared with what Dan had told her. Only, her mother hadn't blamed her own father; in this letter, she'd blamed herself.

Maddy looked at the postmark on the envelope. Emma must have posted the letter the day she'd had the accident. Then Maddy had a terrible thought. If her mum didn't recover, they might never "get together." She wiped her eyes again. This letter might be all she'd be left with. But the thought was transitory, and she pushed it back. Emma, her mother, yes, her mother, was going to be ok. Deep down, she was happy, really happy. She just felt things were going to be alright now. Her mother loved her and always had.

# Chapter Fifty-Nine
# Toby

'She just squeezed my hand,' said Toby as Emma's mother came back into the room. 'I think she's coming round a bit. Her eyelids were flickering, and she was sort of moaning. But she seems to have gone back to sleep again now.'

'Oh, that's brilliant. That is progress,' said Emma's mother.

Toby shared the good news with a nurse, who came back into the room carrying a new saline drip.

'Oh, that's a good sign,' said the nurse. 'We'd expect her to start re-surfacing in the next twenty-four hours, now that we've reduced the drugs, but it'll take her some time. Don't expect too much. And don't expect the old Emma straight away. Patients are often very confused, and they can suffer memory loss,' she added, as she swopped the saline bags over and, at last, stopped the monitor from making an infernal beeping sound.

'Yes, the doctor explained all the possibilities to us,' said Emma's mother. 'I just hope he's wrong about some of them.'

Toby decided not to ask for any more details. The nurse then checked Emma's chart - all her vital signs, blood pressure, pulse, and temperature had pretty much returned to normal – and then she left. That was another good sign; the nurses weren't by her bedside all the time, which meant they were obviously much more relaxed about her condition. But Emma was still linked to a heart monitor, which pulsed away and occasionally made alarming noises, seemingly for no reason. He'd learnt to ignore them, as did most of the nursing staff. The monitor was always re-setting itself, they explained. He wondered how they knew when there was a real problem.

Toby felt that he was establishing a real bond with Emma's mother. She seemed to like him. 'How's Mr Taylor?' he asked.

Emma's mother explained that her husband had just arrived at the same hospital that morning, about an hour ago. She's been with him on his ward, helping him to settle in.

'He's much, much better. The blood transfusion has helped a lot, and the internal bleeding has stopped. He should be discharged in a day or so, and then we can plan the rest of his treatment,' she added.

Emma's mother looked very tired, and the strain was beginning to show. There were dark rings under her eyes. But, despite that, all things considered, she was holding up remarkably well and there had been no tears, at least not in front of Toby.

'Emma means an awful lot to me, Mrs Taylor,' said Toby. The comment almost seemed to make her jump. Toby knew he wasn't very good at saying important serious things.

'Well, yes, I can tell. You're a very good friend to her. She's spoken of how much you've helped her settle in.'

'I'd err like us to be more than just good friends,' he said quietly and a little mournfully.

Emma's mother was quiet for a bit. She looked a bit embarrassed by his remark.

Eventually, she said, 'Well, there's no point in me trying to tell my daughter what to do, as I'm sure you know, but you do seem like a nice chap. And neither her father nor I have ever taken to that Dan fellow. We quite liked Roger, but he appears to be history in the eyes of our daughter.

Before the conversation could get more awkward, Maddy arrived. She tapped on the window of the ward and waved.

275

'There's that girl. That friend of yours,' said Emma's mother, sounding slightly irritated.

Toby went out to see Maddy. 'Hi, you managed to get away then,' he said.

'Yes, Tom has been so good. It's been fairly quiet at the garage, though, since the accident, but I promised to catch up with any work that needs doing when I get back,' she replied. Toby noticed that she was not wearing her glasses again. She looked so different.

Maddy was obviously genuinely elated at the news of Emma's improvement. 'I'm glad to see you so upbeat,' he said.

'I'm feeling so much more positive about everything,' she said.

'Right, well, let's persuade Emma's mother to come for a coffee, and you can err, break the, um, news to her.'

# Chapter Sixty
# PC Reynolds

The Chief Inspector had been adamant. If it was more than just a road traffic accident, they could be looking at a possible attempted murder charge, which meant the case had to be handed over to CID. It probably should have been already, he'd said. PC Reynolds knew the rules and knew she'd stretched them, but she felt that all her hard work so far would be forgotten – and that wouldn't do her chances of a transfer any good at all. But she felt better when she was told that Detective Inspector Terry Marsh would be put on the case. She was sitting in his office now, waiting to brief him. He was making them both a coffee in the station's small kitchen. She'd offered to do it, but he'd refused.

Terry Marsh was the most laid-back detective she'd ever met. Nothing seemed to upset or wind him up, unlike the majority of her colleagues, who could do with regular psychoanalysis. He was a married man with three teenage children – but even that didn't seem to upset him. While she waited, she examined a picture of his family, which sat on his desk. Perhaps his kids were well-behaved and problem free - but she doubted that - few were.

The rest of the office was pretty sparse, just a filing cabinet and a board on the wall covered in neatly pinned notices and a large map of their division. Maybe, cybercrime wasn't the right direction for her after all; maybe she should try CID. If this case went well, and she impressed DI Marsh, it might seriously help her chances.

'There you go, coffee with no sugar. Biscuit?' asked DI Marsh, opening the door with his elbow.

'No, I'm fine,' said PC Reynolds, taking the tray from him. 'You'll have seen my report, sir,' she began.

'Yes, it's a tricky one,' he said, dunking his biscuit into his mug. His slightly bulging midriff suggested it wasn't the first he'd ever had. 'We've got means, well, possibly. Motive, hmm, I guess. And opportunity. But all the evidence is circumstantial. It's never going to be enough for Crown Prosecution. Did you get anything from the fingerprints?'

'Well, yes, but it's not very helpful, I'm afraid. All the people who work in the garage have dabs pretty much everywhere, as you'd expect. We haven't taken Jen Clark's fingers yet, but, having said that, we found no trace of any unidentified prints on the tools.'

'She could have worn gloves. I would if I was going to try to kill someone by messing about with a car wheel. And she probably wouldn't have wanted to get her hands dirty.'

'What 'cos she's a girlie?' teased PC Reynolds, waving her fingers in the air as quote marks.

'I'm glad *you* said that,' said Chief Inspector Marsh with a smile.

'What do you want to do then, sir? I was about to bring her in for questioning when the case was handed over to you guys.'

'Well, the first thing to say is that I'd like you to stay on the case. You know all the people involved and more about this village than I do. I've cleared it with uniform.' That cheered up PC Reynolds considerably.

'What's your hunch on this one, Pauline?' he asked.

Typical Terry Marsh, she thought. All of a sudden, we're on first-name terms. But he did things in such a relaxed way that it didn't really matter. She knew from colleagues, though, that the informality should never go both ways.

'My hunch is that she could well have done it, sir. We've got the alleged vandalism on Emma's flat, the assault on Emma at the gallery - which was heard by a witness - and she was seen entering the garage the night before the accident. I think it's certainly plausible that she took her partner's keys, with or without his knowledge and messed with the wheel nuts.'

'And you think she knew what to do?' he asked.

'I'll assume you're not being sexist again, sir,' smiled PC Reynolds. 'Dave, my colleague, I mean PC David Lewis, went back to talk to the garage manager, Tom, and he told us that Jen had recently been interviewed for a secretarial job at the garage. She said that her partner, Dan, who works there, as you'll have seen from my report, helped her mug up on all kinds of mechanical issues.'

'Ok. But it's still weighted towards the circumstantial and hearsay. I think our only chance is a confession; otherwise, we've not got enough. Of course, she could retract it even if she makes one, but at least it might lead us to other inquiries. So, I say we bring her in under caution. She can have a solicitor if she wants, and he or she might suggest that she keeps shtum. But we'll have to take that risk.'

# Chapter Sixty-One
# Maddy

They found a quiet corner in the hospital canteen. Emma's mother had taken a little persuading, she was anxious in case Emma showed signs of coming around again. But the nurse said she doubted Emma would wake up in the next few hours, as she'd just been given further sedation.

It was now just after three, and the canteen was pretty quiet. A group of four nurses, probably waiting to start their shift, were chatting and giggling at one table. One of them had obviously found something amusing on her phone as it was being handed to each in turn. On another table, a tired-looking consultant was thumbing through a report. But otherwise, the place was virtually empty.

'You said there was something important to discuss, Toby,' said Emma's mother. 'As if there aren't enough important things going on.'

'Actually, it's not me, Mrs Taylor. It's Maddy.'

'Oh,' Mrs Taylor looked surprised and then suddenly worried.

Maddy had rehearsed what she was going to say. But she was more nervous about this conversation than her recent talk with Dan. She guessed it was because Mrs Taylor, her grandmother, was older, and seemed severe and a bit scary. She looked down at her hands – they were shaking again.

'Remember you asked me the other day if we'd met before somewhere?' Maddy began.

Surprisingly, she didn't have to say anything else. Emma's mum suddenly put her hand to her mouth. The shock and surprise on her face were plain to see, as if something momentous had suddenly hit her. 'You're my granddaughter, aren't you?' she said.

'You've got it in one,' said Maddy, grinning from ear to ear, hugely relieved.

'Oh goodness, what a shock, I knew there was something about you. You've got Emma's eyes, it's obvious now. Oh, my goodness.' Emma's mother buried her head in her hands and began to sob. It was as though she couldn't hold back the tide of emotion any longer, it all came flooding out. Maddy didn't know what to do, but tears were welling up in her eyes too. She looked at Toby. He also looked as though he was about to start crying and he squirmed in his seat, looking embarrassed.

'I think I'll go back and check on Emma, I'll leave you two to get to know each other. I'll text you, Maddy, if there's any change,' he said, and with that, he was off. He couldn't get out quick enough, thought Maddy.

Maddy offered her grandmother a tissue which she took and dabbed at her eyes before taking Maddy by the hand. 'I'm sorry, dear; it's such a shock after everything else. Does Emma know? How did you know she was your mother? How did you find her? So many questions, I've, I've, thought about you so many times over the years, wondering how you were growing up.

Maddy wiped her eyes. 'I've a bit of a confession to make,' she began, 'and I hope you'll forgive me. Emma, my mum, didn't, until very recently, know I was here. I've been working in the village for quite a few weeks now. You see, I found out about her after discovering my birth certificate. I tracked her down online. But before I revealed who I was, I just wanted to get to know her a bit first, from a distance. Do you understand that?'

'Yes, I think I can,' replied her grandmother, looking at her with kind soft eyes, which Maddy hadn't noticed before.

'But I've been worrying, these past few days after the accident, that she might not *ever* meet me, you know, properly, if…if, well, anyway, that's not going to be an issue now because she's going to be ok. I'm sure of it.' Maddy paused and produced Emma's letter from her pocket. 'I've also just received this letter from her in the post. She must have sent it just before the crash.'

'Goodness, what does it say.'

'Well, basically, despite what I thought, she had recently guessed who I must be. You see, we kind of met in the office at the garage, and I wasn't wearing my disguise at the time.' She took the false glasses out of her pocket to show her grandmother. 'I'm not sure how effective these were anyway. So, in the letter, she said she loved me and that she always had. And that was all I wanted to hear.'

'Was that all it said?' asked Maddy's grandmother. Maddy said that basically it was, deciding not to reveal any more at that moment. She put the letter away before her grandmother asked to read it. She didn't want to provoke or get into the middle of a family row over the part played by her grandfather. Not when she'd only just discovered them all.

'And, err, what about your other parents?' asked her grandmother.

'Um, well, that's another confession. They don't know I'm here. They just think I'm on a holiday with my friend in Cornwall. But I'm going to have to go home and tell them everything soon.'

'I see, yes, you must,' was all her grandmother said, her voice fading away as if her mind had locked onto some distant thought.

'I've met my dad, Dan, and he knows about me,' Maddy said, hoping that would help the conversation along.

But she could tell from her grandmother's face that it didn't. She was looking into the distance. Eventually, she came back to the present and said, 'Oh right, and what did he have to say? As far as we ever knew, he didn't know about you either. Emma's father thought it was for the best. We thought it was all for the best. Emma was very young. You do understand.'

'Well, I'm struggling with that. I've always struggled with that, but I guess now is not the time and place,' replied Maddy, again deciding that she must not get into discussions which were too deep. Not yet, anyway.

They sat and talked for three-quarters of an hour, and gradually the tension lifted. Her grandmother wanted to know how she'd been brought up. Was she well cared for? Had she been happy? What schools had she been to? What she liked and disliked? What her ambitions were? And so on, and so on. She asked all the obvious questions and one or two surprising ones, such as did she love her adoptive parents, and what had they told her about the past.

At four o'clock, her grandmother suddenly looked at her watch and announced, 'Do you know what, I think it's time you met your grandfather.'

Maddy felt her stomach disappear. She felt like saying, '*But he didn't ever want me. He gave me away.*' But instead, she tried something a bit subtler. 'How do you think he'll react?'

'I think it's going to give him a boost. I think it's what he needs; it gives him something else to fight for. He won't admit it, but he regrets what he did to Emma, how he persuaded her, and what he did to you. There are things you don't know, and it's time you did. And now he's got the chance to make amends and bring our family back together again. He should have done it years ago.'

Maddy was scared stiff. But she was beginning to like her grandmother. She seemed one very determined lady. It was almost, thought Maddy, as if the current crisis in her life had brought out the best in her. What a shame she hadn't spoken out eighteen years ago.

# Chapter Sixty-Two
# PC Reynolds

PC Pauline Reynolds stared into the mirror, looking hard into the eyes of a tired face. She tidied up her hair, which was pinned at the back with a large clip. She took a deep breath, and she was ready - ready for the interview with Jennifer Clark.

She and Dave had collected Jen about an hour ago. They'd been kind to her - in a way - by waiting until her lunch break and allowing her to tell the boss she was going off sick. But now, any kindness would have to end. She suspected that Jen Clark was a pretty tough cookie, and they'd have to be even tougher to extract a confession. DCI Marsh had suggested they play good cop, bad cop. She was going to be the good cop, in the hope Jen would feel her empathy and believe that she'd better understand the lengths to which a woman could be driven.

She left the ladies' cloakroom, walked a few paces down the corridor, and knocked on the DCI's door. She opened it without waiting for a reply. 'Jen Clark is in the interview room, Sir. She's had a cup of tea and has been sitting for about half an hour with Dave, I mean PC Lewis, for company.'

Ten minutes later, with the preliminaries out of the way – an explanation of why she was being questioned and what her rights were - the interview proper was about to begin. Jen had been offered a solicitor, and they'd explained to her at some length, with the digital recorder running, how it would be in her best interests. There were, after all, very serious matters to discuss. But Jen had refused, saying she didn't need a lawyer, that it would be a waste of money, and that she was one hundred per cent confident she could clear the whole matter up. A decision she might regret thought PC Reynolds, but it was what they'd hoped for. Solicitors always made interrogations much more difficult - that was what they were paid to do. Many police officers struggled with the idea that public money, via legal aid, should go towards helping, as they saw it, someone obstructing, or avoiding, justice. PC Reynolds wasn't one of them. She understood the need for representation in a democracy. And that everyone was innocent until proven guilty. She was only interested in the truth.

DCI Marsh began. 'So, Miss Clark, a couple of months ago, a woman called Emma Taylor arrived in the village, when did you first become aware of her, and when did you learn about her previous relationship with your partner Dan Cartridge?'

'Relationship is a bit strong, they were only teenagers,' said Jen dismissively.

'Just answer the question please, Miss Clark,' repeated DCI Marsh firmly.

'Well, I was in the hair-dressers a few weeks back, I think, and one of the girls started gossiping. She just wanted to tease me, so she told me that this Emma had returned to the village and that back in the day, way back in the day as it happened, she and Dan were a big thing.'

'And how did you feel about that? It's always difficult, isn't it, when an old boyfriend, or girlfriend, comes back onto the scene?' interjected PC Reynolds.

'Well, I wasn't too bothered, to be honest. I knew Dan and I were strong together and this was just a school romance, so it was all something and nothing really,' replied Jen.

She seemed quite relaxed and confident, despite the arrest, despite being hauled to a police station for questioning. PC Reynolds was surprised.

'Something and nothing,' interjected DCI Marsh, 'so why did you vandalise Emma Taylor's flat?'

Jen looked markedly less relaxed now, genuinely taken aback in fact. PC Reynolds wondered what she'd do next. Jen didn't know how much *they* knew, of course. Even so, DCI Marsh was taking a bit of a flier and going for the jugular early. If Jen had had any sense, or if she'd had the advice of a solicitor, she would have said nothing, called their bluff, stone-walled them, but she possessed neither. Her composure just slipped away. The façade of confidence and nonchalance evaporated, and to PC Reynold's enormous surprise, she blurted out, 'I guess I just got mad one night, I shouldn't have done it, it was stupid.'

PC Reynolds made notes. They had her on criminal damage of the flat, if nothing else. 'I guess anyone would be upset if they thought their partner was in another relationship. Jen, tell us exactly what you did to Emma's flat?' she asked in a more soothing voice.

Jen was now looking increasingly distressed. 'I wrote "*go, you bitch, go*" on her window.'

'Why?' interjected DI Marsh.

Jen paused for a moment, then said, 'Well, why do you think it's bloody obvious? I hoped it might frighten her off.'

'So, just to clarify, you *were* bothered by her, Jen?' Jen nodded. 'For the tape, Ms Clark has indicated her agreement with that statement,' said PC Reynolds, also writing it down in her notebook. If required, they could try to back up this confession with forensic evidence by obtaining a lipstick sample from a search of Jen's belongings – assuming she hadn't had the good sense to throw it away.

'And did it?' asked DCI Marsh, 'frighten her off?'

'No, well, I didn't seriously think it would. I don't know why I did it, but there was no harm done, not really,' replied Jen, the distress coming through in her voice.

'You suspected that Dan was seeing Emma?' asked PC Reynolds.

'He told me he wasn't, and I tried hard to believe him.'

'But you didn't, did you,' came back DI Marsh. 'Because you also went to Emma Taylor's studio, assaulted and threatened her with these words?' he briefly looked down at his notes. 'You said, "*Something very horrible is going to happen to you.*" And before you answer, Miss Clark, I should warn you we do have a witness.'

Jen rocked in her seat for the second time. She bit her lip and stared up at a small thin window which ran across the top of the room.

'No harm done, Miss Clark? You can't say that, can you?' added DI Marsh, turning the screw.

Jen began to sob uncontrollably now.

'Take your time Jen, it's important that we get to the truth,' said PC Reynolds, soothingly.

'I, I was told by someone that they'd been seen together, and I just lost it, I suppose. But I'm really, really sorry about it. I did only slap her, it…it wasn't an assault as such, like you say.'

'If you strike someone it's an assault, Miss Clark,' said DCI Marsh.

'And I didn't mean the threat,' Jen continued in between sobs. 'It just came out. No one would believe that I'd harm anyone.'

'Well, that's the trouble Miss Clark, it's difficult to know what to believe from you.' DCI Marsh paused again, and again he looked down at his notes. PC Reynolds knew it was all for effect. 'Can you account for your movements on the night of June 24$^{th}$? The night before Emma Taylor was involved in a car accident?'

'Accident being the keyword there,' Jen quickly replied, pulling herself together a little. 'It was an accident. I don't know what you're implying, but it *was* an accident, a bloody accident. I'm sorry it happened, but it's got nothing to do with me. It was that Laser in the garage. He screwed up her wheel. He should be in here, not me.'

'Jen, try to take things one step at a time. Let's just answer the questions as they come,' said PC Reynolds, offering a tissue.

DCI Marsh was unrelenting. 'So, what *were* your movements on the night of June 24$^{th}$?'

'I was at home, at home with Dan, like I am every evening.'

'At home? At home all evening? Think very carefully before you answer, Miss Clark. Remember you are under caution, and anything you say may be used against you in court,' added the Inspector.

'I might have taken the dog out for a walk at some point, I guess. I can't remember.'

'What time would that be?'

'I can't remember.'

'Well, then, let me help. Do you recall, at about eight-thirty, entering the garage in the village, the garage where your boyfriend Dan works, the garage which, on that night, contained Emma Taylor's car?'

'Oh god, alright, you know about that too.' Tears streamed down Jen's cheeks, and what she said next was interrupted by sobs and sniffs. 'Yes, I did go into the garage. I…'

DCI Marsh interrupted. 'And how did you manage to enter the garage on that night?'

'I took his keys. I borrowed Dan's keys.'

'And were you aware that you were, in effect, entering the building without consent - unlawful entry, at the very least? What were you doing there, Miss Clark?'

'I went to look through Dan's things to see if I could discover whether anything was going on with that girl. I just wanted to find out if Dan was lying to me,'

'And that was it?'

'Yes'

'Because, the thing is, Miss Clark, you do *know* about cars, don't you?

'A bit.'

'Enough to understand that if you loosen wheel nuts, they can work free because that's what happened to Emma Taylor's car. That's what sent it careering through a fence and into a tree. That's why she's in a hospital bed in a coma. That's why she might die, Miss Clark.'

'I didn't do anything,' sobbed Jen.

'You didn't *do* anything? You've already confessed to criminal damage, to assault, to threatening words and behaviour and now to unlawful entry, and you didn't *do* anything?'

'I didn't sabotage her car. I wouldn't do that. I wouldn't try to kill someone. What do you take me for?'

'I think you are a desperate woman, Miss Clark, taking desperate measures.'

Jen was sobbing again. PC Clark poured her a glass of water and told the tape she was doing so. The interview had reached a crucial stage.

'What really happened in that garage?' began DI Marsh. 'You went to Emma Taylor's car, didn't you? And you turned on the power, you took the wheel gun, and you un-did those wheel nuts, didn't you, Miss Clark? You didn't care what happened to her, you wanted her out of the way, out of your life.'

Between sobs, Jen kept repeating the words, 'I didn't do anything, I didn't do anything.'

'Jen, it would be much easier for you if you tell us what happened, tell us the truth,' added PC Reynolds.

'I *am* telling you the truth. I want a solicitor, I didn't do anything,' said Jen between the gasps of her sobs.

DCI Marsh glanced at PC Reynolds. She knew straight away that he'd think they'd fallen short of the mark. They had gained additional supporting evidence, and they were further forward than when they started. But they didn't have that crucial confession for attempted murder, or even tampering with a vehicle. They had no choice now but to arrange for Jen Clark to get a solicitor. They'd hold her overnight, and they'd talk to her again in the morning with the solicitor present. But once he or she was involved, they'd probably get no further with a confession. They could hold her under arrest for twenty-four hours, and PC Reynolds knew DCI Marsh intended to use every minute. There was a risk the solicitor would try to claim they'd bullied her into what she'd told them so far. But PC Reynolds was sure they'd behaved within limits. Anyway, it was all on the recording. Ultimately, even if the evidence was only circumstantial, it would be up to the Crown Prosecution Service.

# Chapter Sixty-Three
# Emma

She could just about open her eyes. She could see enough to know she was in the hospital. She tried to move. Too much pain, a sharp pain in her side. Toby was there, holding her hand. Toby, Toby. She knew he'd be there for her. Her mother too. And that red-haired girl. That red-haired girl? It came back to her. Maddy. She was Maddy. My Maddy. She tried to speak, but somehow, she couldn't. She managed to whisper.

'Water.'

'Yes, darling,' said her mother reaching for a glass and holding it to her lips. Then they were all talking at once. She couldn't take it in. She closed her eyes again, and she was sinking again. Stuck in the glue. The incredibly sticky glue. Then she saw a tree. Yes, the tree, the accident. That was why she was in the hospital. She was sinking.

# Chapter Sixty-Four
# Maddy

Maddy decided she was going to the pub. She wasn't much of a drinker, but tonight she was going to have a few. She needed them. The last few days had taken their toll, and Maddy felt wrung out.

Luckily, she had been saved from the additional stress of meeting her grandfather. When she'd gone to his hospital ward with her grandmother he'd been asleep, so they'd gone back to be with Emma, just in time for a few moments of semi-consciousness – that had been a real bonus. It looked like she would be alright. It was a massive relief.

Maddy put some lipstick on, threw on her favourite comfortable sweater and brushed her hair, pulling it back into a ponytail.

Although she was now eighteen, she'd been going into pubs for well over a year, so she could hold her drink pretty well. She'd always looked older than her age, and if a landlord was known to ask questions and seek identification, she'd just persuade someone else to buy a drink for her. Consequently, she'd only been into a pub on her own once before, at Dan's concert, so she felt slightly awkward. She looked around the bar. There was one familiar face; Deano, the garage apprentice. At least he was someone she knew, and he was alright, really. In fact, she quite liked him now. She walked over.

'Mads, watcha, how ya doin,' he said. It was obvious he'd already had a few. 'Let me get you a drink.'

'Double rum and coke, if you're asking – I need it.'

'Not the only one,' replied Deano.

'Yeah, it's been a hell of a few days.'

Deano ordered her drink and bought another whisky chaser for himself.

'How's Emma?' he asked, only he ran the words together, so it came out, 'Howzemma.'

'Well, there's some brilliant news, she woke up for a bit today. She was still pretty much away with the fairies and didn't really seem to know much of what was going on, but she was able to ask for a drink of water. So that's real progress. Everyone is delighted.'

'Who's everyone? Wazz Dan there?'

'Err, no, surprisingly, perhaps. Just me, Toby, and her mum. There's been no sign of Dan,'

'He's going to fuckin' kill me,' slurred Deano.

'Why?'

'Never mind.' Deano seemed to check himself. He took another drink, sat up on his stool a little and looked her up and down.

'D'ya know what, Mads? You're alright, you know. You look really, really great.'

'I don't, I look a wreck.' Despite the fact he was quite drunk, she was in the mood for a compliment.

Deano had seemed a bit of a jerk to her at first, a good-looking jerk, but nevertheless, a jerk. But he'd grown on her, with his frequent visits to her office and hammy chat-up lines. And now, partly because she wanted a drinking partner, she was determined to enjoy his company. He gestured to her to come close, and then he whispered in her ear.

'I want you,' he was trying but failing to look serious.

The nerve! Nevertheless, a delicious tingle shot through her. Bizarre though it seemed to her inner common sense, the idea of her and Deano tonight didn't seem like such a bad idea.

She whispered back in his ear. 'Let's get wasted, get me another drink.'

Two drinks later and they'd moved to the back of the bar. She had a job keeping Deano's hands off her. She wasn't drunk enough yet to be oblivious to embarrassment and they were getting one or two looks from other customers. She decided she'd try to slow things down a bit.

'Why will Dan kill you?' she asked.

'He just will.'

'But I think he quite likes you, Deano, despite the way he goes on sometimes.' She had no hard evidence for this assertion.

Maddy had noticed, with relief, that Deano hadn't said anything about Dan being her father, so hopefully, he hadn't told anyone. She wasn't surprised by that. Dan wasn't a great talker anyway, and he'd want to keep it quiet for now, at least until he'd explained things to Jen. That was going to be one hell of a conversation.

'It was down to me, you know,' said Deano, bringing her back to the present with a start.

'What was Deano?' she was getting very curious about where this conversation was going.

'I did it, y'know,'

She took him by the shoulder and looked straight at him. He was swaying slightly from the waist up. 'What are you saying, Deano?'

'I didn't finish off the nuts, Mads, I didn't finish the job. Laser left me to do the health check, that's what we call it, and I fucking didn't do it properly. I forgot to tighten one of the wheels, I got distracted. I nearly killed Emma. And now Dan says they've arrested Jen. They think she did it, they've got her in a cell.'

Arrested Jen. Maddy could see why they might. But although Jen seemed a bit off her trolley, she didn't seem capable of trying to kill someone.

'Christ, Deano. Have you told the police?' she said.

'No, I can't, if it comes out, Dan will kill me.'

'He'll kill you if you don't. Can't you see that?'

'Oh fuckin' great, he's going to kill me either way,' Deano started to laugh.

'Listen, Deano, pull yourself together. You're going to have to tell the police first thing in the morning.' Her own head had suddenly become crystal clear. 'Right now, Deano, I think we need to get you home. You've had enough.'

'I can't ride my bike, I don't think,' said Deano, pulling on his leather jacket.

Maddy thought for a moment. A taxi to take him home to the neighbouring village would cost a fortune. She gulped down the remains of her third double and made up her mind.

'You'd better stay with me then; we can get into my digs the back way if you're quiet.'

Deano just grinned from ear to ear.

# Chapter Sixty-Five
# Jen

Jen lay on the flimsy mattress staring up at the ceiling. She'd hardly slept. No surprise, really. A mixture of terror and the cold had left her shivering most of the night. She'd only been allowed one blanket. She looked around the sparse, bleak cell, which consisted of the bed where she lay - a concrete slab with a thin plastic-covered mattress - a toilet, a small washbasin and a simple wooden table and chair. Her breakfast container lay on the floor – she'd only been able to nibble at the dried toast. She wasn't hungry. Her stomach remained in a tight knot.

Every hour an officer would open a little hatch and peer in – presumably to check she hadn't managed to do herself any harm. She'd been awake for several of these checks. Jen never imagined she'd see the inside of a police cell, let alone stay the night in one.

She knew it didn't look good. Of course, she hadn't done it. She didn't want the bloody woman dead; she just wanted her to go away. Now she was the one who might be going away – for a very long time.

But her solicitor, when he arrived, had been good at his job. And at least *he* seemed to believe her. He'd told her that he doubted the police would be able to put a case together on the evidence they appeared to have. He'd also agreed it didn't look good; the vandalism, the assault, entering the garage the night before the accident. But if she stuck to her story, the truth - and the police had no forensic evidence that she'd tampered with the car - he doubted they'd charge her with the more serious offence. And even if they did, he doubted a jury would convict her.

But she wasn't so sure. She wondered who'd seen her go into the garage? Surely, Dan hadn't followed her that night. He wouldn't have inadvertently told the police, he hated the police. She was comforted by the fact he seemed to be genuinely mad with Emma about the baby revelation, and she felt a lot better about him, a lot more secure, a lot more confident. Strange, really, she thought, that *she* wasn't upset about Maddy. But the thing was - she'd met Maddy. She *knew* Maddy; Maddy seemed a nice girl, attractive, sassy and intelligent. Anyone would be proud to have her as a daughter. And she'd be proud to have her as a step-daughter. The cell door opened, and the sergeant stepped in.

'Right, Miss Clark, you can go.'

'I can go,' she said, suddenly sitting up. What had changed?

'Yep, we've had new information about the car, and you're off the hook. But we will be putting you on police bail while we continue investigations on the other matters - criminal damage, assault and unlawful entry.

Jen's possessions were returned to her, which only consisted of her coat and handbag, and she made her way to the front desk of the police station. There, waiting for her, hands in pockets, and with a wide grin on his face, was Dan. She rushed into his arms, sobbing. He was there for her, her Dan.

Back home, each with a mug of tea sat at the kitchen table; Barney tucked up in his basket, and Jen explained to Dan that she might still face three charges.

'Well, they're only minor. Minor compared to attempted murder,' said Dan.

'Well, they might not be. They're still potentially serious, and my solicitor said I could still go to jail. But he thought it more likely, if I plead guilty, and given they're first offences, that I'd get community service or a suspended sentence at worst.'

'I don't care, Jen, you are home,' said Dan.

'What happened? Did Laser own up?' asked Jen.

'No, Maddy rang me this morning to say that Deano, the little wanker, had confessed to the police that it was his fault. Laser had asked him to do a health check. He'd looked at the brakes, which was surprisingly thorough for him, but he'd forgotten to tighten the nuts, which is entirely typical of him. He's such a fucking airhead. I'm sure Tom will have to sack him now. And Laser shouldn't have left him to it, or at the very least, he should have checked his work. And he should have come forward to say that Deano was the one responsible. He was trying to protect him. He didn't want to get either of them into trouble.'

'Well, at least Deano had the courage to own up and tell the police.'

'Eventually. I think he only did it because I was in such a state about you being arrested.'

'How did Maddy know?'

'I don't know. Deano must have told her, I suppose. I'm not sure when. I didn't think they got on particularly well.'

Jen took a sip of tea. 'You didn't doubt me, did you?' she asked, looking up at him.

'Not for a moment,' said Dan. 'What we need to do now is put this all behind us and start again.' he added. And this time, she believed him. Jen felt herself calm down a little. In fact, she felt calmer than she had for weeks.

# Chapter Sixty-Six
# Emma

Emma had woken in the middle of the night, and this time she'd stayed awake. There were vases all around; red roses, yellow roses, iris, carnations, and some strongly scented freesias. A nurse had held her hand and patiently told her exactly what had happened while she'd been in hospital; what they knew about the accident; how long she'd been unconscious; what her injuries were; what treatment she'd had; who'd visited and who'd left messages. The nurse made a special point of telling her how Toby had spent as much time with her as possible. 'He's so sweet,' the nurse had said.

Emma had replied that she'd always underestimated him, 'I think I always have,' she'd said to the nurse, adding, 'When I was in the coma, having dreams, a lot of things seemed to fit into place.'

Now, after a small amount of breakfast, in a new private room, which sat at the end of a general ward, she was feeling a bit more like herself. She tried to change position to get rid of some of the stiffness in her side. Her ribs really were very sore. They'd given her painkillers, which helped a bit, but they also made her feel drowsy. The main thing, she thought, as the perfume from the freesias drifted across, was that she could smell again, she could see again, she was alive. She knew that must be something of a miracle because when she closed her eyes, she could see the tree coming towards her at tremendous speed; in the few seconds she'd had before the crash, she'd thought she was going to die.

'Your friend Toby brought most of them,' said the nurse rearranging some of the flowers. 'We couldn't display them in intensive care, so we've been keeping them at the nurses' station. Beautiful, aren't they? So, is he your boyfriend, Toby?'

Instinctively, Emma was about to say no. But she stopped herself. The idea would have been preposterous once, but now? Well, she wasn't so sure. 'Possibly,' she said with a weak smile. 'Who else has been to visit? I have a vague memory of seeing my mother?'

'Yes, your mother and your daughter.'

'My daughter? Oh, you mean Maddy.'

'Yes, she came with Toby every day, I think,' replied the nurse, looking a little puzzled.

'Any other visitors?'

'No, I don't think so. Not on my shifts anyway,' said the nurse. Then she left, pushing the drugs trolley ahead of her.

Emma had an image, in her mind, of Toby clutching her hand, looking *so* worried. It was when she'd fought and struggled up from that deep place. She didn't want to go back there. Toby? Images from the last couple of months flashed through her mind; restaurants, the cinema, around at her hers, around at his; laughing together; how happy she'd been to see him after the vandalism on her flat; how he'd dealt with Jen after she'd been slapped; the look on his face when he'd won that commission; the look on his face when she'd been with Dan. He'd made her laugh, but all the time, she'd just made him sad. And despite all that, he was still there for her.

And what about Dan? Well, he clearly hadn't come to visit. It all came back to her, the argument in the garage just after she'd heard about her father's leukaemia, and just before she'd got in the car and begun that drive up Lakey Hill. How horrible he'd been. How angry he'd looked. Like a stranger.

Yes, of course, she could and should have spoken to him earlier about the baby, about Maddy. But didn't he understand that she'd obviously come back to the village in order to tell him, to tell him everything, to be with him? That wasn't going to happen now, and for the first time, she realised she didn't want it to happen. It was as though she'd gone through some kind of epiphany whilst in the coma. She felt different, she felt calmer, and in fact, she felt like she really, really, knew what she wanted to do for the first time in years and years. She'd been deceiving herself. There would be no more clinging on to the past, clinging on to what once was; her obsession with Dan, driven by a need for redemption, for forgiveness. It was over? Whatever connection they had now, it wasn't love, not any more. Not if she was really being honest with herself. Time changed people. That was then. This was now. Dan had moved on, he wasn't the same person, and neither was she.

There she'd said it, at least to herself. She was finished with Dan. Her plan would be adjusted and rewritten. Some of it had worked. She'd found him, she'd re-discovered who he was, and she'd found her daughter, or rather her daughter had found her. No, it simply wasn't going to work out being with Dan; she could see that now. Suddenly her eyes felt heavy. Thinking was exhausting. She was tired, very tired.

When she woke up again, they were all there - her mother, Maddy, Toby, and her father. He looked pale, not helped by the beige dressing gown he was wearing. He was holding her hand, and with the other hand, he caressed her cheek.

'Hello darling, how are you feeling?' he said. It seemed to Emma the kindest voice she'd ever heard him use.

'I'm fine, Dad. I'm going to be ok. How are you? Why are you here? Why are you in a dressing gown?'

He smiled. 'Oh, I've been getting better myself. They moved me down from the hospital in Scotland so that I could be here with you. I need some treatment, but I'm going to be alright. I know I am.'

'Toby,' she said, reaching out her other hand towards him. He took it and kissed it, and she smiled. 'And Maddy.'

Maddy came forward, and Emma could see that she was shaking. Things had to be said, never mind if it was awkward for everyone. 'Maddy, I guessed when I saw you in the garage,' Emma began. 'I'm so sorry. Sorry about everything. There's so much to explain. I've been looking for you, but in the end, you found me. Did you get my letter?'

'I did. I did. It was wonderful. I should have told you about me earlier. But I wanted to find out about you first; that's why I came here. That's why I took the job in the garage. I hope you understand.' Maddy took hold of her hand, and Emma felt a surge of happiness.

'Of course, I do. But I hope we can really get to know each other now. I've missed all of your life so far, but I want to be a part of the rest. I really do. I want to make it up to you. I never wanted to give you away,' she glanced at her father, who was looking down, but she could see tears streaming down his face. 'I was so young; it was very difficult,' she added.

'I know it must have been, well. Actually, I don't know, but I guess they were different times. Anyway, I want you to get well, for us to talk, and to sort everything out for a new beginning. A new life for both of us, and with my grandparents, and my new dad, I guess.'

'Oh, you know about him as well?' said Emma.

'Yes, we're cool about it.'

'Yes, well, I bet he is,' said Emma, remembering his angry face again.

'Not that sort of cool, we'll be fine, err, Mum. Can I call you mum? From now on, I'm just going to have to have two people I call "Mum" and two people I call "Dad," I think,' laughed Maddy.

'It sounds very strange, but yes, of course, you can,' said Emma, her heart beating faster. How long had she imagined this moment? Too long. But she'd never imagined these circumstances. She felt very tired; again, it was all too much.

A nurse came in, and the four members of Emma's family stood back as she approached the bed. It was the Scottish nurse. 'Let's get you sitting up a wee bit better,' she said, picking up the bed's remote control. The bed began to move up slowly, and Emma grimaced as her ribs re-adjusted to the new position. Toby squeezed her hand ever more tightly.

'So, Mum, Dad, do you know about Maddy as well?' asked Emma.

'Yes dear, we've all had a big talk this morning, and everything's fine,' said her mother, who seemed to have a permanent smile on her face.

'Everything is fine,' repeated Emma lying back on her pillow. She knew her mother meant well. But could it really be written off so easily, eighteen years, just like that; eighteen years of hurt, guilt, trauma, a broken marriage; a humiliating attempt at reconciliation with Dan; an assault by his girlfriend; a car crash? Not to mention or think about everything Maddy had been through. What had her life been like?

But Emma quelled those thoughts for now and looked at the four smiling faces clustered around her bed. She resolved that this was not the time or place for an argument, and anyway, maybe, her mother was right... *everything was fine*. Maybe, it was just time to move on.

'Everything is fine,' she repeated.

'Well, it will be as soon as I can get back on my feet again,' chipped in her father, in his usual self-centred way. 'I just need to find some suitable bone marrow from somewhere.'

'Mr Taylor, I mean Grandad,' said Maddy. 'Can I help with that, seeing as I'm a member of the family, you can have my bone marrow?'

Emma was stunned. And she could tell her father was even more affected by Maddy's offer. Tears welled up in his eyes again. Emma had never seen him like this. He was always so strong, so intransigent, a bully, never the kind, gentle, supporting father she'd wanted. He'd told her what to do, what to think, how she should live her life, but here he was, a broken man, certainly a humbled man, shaking and sobbing into a handkerchief.

'Don't cry, Dad,' was all she could say as her mother put her hand on his shoulder.

'He'll be fine dear. It's all a bit too much for him.'

Emma looked at Maddy. She was so very proud. Here was her daughter who had been given away by her grandfather, although she probably didn't know it, now willing to donate her bone marrow to save him, to save his life. The irony was obvious.

Emma's mother turned to Maddy. 'That's a lovely, lovely offer, Maddy. But you wouldn't be compatible. It's only siblings, brothers and sisters, who can help and even then there's only a one-in-four chance of a match. Otherwise, it's just a question of waiting for someone off the register.'

'What about Aunt Harriet, Dad's sister?' asked Emma. 'I know we don't talk to them anymore, I can't even remember why, but couldn't she help Dad?'

'We've been in touch. I sent her a letter,' said Emma's mother. 'But I don't know if it will do any good. We've not spoken for, well, a long, long time.' She looked awkward.

'We can certainly give it a good try,' said a woman who'd just entered the back of the room.

'Harriet,' shrieked Emma's mother.

'Mum. Mum and Dad,' gasped Maddy as the couple came into the room. She rushed into their arms. 'What are you doing here?'

Now Emma was more confused than ever. Her head was spinning.

'Never mind us, what are *you* doing here? You're supposed to be in Cornwall,' said Aunt Harriet as she hugged Maddy.

'Will someone explain to me what is happening?' said Emma, feeling weaker than ever.

'Agreed,' said Maddy. 'What's going on?'

There was a moment of stunned silence as if the world stood still, and everyone tried to take in what had just happened. Emma couldn't speak.

'Oh god, I'd better try to explain,' said her father, drying his eyes and blowing his nose in a rather loud way so that he sounded like a cross between an elephant and a trumpet. 'Maddy, you were adopted by my sister and her husband. We thought it was for the best.'

Emma couldn't believe what she was hearing. Her hand was over her mouth. She was shocked.

Her father continued: 'But stupidly – and I know it was all my fault - we fell out, we had a massive argument about everything, and I cut ties, I didn't keep in touch. In fact, we didn't speak at all, did we, Susan? So, we never knew how you were doing.'

'Wait a minute,' said Emma. She was fully awake now. 'Aunt Harriet and Uncle Stephen brought up Maddy. And no one thought to tell me.'

'We thought it for the best,' said her mother.

Aunt Harriet, Maddy's adoptive mother, came forward and stood at the end of Emma's bed. 'We agreed to keep it a secret. That was the deal, and I stuck to it even after the argument. In fact, if I'm honest, it was partly because of the argument. I'm sorry, Emma, if it was wrong. If I'm honest, I was scared of losing Maddy, I'd always longed for a baby.' Then turning to Maddy, she reached out and held her hands. 'And Maddy, we should have told you much earlier than we did that you were adopted. And we should have told you who your mother was.'

'But I don't understand,' said Maddy, looking pale and shocked by the sudden turn of events. 'How can you be my grandad's sister? Your maiden name isn't the same.'

'I'm afraid I told a fib about that,' replied Aunt Harriet, looking to the ground. Her husband clasped her hand. 'Again, we're so sorry if we did the wrong thing.'

'Of course, it was wrong, Aunt Harriet, Mum, Dad, you were all wrong. What were you thinking?' said Emma, the energy draining from her voice. 'And if anyone says they thought it was *for the best* again, I'll, I'll…' It was all too much for her, and she just collapsed back on the pillow and closed her eyes. Her head was spinning.

# Epilogue

The sun's rays sliced through the kitchen window. On that bright, happy, glorious, blue-sky morning, it lifted her soul. She stood, almost hypnotised, her eyes locked onto the two dancing, jumping, skipping children. For a moment, her heart ached with joy, so much so it almost hurt.

It was the first day of the long school summer holidays, and the two children, like newborn lambs discovering fresh air and green grass for the first time, embraced freedom. She loved to watch them play like this - together. They were barely fourteen months apart in age, and, mostly, they got on really well. They were so happy and innocent, their lives before them. So much joy to find; so many mistakes to make or avoid; so many discoveries ahead.

Emma returned to the mundane - washing up the breakfast things, but as she did so, she caught herself in the small mirror on the windowsill. She tucked a strand of hair behind her ear. Was that a hint of grey? No surprise, really, for a forty-three-year-old mother of three. She felt two arms circle her waist and a tousle-haired head nuzzle into her neck.

'You're tickling my ear,' she protested.

'I love you, Emma Taylor,' said Toby.

'It's Mrs Emma Forbes to you, if you don't mind.'

'So, what shall we do with these two scallywags, take them out for the day, or just let them frolic about in the garden?'

'You've forgotten, haven't you? Typical. Maddy and Dean are coming for lunch. Maddy wants to show off her engagement ring and talk about their wedding plans and everything, so I don't really think we've got time to go anywhere.'

'Oh right, yes, err, ok. I'd better go and frolic for a bit then,' said Toby.

Emma was pleased that Isla and Charlie were going to spend some time with their father. Toby had been a bit obsessed with his latest commission, and she thought he needed a break. She watched as he ran out into the garden, and then she returned to the dishes, singing to herself.

Toby sat down on the bench. He'd only been playing with the children for half an hour. It seemed they could keep running about all day, but he needed a break for ten minutes. He wasn't as fit as he thought.

'Lazy bones, lazy bones,' the children chorused, before heading off to climb into their tree house.

He soaked in the sun, tilting his head to let the warm rays caress his face. Thanks to the gulf stream, the lowlands of southwest Scotland often enjoyed days like these. He was glad he'd allowed himself a day off. When you were your own boss, it was always a tough negotiation. But he was ahead of where he expected to be on his latest sculpture, so he'd earned it.

Moving north and joining a new art gallery had been a big move for Toby and Emma. Emma was now working again, part-time, and despite the four years out having and bringing up the children, she was doing well. Less seemed to be more when it came to her paintings, and she was fetching better prices at the gallery and online. Toby's contacts had also helped open doors for her to some bigger city-based galleries. Her father had continued his support, too, often sponsoring her exhibitions, even though Toby had told him they could manage. Emma still called it guilt money.

Toby drank in more sun. Things couldn't be much better. He'd had a succession of lucrative commissions, mostly from corporations in London, Manchester and Glasgow. His reputation had grown, and he was now written about in the right magazines. He was developing a national reputation, so it didn't really matter where he based himself. He quickly touched the wood of the bench where he sat as an insurance policy.

The move north also helped Emma escape her memories. She'd left the village, and Dan, on what could only be described as acceptable, rather than amicable, terms. They'd had to be civil for the sake of Maddy, but it was clear their relationship couldn't recover. Dan wasn't going to forgive Emma for concealing the truth about Maddy, and Emma wasn't going to forget how he'd treated her on the morning of her terrible car crash. History now. And it had provided Toby with the chance he never thought he'd get. He often joked that winning Emma was a race between the hare and the tortoise.

'Daddy, daddy, come and find us,' a shrill voice cried from somewhere up a tree.

'I'm coming. I'm coming to get you,' he called back.

Maddy paid the taxi driver. Turning away from the cab, she asked, 'How do I look?'

'Ugly and disgusting,' replied Deano, putting his arm around her waist and kissing her on the cheek.

'Like normal then, good, right, here we go.'

They walked up to the door. Maddy always felt apprehensive whenever they met up with her mother and Toby. For starters, there was always the greeting to get over - it still felt a bit awkward even after seven years. It had been agreed, after some debate, that she should call her real mother Emma rather than Mum. It was Emma's idea. She'd argued that because Maddy was an adult by the time they met, it changed things. Also, she was used to calling her adoptive mother Mum, so it made sense, there'd be no confusion or conflict. But Maddy felt awkward about calling her real mother by her first name, so, most of the time, she tried to get away with not using any name at all. She'd usually wait until she could catch her mother's eye before speaking.

Deano never felt awkward about anything very much. He called them Emma and Toby like he'd known them all his life. Emma, meanwhile, always insisted on dropping the 'o' and calling him Dean. Maddy thought that maybe it helped her think of him as a different more mature person, and not the hapless mechanic who'd nearly killed her. Deano worked in marketing now; he'd recently been promoted, and he earned a decent salary. He'd followed her to university, and their relationship - which began on that drunken night in the village - had developed into a full-blown love affair, which resulted in them living together before and after graduation.

'Hi Maddy, hi Dean, how are you? You're both looking well,' said a smiling Emma, as she opened the door.

'We're fine. Yourselves?'

'Run ragged by these monsters,' said Toby as he was pushed aside in the hallway by two unstoppable, excited children.

'Maddy, Deano,' they squealed, jumping into their arms.

This was the best bit of any visit, thought Maddy. She loved her step-brother and sister to pieces. And she gave them both an enormous hug.

'Come and see our tree house,' said Charlie. 'Come and see, please, please.'

'I'll go,' said Deano. 'You get settled in first.' Maddy loved him. He always thought of how to make her more comfortable. Anyway, she also knew that he'd rather play with the children than sit and talk.

After the tea was poured and they'd settled down in the lounge, Emma said, 'Well, show me your ring then?'

Maddy thrust out her hand to reveal a small gold band with three tiny diamonds. She'd insisted that Deano didn't spend too much on it, so, in truth, it wasn't that impressive. But Emma made all the right noises, saying how lovely it was, and they settled into discussing the rest of the wedding plans.

Eventually, Maddy came to the difficult part of the conversation. There were just the two of them now, as Toby had joined Deano and the kids outside.

'I've, um, been to see Dan to ask him to give me away,' she said.

'Oh,' said her mother. There was a pause. 'Not Uncle Stephen, I mean, your, um, other dad then?'

'No, it was his idea, actually. He thought it would only be right and proper if it was my real father. It's all been a bit awkward. But they both seem to be happy about it.'

'Dan was *happy* about it; I didn't think he liked parental responsibilities,' said Emma, tartly.

'Oh, I don't think that's entirely fair. He's always been willing to help me if I needed it.'

'It's just that you've never actually asked him, and he's never offered.'

'Well, no, but he's always said he'd help me, and he sends me birthday cards, and we talk on the phone every now and again.'

'Has he ever actually phoned *you*? I bet not?'

'Well, no, but then he doesn't know whether I'll be busy. It's fine. Anyway, don't make a thing of it, please.'

'How are Dan and Jen, anyway?' asked Emma.

'Oh good. Dan gets a bit stressed now that he's in charge of the garage. Jen loves being at home with little Milly, but she's due to start school next month, and Jen's going back to work part-time.'

'Oh right, good, good, that's good to hear,' Emma's voice tailed off. She made her excuses and went into the kitchen to make the lunch. Typical, thought Maddy, the conversation was always quickly closed down when the past reared its ugly head.

Anyway, thank goodness that chat was over. Maddy had known that Emma wouldn't be too happy about Dan's involvement in the wedding. She wished her real parents had a better relationship, but she knew it wasn't going to happen now.

She sat in the quiet of the room for a time, and her mind slipped back to the time after that unbelievable day in the hospital when all the secrets came out. Her grandfather had taken most of the blame. Later, when he was well again after his successful bone marrow transplant, he'd fully explained things to her. He'd admitted to Maddy that when Emma revealed she was pregnant, he'd been so stuffed up with pride he'd been a terrible bully.

But the horror of nearly losing Emma in the car crash, coupled with his own possible demise, had shocked him into realising what he'd done wrong. Maddy had long since forgiven him. They had quite a special relationship now, and she went to see her grandparents as often as she could.

On one visit, he'd explained more about her adoption by his much younger sister, who couldn't have children herself. Maddy also learned that the adoption was actually, technically, illegal. It should have been arranged through the proper agencies. Instead, it became a private, secret, family matter. In those days, apparently, it was easier to do. There were no proper identity checks when a child turned up at a health centre, or a school, for example. No one demanded to see a birth certificate.

After listening to everyone's story, Maddy had easily forgiven them all, most importantly her own real mother, Emma. She eventually understood why she'd felt compelled to do what her father suggested. But Maddy also knew that she'd never have done it herself.

'Lunch is ready,' called Emma from the kitchen.

That evening Emma was happy. The day had gone well. Deano had exhausted the children, running about the garden all afternoon. They were now sound asleep in their beds. The lunch had gone well, and, overall, she and Maddy had got on.

'Drink?' asked Toby, pouring a glass of red wine.

'God, yes, several, please,' replied Emma, almost snatching the glass from his hand before he'd finished pouring.

'I suppose we ought to be having champagne to celebrate Maddy's rather startling news,'

'Yes, I suppose we should,' replied Toby sitting back in his favourite chair wearing his favourite old jumper and his favourite tatty slippers.

'Just think, I'm going to be a grandmother. Once, I wondered if I'd ever have a baby of my own – and now I'm surrounded by children.'

'I'm surprised she told us, actually,' said Toby. 'I thought she might keep it a secret for a while.'

Emma glared at him, but she could see a smirk on his face and a twinkle in his eye. He was poking fun.

'That's in very poor taste, I've told you our family motto is *no more secrets*.'

She threw a cushion, which hit him smack in the face.